PENGUIN B

THE TERMITE QUEEN

Tạ Duy Anh (1959–) is a prolific writer from Hà Nội who has published in multiple genres and won numerous awards for his literary writing in Việt Nam. His novel *Lão khổ* (*Mr. Misery*) has been translated into French and published in France under the title *Sur le dos du buffle* while some of his short stories have been translated into English, French, German, Russian, Chinese, Japanese, and Thai.

Quan Manh Ha is professor of American Literature & Ethnic Studies at the University of Montana. His research interests include multiethnic US literatures, Vietnam War literature, critical race theory, and literary translation. He is the translator of *Other Moons: Vietnamese Stories of the American War and Its Aftermath*, *Luminous Nights: Pioneering Vietnamese Short Stories*, and *Hanoi at Midnight: Stories* by Bao Ninh. He believes that literary translation is a political and an ethical act, and thus besides publishing several scholarly articles and essays in journals, he is committed to translating Vietnamese literature to promote cross-cultural understanding and global discourse on colonialism, imperialism, and the Vietnam War from all sides of the conflict. His short-story translations have appeared in various journals, such as *Metamorphoses*, *Southern Humanities Review*, *Asian Literature and Translation*, *CIRQUE: A Literary Journal for Alaska and the Pacific Northwest*, and *DELOS*.

Charles Waugh is the co-editor and co-translator of two collections of short fiction by Vietnamese writers: *Wild Mustard: New Voices from Vietnam*, and *Family of Fallen Leaves: Stories of Agent Orange from Vietnamese Writers*. He is the associate editor for fiction at *ISLE*, the journal of the Association for the Study of Literature and Environment, and professor of English at Utah State University, USA.

ADVANCE PRAISE FOR *THE TERMITE QUEEN*

'*The Termite Queen* deserves to be placed on the same pedestal with the greatest novels written during the golden period of Vietnamese fiction, 1930–1945. Strangely, the government's official, blistering criticisms of the novel's content and characterization turn out to be accolades. A marvelous and admirable book!'

—Bảo Ninh, author of *The Sorrow of War* and *Hà Nội at Midnight*

'The novel offers a chilling look at the most divisive issue in contemporary Vietnam—the great on-going land grab that has displaced millions of poor Vietnamese. This culturally important work should not be overlooked.'

—Andrew X. Pham, author of *Catfish and Mandala* and *The Eaves of Heaven*

'Tạ Duy Anh's book is a poignant fictional account of economic and political dynamics in Vietnam that, for some Vietnamese, have been all too real. Quan Manh Ha and Charles Waugh's translation of the story is superb.'

—Benedict J. Tria Kerkvliet, author of *The Power of Everyday* and *Speaking Out in Vietnam*

'Tạ's novel, a rollicking tale full of corrupt officials and avaricious businessmen, is finally appearing in a masterful translation that opens a window into some of Vietnam's biggest scandals.'

—Thomas Bass, author of *Censorship in Vietnam*

'The novel demonstrates Tạ's astute perception of how things operate in Vietnamese society, of people's innermost feelings, and of the contradictions that corner the common people. The book gives voice to the people's endless aspiration for peace and justice.'

—Joseph Ngô Quang Kiệt, former Archbishop of Hà Nội

'*The Termite Queen* exposes dark realities and degradation in Vietnamese society under an authoritarian regime. Undoubtedly a brave novel.'

—Đinh Quang Anh Thái, reporter and former content editor at Radio Free Asia (RFA)

'Daring, disturbing, moving, and unforgettable, *The Termite Queen* establishes Tạ Duy Anh as one of Việt Nam's greatest novelists, one whose work deserves to be read, studied and discussed for many years to come.'

—Nguyễn Phan Quế Mai, author of *The Mountains Sing* and *Dust Child*

The Termite Queen

Tạ Duy Anh

Translated by Quan Manh Ha
and Charles Waugh

PENGUIN BOOKS

An imprint of Penguin Random House

PENGUIN BOOKS

USA | Canada | UK | Ireland | Australia
New Zealand | India | South Africa | China | Southeast Asia

Penguin Books is part of the Penguin Random House group of companies
whose addresses can be found at global.penguinrandomhouse.com

Published by Penguin Random House SEA Pte Ltd
9, Changi South Street 3, Level 08-01,
Singapore 486361

First Vietnamese edition published in 2017 by Vietnam Writers' Association
Press

First published in Penguin Books by Penguin Random House SEA 2023

ISBN 9789815127157

Typeset in Minion pro by MAP Systems, Bangalore, India

www.penguin.sg

Foreword

Quan Manh Ha and Charles Waugh

Tạ Duy Anh (1959–) is a prolific writer from Hà Nội who has published in multiple genres and won numerous awards for his literary writing in Việt Nam. After graduating with the highest distinction from the Nguyễn Du School of Creative Writing and producing many well-received works, Tạ became a member of the Việt Nam Writers' Association, and served as editor for its publishing house until he retired in 2020. Despite his well-regarded career as writer and editor, a few of his works have been censored in Việt Nam. His novel *Đi tìm nhân vật* (*Looking for a Character*) was banned in 2002 after the government condemned it for 'portraying a dark and negative picture of society'. Fifteen years later, the book was reassessed and approved for republication. Many of his short stories have also been censored. Banned in Việt Nam, his novel, *Sinh ra để chết* (*Born to Die*), was published in the United States in 2018. In 2017, the Việt Nam Writers' Association Press published this novel, *Mối chúa* (*The Termite Queen*), with Tạ using the pseudonym Đặng Khấu. Six months later, the Ministry of Information and Communication banned it, saying:

> The novel addresses major issues in today's society. The author exposes social ills and social injustice. However,

the majority of the novel's characters, from lower to upper class, are negative, miserable, and desperate. The characters' narratives present a society that is governed by stupid, greedy, and malicious people. The government acts cruelly and immorally: it oppresses farmers, destroys its own members, and murders dissidents for monetary reasons. Some details are presented sarcastically and acerbically with exaggerated and negative depictions that make reality appear dark and depressing. The pages that depict how the government coerces farmers into sacrificing their land for investment projects exaggerate the conflict between the government and the citizens—the oppression is described like a carefully thought-out, fully armed battle.

According to writer and critic Phạm Lưu Vũ, *The Termite Queen* is a Kafkaesque story within a story, and the Ministry of Information and Communication's criticism and assessment 'summarize the book's themes and meaning accurately'. Thus, he argues, it has been censored for too directly exposing the truth.

The Termite Queen is told by a first-person narrator who returns to Việt Nam after completing his higher education in England to take over as chairman of the successful company his recently deceased father had built. The role demands he find the secretive and powerful person truly in control of the company's investment projects and lucrative business contracts. In his search for the shadowy Mr Big, he encounters significant corruption and issues related to industrialization, urbanization, greed, immorality, corporate overreach, official malfeasance and toxic masculinity, as well as the heartbreaking fate of the vulnerable farmers. In particular, the novel focuses on widespread land reform, which involves powerful investors working together with government officials to force people out of their homes and properties. Land expropriation has had a long history in Việt Nam, from before the colonial era all the way to the present.

Long considered a realist writer, Tạ has said that he has fabricated nothing in the novel: he has only written about what he witnesses on a daily basis in Vietnamese society. Thus, it could be argued that *The Termite Queen* is a historical novel, albeit a present history, with the book coming out at what Tạ calls, 'a very important period in Vietnamese history'. It may also be argued that in such extreme times, satire is the only realistic way a socially engaged, realist writer can approach the absurdities of the moment in which he finds himself living. In an interview with Radio Free Asia (RFA), Tạ says, 'I am deeply concerned about my inability to do anything to help the community. Personally, I feel that voiceless civilians are the most disadvantaged. The people who take away people's lands are not just state officials or powerful authority figures in the government—they are also extremely wealthy people. [...] As a writer, I use my creative writing to portray that reality with the hope that it will somehow have an impact upon the community.' When asked if he worried about the novel's censorship, Tạ said, 'I want to have freedom of expression in my writing. I must create my own freedom and I'm not concerned about awards and recognitions. That's how I have my freedom. Now and in the future, I'll always write with that philosophy in mind.'

Since the book was banned in 2017, an unauthorized PDF version of the novel has been made available online for the many interested Vietnamese readers willing and savvy enough to seek it out. In June 2018, the California-based press, Người Việt Books, published *The Termite Queen* in its original Vietnamese, recognizing that it raises important issues of social and environmental injustice, ills related to economic disparity and conflicts between the government and various civilian groups. But the novel is also unprecedented in its portrayal of the kind of toxic masculinity that seems to be behind all these other woes. The hyper-competitive, hyper-consumer-driven world the novel describes results directly from the behaviour of the male characters who must possess everything, including the women and the land around them. No other contemporary fiction cautions readers of these aspects of the recent development of Việt Nam's hyper-capitalist culture in quite this way, or in any comparable way, really. This edition is the first novel-length, English translation.

The Termite Queen and Its Socio-Historical Context

Benedict J. Tria Kerkvliet

Because land controversies are central to Tạ Duy Anh's novel, some background about land use in contemporary Việt Nam may help readers of this English-language translation to better understand and appreciate the story.

The use and distribution of land have long been contentious political issues in Việt Nam. Rural unrest rooted in land inequality, landlords' abuses of their tenant farmers and agricultural workers and onerous taxes on villagers contributed significantly to popular support for Việt Nam's Communist Party (VCP) and the war Vietnamese people fought (1946–1954) against French colonial rule. During that war, the VCP reduced the rents tenant farmers paid to landlords, confiscated some land from large landowners and distributed it to landless families. After the French were defeated in 1954, land redistribution continued, especially in the northern half of the country that the VCP governed.

By the late 1950s, the VCP government in the north embarked on another method that its leaders argued would prevent land inequality, increase agricultural production and markedly improve villagers' lives. That method was collective farming. In each village or cluster of villages, nearly all agricultural land as well as farming implements, work animals and ponds and small lakes were amalgamated into one large farm. Villagers were organized into teams assigned by each collective's managers to do specific tasks for each crop and throughout each season. Some of what the collective produced was given to the government for distribution to factory workers, soldiers and other non-farming citizens; the rest was shared among collective members according to complicated formulae.

Initially, several collective farms were reasonably successful, although few matched leaders' expectations. By the mid-1970s, however, production levels were falling, living conditions were worsening and rural discontent was brewing beneath the surface in much of northern Việt Nam.

Nevertheless, in 1976, after Việt Nam was reunited because the VCP regime prevailed in wars against the government headquartered in Sài Gòn and the military forces of the United States and its allies, authorities attempted to collectivize farming throughout the nation. But, with few exceptions, the attempt failed. Meanwhile, most collectives in northern Việt Nam were collapsing as well.

The demise of collective farming and the spread of discontent, poverty and hunger throughout the country pushed authorities in the 1980s to embrace family farming, which is what most villagers wanted.

At the same time, Vietnamese officials, and most farming households as well, wanted to avoid repeating a history of rural unrest arising from extreme land inequality. So, in the late 1980s and early 1990s, local and national authorities oversaw a process that reallocated rather equitably nearly all agricultural land to farming households. National authorities also made laws aimed at trying to maintain a more-or-less equitable distribution of agricultural land. Consequently, according to Việt Nam's laws since the late 1980s until today, farming households have the right to use, not own, land for twenty to fifty years, depending on location and type of crops. (Other entities such as companies and religious groups may also have use rights to farmland.) Ponds and small lakes may also be assigned to households and other private groups for specified time periods. Holders of use rights must pay certain fees and taxes but otherwise can keep or sell whatever they produce on the land or water allotted to them. They may also lend or bequeath their use rights to someone else and use their rights as collateral for loans.

Laws do allow the government to cancel use rights and reassign land and bodies of water to 'national defense, security, national interest, public interest, and economic development' projects.[1] Such cancellations became frequent as Việt Nam's diversifying economy required converting more agricultural land to land for urban and industrial purposes. Revoking use rights and taking families' farms, though, has often been highly controversial and tumultuous. Such is the context for this novel.

From 2001–2005, authorities took 366,400 hectares of agricultural land from households; by 2010 the total had risen to roughly 745,000 hectares, affecting some nine million farming people, or about 10 per cent of the country's population.[2] What proportion of those people objected is unknown but the

---

[1] *Luật Đất Đai Năm* 2003 (Đã được sửa đổi, bổ sung năm 2009–2010) [Land Law of 2003, with modifications made in 2009–2010], article 38, clause 1. Similar provisions were included, with more elaboration, in the country's revised land law of 2013, article 61.

[2] My figures draw on World Bank, *Compulsory Land Acquisition and Voluntary Land Conversion in Vietnam* (Hà Nội: World Bank, 2011), 16; Hiếu, Lê, 'Về vấn đề chuyển đổi mục đích sử dụng đất nông nghiệp trong quá trình công nghiệp hóa, đô thị hóa' [Regarding the Changing Use of Agricultural Land during Industrialization and Urbanization], *Tạp chí Quản lý Nhà nước* [Journal of State Management], no. 174 (7, 2010): 34–35; Sơn, Đặng Kim and Nguyễn Đỗ Anh Tuấn, *Chính sách Đất đai cho phát triển tại Việt Nam: Cơ hội hay Thách thức?* [Land Policy for

volume of complaints and protests against farming areas being appropriated suggests it was significant.

In the four years from 2008 through 2011, the government received nearly 1.6 million batches of petitions, accusations and other criticisms from citizens, a 26 per cent increase over a previous comparable period.[3] Some complaints come from individual families, but several were signed by numerous households from the same community. So, the 1.6 million figure represents at least a few million people. Over 70 per cent of the criticisms—some reports say 90 per cent—were about land, especially its appropriation and the low compensation paid to those who held the rights to use it.

About 42 per cent of the complaints were reportedly resolved. That often meant that the affected farming families agreed, often reluctantly, to give up their use rights in exchange for compensations such as money, relocation to different farming areas and/or promised employment in the enterprise or entity to be built on the retrieved land. Typically, the compensations came from local governments and the companies that had high-level governmental approval to obtain land to build factories, urban housing and other projects. Frequently those companies had close connections to key government agencies. Sometimes

Development in Việt Nam: Opportunity or Challenge?], (Hà Nội: Trung Tâm Tư Vấn Chính Sách Nông Nghiệp, 2011), 63.

[3] 'Tố cáo khiếu nại' [Denunciation Complaint], 2 May 2012, BBC, accessed 19 July 2012, www.bbc.co.uk/vietnamese/vietnam/ 2012/05/120502_land_dispute_conference.shtml; Tấn Phát, Nguyễn, 'Những bất cập hiện nay của chính sách đất đai và thách thức đối với phát triển tam nông ở Việt Nam' [Land Policy Shortcomings and Challenges for Three-Pronged Agricultural Development in Việt Nam], Nghiên Cứu Kinh Tế [Economic Research], no. 366 (11, 2008): 65–66; Lê Quân, Viết, 'Câu hỏi sau vụ chống cưỡng chế ở Hải Phòng' [Questions after the Resistance to Coercion in Hải Phòng], 10 January 2012, Vietnam.net, accessed 13 January 2012, http://tuanvietnam.vietnamnet. vn/2012-01-09-cau-hoi-sau-vu-chong-cuong-che-o-hai-phong.

the companies were the creations of shady or illegal deals made in the 1990s when numerous state-owned enterprises were privatized.

Meanwhile, over half of the complaints went unsettled because use right holders were refusing to surrender their farms. People in these cases frequently resorted to public demonstrations, which, by about 2010, had become common in Việt Nam. The vast majority of demonstrations were by people from the same village or subdistrict (called 'commune' in the translated novel) who used legal methods to oppose authorities' decisions and actions against them and their farms. Initially, they submitted written complaints and protested at district offices, the lowest levels of government responsible for managing land. Getting no relief there, they continued to speak out, sometimes for months, even years, by demonstrating at and sending protest letters, petitions and other documents to district, provincial and national government agencies and to the land-development companies that were often participants in the land retrievals. Villagers demonstrated peacefully, typically doing little more than quietly sitting and standing while holding signs, photos and patriotic symbols. To broadcast their demonstrations, they commonly contacted Vietnamese news media; some also reached out to foreign media, the United Nations, Human Rights Watch and other international entities. Many arranged for their petitions, videos and pictures to be put on the internet. Sometimes they asked lawyers to help them file complaints.

Occasionally villagers from different communities helped and reinforced each other's demands and demonstrations. Once in a while, protesters from numerous different areas converged at the buildings and offices of targeted government agencies and businesses to create demonstrations that had hundreds of people, even over a thousand, objecting to their

xvi   The Termite Queen and Its Socio-Historical Context

farms being confiscated. Some of those demonstrations lasted for weeks. Sometimes protesters resorted to violence, usually in reaction to clubbing, tear gas and acid throwing and other physical force by government police and thugs hired by land-development companies.

Villagers' overall demands have been justice, fairness and the means to make a decent living. Usually, they wanted to retain their farms so that they could support their families. Some agreed to surrender their fields but only for compensation that was fair, for which they had a couple of measures: one, was to provide as well for their families in the future as they could now from farming; the second, was the purpose for which the land would be used if they were to leave. Villagers were known to say that they would surrender their land for less compensation if the state needed it for the good of the country. But if, as was frequently the situation, the land was for the benefit of companies, investors, home buyers and so on, then the compensation should be equal to what the land was worth in the real-estate market plus pay relocation expenses and help households find decent employment. To identify that acceptable compensation, villagers typically wanted to negotiate with those who would get the land; they objected to government authorities and companies imposing an amount on them. They suspected that buyers, after paying them a small amount, would later sell the land for considerably more and keep the difference or in some other way personally benefit.

Suspected corruption has been one reason why protesting villagers argued that district and provincial officials often acted illegally. Another reason, they said, is that authorities violated laws and regulations about land retrievals and compensation amounts. Many also claimed that authorities and their partner companies used intimidation and violence against peaceful demonstrators.

Protesters' demand for fairness and justice has gone beyond applying existing laws and regulations. They claimed that it was wrong to take land against the will of families who had served and died for their country and for the very government that was now mistreating them. Such disregard of people's sacrifices was vulgar and immoral. Another claim was that summarily confiscating land greatly favoured those who would end up getting it at the expense of those who were currently using it. Even minimal justice, villagers insisted, requires an equitable outcome for all concerned. Often villagers rejected laws authorizing the state to unilaterally reclaim farmland. Their demand to negotiate a price included the possibility that farming households could ultimately decide not to sell their land use rights, another stance at odds with national laws. Indeed, according to these claims, a family was entitled to refuse to sell regardless of price, not only because it held use rights but because it needed the land for its livelihood, it simply preferred to farm, or it had shed blood for the country.

Often authorities' initial reactions to angry villagers' complaints and demonstrations have included toleration and accommodation. District officials reacted to letters, petitions and other protests with degrees of disregard and indifference but also with conversations and meetings where people questioned the development plans, refused offered compensations and pleaded to retain their fields. Villagers' arguments and resistance caused some officials and land-development companies to increase the amount of compensation. When villagers protested outside office buildings, police usually stood by, watching and keeping participants from blocking entrances or obstructing traffic but not attempting to stop the demonstrations. National authorities, too, were often tolerant and responsive.

Land protesters have taken their complaints to national offices expecting favourable reactions there. To an extent, their expectations were realized. Beginning in 2000, national authorities sent several problem-solving teams to places generating persistent opposition to retrievals of farms, low compensation paid to holders of use rights and other land issues. Meeting with villagers, local officials and investors, these national teams and sometimes provincial ones resolved numerous contentious cases. They often found merit in villagers' criticisms and demands. So did several national agencies. In 2012, for example, the Government Inspectorate reported that nearly half of all citizen complaints (70 per cent of them concerning land appropriations) between 2008 and 2011 were entirely or partly valid.[4]

Due in part to people's criticisms and demonstrations, national authorities have revised regulations regarding land appropriation, compensation and assistance to affected people. Broadly speaking, the legal and administrative changes gradually resulted in compensation amounts to approach market values and be determined by negotiations between land-use holders and developers. In 2013, the National Assembly, partly in response to public pressure, wrote a new land law 'that effectively addressed some of the issues ... raised by experts, civil society advocates, and the media, as well as by farmers themselves' and may have contributed to fewer land repossessions in 2014–15.[5]

Besides being responsive and tolerant, however, authorities have also been repressive. Authorities have harassed those who

---

[4] 'Hoàn thiện cơ chế phối hợp giải quyết khiếu nại, tố cáo' [Improve Mechanism to Coordinate the Resolution of Complaints and Denunciations], 2 May 2012, Quân Đội Nhân Dân [People's Army], accessed 24 July 2012, http://qdnd.vn/qdndsite/vi-VN/61/43/10/50/50/186900/Default.aspx.

[5] Wells-Dang, Andrew, Pham Quang Tu and Adam Burke, 'Conversion of Land Use in Vietnam through a Political Economy Lens', Journal of Social Sciences and Humanities 2, no. 2 (2016): 139–40.

refused to give up their farms and mobilized police to break up large demonstrations, arrest participants and on numerous occasions forcibly evict villagers from their fields. For example, in April 2009, district authorities in a rural area of Hồ Chí Minh City used bulldozers and police to destroy homes, crops, fishponds and other property belonging to about 400 families. They were the last of 4,000 households in the area who had protested for years against replacing their fields with an industrial park. In an extreme case of violence, authorities in January 2020 sent hundreds of heavily armed police into a village southwest of Hà Nội where residents since 2016 had been resisting government efforts to retrieve their fields. In the event, police killed the protesters' elderly spokesman and arrested his sons and other villagers. Three policemen were also killed, possibly accidently by their fellow officers.

Việt Nam's laws and regulations make provincial and district authorities the agents responsible for repossessing land and compensating people. Because the rules and regulations governing these actions are complicated, evolving and often contradictory, these local authorities were frequently ill-informed and confused. At the same time, many officials were eager to attract investors who proposed projects that promised to diversify local economies; and a key to getting such investment was low-cost land. This helps to explain why many district and provincial authorities, instead of aiding discontented villagers and thereby avoiding protests, minimized compensation payments and ignored or dismissed villagers' demands.

Other considerations, too, have motivated officials' behaviour. Land acquired from current users at a low price could be sold to companies and investors at a higher price. With that profit, authorities could augment local government revenues for public services like healthcare and education but also maybe take some of the money for their own use. When companies dealt directly with villagers, they too strove to keep compensation low in order to reduce the project's costs. Often district and provincial officials expected, even demanded, payments from those companies. That money could be for community improvements, but some could be for the authorities themselves. Indeed, the numerous opportunities for authorities to benefit personally from land appropriations were often reasons why officials shunned villagers' claims.

THE TERMITE QUEEN

Prologue

With no literary talent, I never aspired to become a writer, and always assumed I'd follow my father's advice to study finance. As the son of a rich and famous businessman, I could study at any of the world's best universities, but as it was, literature determined the country where I would go to school.

During senior year of high school, my literature teacher taught so passionlessly, each lecture was deadly dull. But she also told us stories. I have travelled all around the world and have yet to find another storyteller as great as her. Her shoulders were slightly hunched, but she had a mesmerizing face. Whenever I think about the Virgin Mary or a goddess, my teacher's holy face fills my mind. When she told a story, each student in class looked at her beautiful lips attentively, and our hearts leapt. I personally felt a sharp pain somewhere in my tiny blood vessels and assured myself that she must be an angel. No earthly human could have her eyes, her lips and her clear, vibrato voice.

When my teacher read to us Charlotte Brontë's *Jane Eyre*, I dreamed about the day when I could visit England. Brontë herself is also an angel to me—as is her sister, Emily. I have somehow been hypnotized by their writing. When my father gave me a list of the schools he approved of where I might study, I didn't make the connection explicitly at the time, but only felt strong winds blowing me toward the moors of northern England, as depicted in Emily's *Wuthering Heights*.

I say this simply to try to articulate my strange relationship with literature. I discovered I had been fated to become a writer, albeit reluctantly, after I finished reading a book called *The Termite Queen* in a single night. Its author lived a reclusive life and rarely appeared in public, preferring instead to keep his anonymity through the use of a pseudonym. But the book challenged my courage and self-control. That night, and every moment since my father passed away, my emotions had been in absolute turmoil. Reading the book felt like reliving a painful period not only in my own life but also in the lives of those I love.

When I read the original *Termite Queen*, I identified with the character named Việt. Several passages made my face burn as hot as if I had looked into a mirror before a date and noticed pimples I needed to hide. I could even see my own thoughts in those of that character. I don't know how the author could have gained such intimate access to every single detail of my romantic experiences. But it was the sections about my father, honestly speaking, that shocked me. The author intentionally revealed the true identity of the book's main subject, despite using an abbreviation for my father's name. Any reader might find themselves drawn to such an intimate portrayal and read with great curiosity, simply because he was a famous figure who had lived an enviable life. But the book, despite being sold as nonfiction, exaggerated and fabricated his life, whether with good intentions or bad, I do not know. I didn't care much for reading about many of the narrated events, especially my father's sex scandals, which the media had already discussed to death. According to the author's note, he worried the reader might come to regard my father sympathetically, as a modern-day Red-Haired Xuân, the protagonist of Vũ Trọng Phụng's satirical novel *Dumb Luck*, an individual embodying a new epoch, an intellectual businessman who should be honoured for having overcome various tragedies in his life and who established a whole new system for doing business in my country.

I do not doubt the author's sincerity, but the book reveals his lack of talent to do the subject justice. Perhaps it was the calibre of the character and his complicated social networks that baffled the author and made him lose control of his depiction. Apparently, this is very common in creative writing. I believe my charismatic literature teacher said as much several years ago, but back then I hadn't been paying much attention. What I do recall clearly is that, when a real-life character is actually larger than life, the author can become intimidated and the work suffers.

In the Preface, the author discusses with modesty the possibility of this particular failure. But I believe the author lost direction in part because his protagonist, Mr N., had been based on distorted and even false information from a biased source who deliberately presented mistruths. The character is therefore a kind of replica of my father, in regards to personal background, mannerisms, attitude and mindset, but how it presents his path to fame and fortune looks a lot like the way the character, Red-Haired Xuân, changed his own life. Because the book is presented as nonfiction, the verifiability of all events, which actually did happen, and their contexts, is important. However, the work suffers from a careless verisimilitude. Many events have been twisted by prejudice, whether intentionally or not.

I didn't begin reading with the intention to comment on the matter, nor did I want to confront the author in person, hoping that he would make the necessary adjustments in the next edition. But as I read further, I realized that if I did not set the record straight, it would be regarded as tantamount to admitting my own weakness and irrationality. Despite all this, and ignoring the previously stated problems, the book is worth reading. I was interested in how certain events were depicted, because although they were beyond my reckoning, they were at least logically believable. The book certainly gave me a better understanding of several involved individuals, and as an insider, I knew I couldn't be objective. Thus, *The Termite Queen* bestowed upon me a better-informed perspective on the actual people who were very close to me on a daily basis. And one of those people would forever affect our family's lives, haunting us even after death.

Generally speaking, however, I could not let stand the original content of the book, especially when considering the issues directly related to my family. The question was, how could I successfully refute its many inaccuracies and misportrayals? It would be useless to write an ordinary critique, like a book review in a newspaper, because although the author wrote his book about us, as well as about actual people, events and details from our personal lives, the acronymic characters were not, legally speaking, us. I could not accuse the writer of slander and make him accountable for what he wrote.

Perhaps it was my old teacher who had told me that since literature first appeared, it has been paying the price for its ability to distort the truth and arouse suspicions. Bear in mind that a totalitarian who can burn Rome in a single night or hang any writer or philosopher on a whim is still absolutely powerless to make people reject a literary work that infuriates him. And I am a nobody, of course. So, finally, I decided to set the record straight by rewriting my father's story in my own book.

This very book you are about to read.

Rewriting was a difficult task because after everything happened—i.e., the plot of my narrative—journalists and business partners hounded me relentlessly. But the difficulty was also psychological. Would I present a version of my father even worse than his portrayal in *The Termite Queen* if my narrative was incoherent, fragmented and unreliable? Maybe it would be better to allow readers to see my father the way *The Termite Queen* showed him, rather than muddy the water with a rewrite that failed to improve upon the original. This frustrating thought consumed a great quantity of my time.

Fortunately, in the midst of my struggle to place words on the page, a writer named L. offered me invaluable help (respectfully I have abbreviated his name). He intimidates women but never equivocates and has always been utterly straightforward in his suggestions for revision. In fact, there were only a few times he tried to interfere with the plot of my book, but at all times he was obnoxiously critical. More than once his miserable face made me want to give up. Based on my experience with him, I now know writing is not a career for those who seek fame or the psychologically feeble.

I would not call my narrative a work of literature. Rather, it is an appendix to the original *Termite Queen*—my attempt to add the additional necessary details and to correct misrepresented information, depending on the event or situation. I rewrote *The Termite Queen* in my own way, based on facts that often only I was privy to. I quoted certain passages from the original verbatim when I could not rewrite them any better, and I cited them properly to avoid confusion. I apologize if the readers of this narrative are sometimes uncomfortable with the two distinct voices presented in my book that work independently of each other because they come from two unrelated narrators.

I also chose to name my book *The Termite Queen* because I wanted to pay respect to the author of the original. At the very least, he took the time to research my father and my family with apparently good intentions, and my book would not exist without his. Please consider my book, the *Termite Queen: Version Two*, or the real *Termite Queen*, which intentionally follows the *Termite Queen: Version One*, or the original *Termite Queen*.

Chapter I

I felt fortunate to be by my father's side at the moment he died.[1] I felt there was something tearing at my father's heart, even as he lay dying. I know of no other world, as people often suggest, than this world. But if there is an afterlife, my father must still be thinking about the burdens he carried with him to his grave.

I had always felt I could read most of my father's thoughts. Sometimes, when on his deathbed, he asked to see the photo of my grandparents that usually sat atop our family altar, I nearly asked him what he wished to tell me, but I never did because I kept hoping a miracle would bring him back to this world. His eyes held a secret, something surely related to my mother, my younger sister and me.

But, as I said, he took all his secrets with him to the grave.

His funeral was regarded in the media as a social event because of all the public attention it received. The shopfronts that faced the main thoroughfare voluntarily closed when my father's hearse passed by. In life, my father had been magnanimous with everyone, especially on big holidays like

---

[1] In the original *Termite Queen*, the author named the son Việt, which is my name, and had him discussing a business contract with an international hotel partner in Europe when he took the call informing him of his father's death. The son fainted, and the hotel staff had to revive him with smelling salts and a glass of water. I find this passage particularly ridiculous, as I have never fainted in my life.

the Lunar New Year, or any time donations were needed. Thousands of people came to the funeral to say farewell, and the lines of people wanting to show their gratitude stretched for kilometres down and around the block. Newspapers wrote captivating headlines about it, as if my father were a celebrity. Politicians and most of the country's extravagantly wealthy businesspeople came. Many of them were his former partners, and others were his rivals. The latter came to say farewell to the man who would no longer stand in their way or scheme to supplant them. Many people remained his good, loyal friends until the day he died. I could tell by looking at their faces. Most of them realized a door had just been shut in their faces, and hungry wolves now surrounded them. They projected both sympathy and anger, having all taken the oath to *Live together, perish together.*

But what the public wanted most desperately to know was how the regime Mr Nam—abbreviated to N. in the original *Termite Queen*—had established would survive after his death, and who would inherit his tremendous empire.

The media was ravenous for information. I must remember that.

When I came to terms with the enormity of the inheritance he'd left me, I realized just how extraordinary a man my father had been. I had lived an insulated, almost naïve childhood and thus had to ask myself: how did he manage such an extremely complicated system so smoothly that it could generate so much money every day? A great amount of money. A stupendous amount of money!

Often, the situation surprised my father, too. Those not from our generation and those who still struggled to eke out a living by saving a penny each day would never be able to imagine how my father could take money from other people so easily. But, of course, everyone wished to be in his shoes.

I saw that every time I looked into the eyes of his friends, or my friends' parents, or his business partners. They all envied him and despised him in equal measure.

After his demise, I recalled that my father had once asked me to go with him to some forested land where he had made plans to build a five-star resort. Whenever he revealed an intention, it was only a matter of time until that intention became reality. But that day, he didn't behave as usual, with his characteristic intensity of purpose. Rather, he devoted the whole visit to enjoying the tranquillity of the woods. He watched as a flock of birds flew off into the distance. Then he sighed, and I heard him mutter as if reading a line of surrealist poetry, 'Eventually, we'll all meet in that great beyond.'

With genuine curiosity I asked what he wanted to tell me, and what that far-off place was, but he answered me with a question, instead.

'Do you have plans for your future?'

Noticing I wasn't yet capable of an answer, he waved his hand.

'No need to answer now. I want you to think carefully and seriously about the path you'll choose for yourself.'

I nodded, and then asked, 'Are you pleased with your own choice?'

He threw the stone he'd been holding into the lake. He cried out cheerfully as a child as it skipped over the surface several times before sinking. The lake would be the resort's primary attraction.

'When I was a kid,' he said to me, 'we had to create our own games. I was so poor that my clothes never fit right. We had no toys. Skipping stones cost nothing, and it exercised the body and eyes. You have to have some skill to do it well. I could skip stones all day with a friend and never get tired.'

He flung another stone, this one making ten, eleven, twelve skips before it sank.

'Let me tell you a story, one you should give some thought to,' he said. And then, as some other impulse crossed his brow, he changed his mind. 'We'll save it for another day,' he said. 'We should just enjoy our time together. It's been so long since I did something just for fun.'

My father never did anything on a whim. I think he had been about to tell me, his only son in whom he had placed so much hope, something very important. But after considering it alongside our light-hearted mood, he changed his mind. I had just finished my first year at university and had returned home for summer vacation. I did not yet have any serious thoughts about what I wanted to do with my future, including marriage. All I wanted was to explore new things. When a problem arose, I often thought about it for a long time and came up with a satisfying solution. For example, many years ago, when I was a kid, I needed to manage many difficult issues. Back then, newspapers talked about projects that my father planned to invest in, and I didn't know whether they were praising him or warning him of the risks. One night, my father came home after midnight, looking exhausted and depressed. He stood motionless as my mother helped him out of his coat, and then fell right into his favourite chair, a gift from a business partner and upholstered with Spanish leather. He loved to caress the leather—like a cattleman grazing his fingertips along a heifer's flank to estimate how much it might be worth. But that night, he could not get comfortable in the stiff leather chair, so he shifted his weight from one side to the other, as if something hard lurked underneath. He gulped down a glass of water my mother brought him, and then blew out a deep breath and launched into a complaint. I rarely saw him do this.

'I want to give everything up,' he said. 'I'm so exhausted.'

My mother knew what to do in such a situation: she just sat beside him quietly. It was the best way she could alleviate his anger and frustration. She was fully aware of everything happening in the world, especially the things related to my father, who always said he was grateful to her for all she did, including giving birth to two children, whom he loved dearly. She let him say whatever he needed to say when he experienced a predicament. In this money-driven society, a lot of young, beautiful women wanted to be his mistress, especially given his wealth and reputation. My mother was fully aware that he had cheated on her with many beautiful women at resorts, both here and abroad. She even knew who some of the women were—famous actresses, singers, models, journalists and even beauty queens.

My father was very generous with women.

So, I couldn't imagine what my parents were thinking when she would rest her hand on his arm like that, or what they would even talk about, considering she heard rumours about him pretty much every day. But one thing I knew for sure was that, despite his affairs, he loved my mother the most.

That night, after sitting quietly next to my father, my mother prepared clean pyjamas for him and ran him a hot bath. Then, she went to bed. Perhaps, I thought, as usual, she knew that he needed her to comfort him. No one could do it but my mother.

But I was wrong. That night, she slept by herself in another room. The following morning, she got up early, prepared his clothes for the day, put a few pieces of ginseng and a multivitamin into his pocket because he didn't always get to eat at mealtimes, and also some ultra-soft tissues that luxury hotels often used. It was the first time I became curious about all the things she did for him and why. It was as if my father was preparing to take a competitive test.

Incense wafted from the altar room where he stood in his expensive suit whispering prayers I could not hear. On the altar rested the photo of my grandfather, who I later learnt had no blood relationship with me, and a totemic figurine of a very important person. When he knelt in front of the altar and looked up so reverently, did he pray for anything in particular, or believe that his prayers would be heard? I didn't know then and will never know. But when he emerged from the altar room, he looked as if a burden had been lifted from his shoulders.

He asked my mother a few questions, obviously quite pleased with the things she had prepared for him. He picked up his briefcase from the floor, popped open the lock, looked inside for a few seconds and then closed it. He thought about something for a few moments and then opened the briefcase again. This time, he removed a stack of envelopes of varying thicknesses. He sorted them out into smaller stacks and calculated something in his mind. Then, he instructed my mother to prepare five more envelopes for him. He changed his mind and said, 'No, not five. I need ten.' As she left the kitchen to get the envelopes, he mumbled, 'Such a bunch of bastards! They can smell money from a mile away!'

My mother said nothing because she knew what was going on and she was used to this. It didn't take her long to come back with a stack of money and envelopes, arranged evenly into little bundles she held between her fingers. She put a sheaf of bills into each envelope and licked them shut. She did everything skilfully like a fan artist. While she finished with the envelopes, he was calculating something with his fingers. They knew what to do just by looking at each other's fingers.

My father sat down to drink a cup of coffee and eat a small bowl of bird's nest soup, and then he went into his room to retrieve a square parcel wrapped in pink paper that he carefully slid into his jacket pocket.

What is that? I wondered. *Why are there envelopes filled with money and a square parcel?* I heard a car start and then idle softly on the street.

My mother adjusted my father's jacket collar and wished him good luck. He murmured back, 'I hope so,' before stepping out the door.

I crept back to bed and rested my face on the pillow. I truly did not want to think about it. The last few stars were about to vanish from the sky.

The car door shut gently. My father normally didn't shut the door like that. The sound of the car shifted and then faded. I leapt from the bed and through the window saw the car's red taillights disappear at the end of the block. It was still dark and cold outside. I didn't know why he had to leave so early.

Where is he going? I wondered, *and what will he do there?* My mother's silence and anxiety from the moment before, as well as the bitterness my father had tried to suppress as he repacked the envelopes came to my mind. *Why does he need those envelopes, and that parcel?*

He came home that evening and as before slumped his big body into the leather chair, letting the briefcase topple to the floor. Very early the following morning, I peered out from my bedroom and secretly observed my parents as they went through nearly the same routine. The look on my father's face seemed to say he wanted to give up. He embraced her and she asked, 'Must we do this all the time? We have everything already.' He nodded and said to her, 'We have so much, but I am never happy. Have I made your life miserable?'

She leaned her head against his chest and patted his shoulders.

'You'll be lucky today,' she said. 'You don't live just for yourself.'

He leaned away from her and said softly, 'Thank you, dear.'

That morning, he stood for a moment at the front door but then turned back and hugged her tightly. He kissed her, and his body trembled as if it would soon explode.

'Let's move somewhere far away,' he said. 'A peaceful place. Just the two of us and our children. Let's leave everything behind. I'll tell them I'm quitting to take care of my health. I don't care who'll get stuck. We can go to Europe, Japan, even Africa ... let's run away. Just say the word.'

'I married you when you were penniless,' my mother said. 'God knows that! And we were so happy back then. You can look at our children and see what I said is true. They look like you. They are smart, good people. Now you are rich, and we all have benefited from your wealth. But do people think I'm the one who never feels it's enough? That I keep pushing you to chase after more? I don't care what they think. But if you think about me as they do, my life would be over.'

She looked stricken, and he had to apologize. He held her and kissed her face as she struggled to hold back her tears. Then he picked up his briefcase, adjusted his collar and looked excited again. Only after he got into the car and it raced away into the quiet, foggy morning did she sit down and cry.

Many mornings were like this when I was a child, and I asked myself, *What is going on with my parents?*

***

After my father passed away, I inherited his role as president and CEO of the company because the majority shareholder stocks he had held were now in my name. Naively, I felt mature enough to accept the position. He had been preparing me for precisely such a moment since I was a college student so that, when the day came, I would not fear to sit in his chair. Even so, I never desired the position. And as it turned out, it proved too much for me to handle.

My education took place in a country where transparency reigned. Now I had to get used to acting in ways I detested. Sitting in his chair, I realized he had not been as powerful as he had seemed. The people who actually ran the company always remained in the shadows, and even I did not know who all of them were. Everywhere I turned, I found yet another schemer trying to take over. They would destroy everything my father had built in a single night. My mother didn't have to tell me this. I knew it. These cutthroats were in fact my father's partners, and it was they, I assumed, who caused his death. This assumption made me braver. My father had shed blood, sweat, toil and tears to make the company prosper, and I would not let it fall into someone else's hands so easily.

I decided to take on my father's role despite their resistance. There were also others in the shadows who couldn't care less what I did, because to them, I had his title but no power. I swore to myself that I would make anyone who tried to intimidate or manipulate me pay a hard price. I had inherited my father's genes and surprised many people with my capability to do the job.

As my first task, I went through the mountains of paperwork that my father had left, which gave me a deeper understanding of all the work he had done and that I would do from now on. I became fully aware that I existed only within a world that he had created. The paperwork revealed to me many of the secret business deals my father had made and bribes he had paid, as well as the identities of some of his shadow partners. In the company, these secret partners were regarded as godfathers. Many of them had invested their power or connections or social status, rather than actual money. I had learnt in school that such arrangements were common in developing countries, but in reality, the situation was far more complicated than a textbook could express. The godfathers were, in fact, vultures who had no sympathy for their prey, even after it had been torn to pieces and began to rot. Many of them reached out to me after my father's funeral to offer condolences and to warn me to stay out of their way. I needed only to carry out my official duties, while they would make the important decisions behind the scenes.

Only later did I realize how long this arrangement had been in place.

Soon after I took over my father's role, the board of trustees—the godfathers—the old wolves—drew my attention to a golf course project that the company had begun. When complete, the project would earn a huge profit and bring a lot of prestige to the company. The initial paperwork had nearly been finished. The golf course would be the key attraction for a tourist resort community planned by the government. The community masterplan had already been approved and the golf course contract would be issued to the developer that satisfied the financial prerequisites and that had the best strategy for the construction, technological solutions and environmental protections. That meant, in theory, the project would be very competitive. But in reality, my company would certainly win the contract thanks to the intelligence and vision of people who understood that *Money offered first is best.*

We anticipated all parts of the project from the beginning: planning, resettlement, compensation, risk assessment and training for citizens who would need new jobs. But our thoroughness, which we publicized, did not guarantee we'd get the contract. I was told that our shadow partners had invested an enormous amount of social and political capital in addition to their money and that many people had been involved so that our company would prevail, and the business 'regime' named after my father would remain unvanquished.

My father had grown famous for seizing opportunities and seeing potential that no one else did. He had developed countless ways to find out which projects would become gold or diamond mines. The golf course was one such place.

Ten years ago, it was just another backwater no one cared about. The people living there didn't even have enough food to eat. Only my father and his partners had known that the town had been designated as the site of this future resort development. Of course, he had to spend a lot of money to get this information. Technically, the rural area would be classified as a suburb according to the confidential zoning plans. The zoning map had not even been drawn yet when we began, and it would probably take a long time for the project to become a reality. But eventually, it would be realized. My father had been certain about this and as an experienced businessman—along with the shadow partners' assistance and advice, of course— would never let such a lucrative opportunity go to anyone else.

Only a juggernaut of an operation like his could dare invest. My father recognized there was a certain amount of risk, but he knew how to bide his time. What if the golf course hadn't been approved by all the necessary parties? What if the project's proponents were no longer powerful because they died or were forced to step down? What if some busybody changed the zoning plan, and there would be no golf course at all? Anything was possible.

My father had been successful because he had been forward-looking, adventurous, self-confident and self-determined. But the real reasons that forced him to take action, as far as I could tell, were not what people imagined.

I needed to retrace my father's footsteps and learn from him. First, I called a board meeting that my mother also attended because she was—of her own accord—a primary shareholder. I spoke briefly about the project my father had not yet completed. The board reminded me that the project had already consumed a vast sum of money but had not yet accomplished anything. Of course, we would earn that money back and more if we could obtain the final permit and complete the project. Everyone knew that—it went without saying. However, I wanted to be careful and hear the board's opinions whether we should continue and what they thought the next steps should be, even though I already knew the answers. I think the board members could tell I had called the meeting just to reassure myself. They knew as well as I that we were sitting on an untamed elephant and whoever wanted to give up and jump off would end up trampled.

In the car on our way home, my mother buried herself deep in thought. Then at last she sighed and said, 'If you need anything, let me know. I handled everything for your father. I can do the same for you.'

Did she mean the envelopes and the money I had seen so many times when I was a child? I could not bring myself to ask. I did not want her to be involved.

During my first week at work, I had to compose respectful letters to the company's many business partners to assure them of my eagerness to continue our work together. Nothing would be affected by my father's sudden death. I had no difficulty writing the letters, which were replied to rather quickly. Everyone congratulated me on my new leadership position. 'Like father, like son,' they said. They sounded sincere as they expressed their desire to continue our cooperation.

I had never met most of the people who sent me responses. Most replied as individuals and did not mention their positions or affiliations. I paid close attention to a letter whose scribbled print was like water bubbling up from a spring. Below it was the simple signature, Mr Big. The letter[2] read:

---

[2] In the original *Termite Queen*, this letter does not exist despite being a very important detail that greatly impacted what would happen to me.

Congratulations on the maturity you've shown in your recent letter!

In all things, you should try to emulate your talented father, who was respected by everyone and admired for his lifelong dedication to the company and for maintaining the welfare of the shareholders and his own family.

I look forward to meeting you in person one day soon.

I studied the letter, trying to conjure memories of this man, but I could not picture him. My vision became blurry. Was Mr Big a part of my life? His name seemed so familiar, but who was he? I debated whether to ask my mother. When I finally did, she said that she had never been introduced to anyone with that name (she hesitated before her answer) but believed he had come to our house several times, dined with us and had taken part in many important decisions about the company. Whether at dawn or in the twilight, she felt she could always just barely perceive the shadow of an invisible person like him whose real name she could not recall. Sometimes, she said, it felt as if he was the shadow of a giant. But it was just a feeling, she said, and then provided no specific details. How could she have any evidence of him if his actions always remained behind the scenes? And then, as I had done, she tried to recall every single face she had ever met through my father, trying to figure out which one belonged to Mr Big, or when his actions may have been perceptible. The times when my father had hurriedly left the house in a panic and seemed as if he had been called to meet his maker. The others when, in their bed late at night, my mother would wake to find my father restless, consumed with concerns. She said those were the times she'd hear him mumbling a name that now she remembered as being Mr Big. It seemed to her now, she said, that without Mr Big, nothing could have been accomplished.

It was then that I realized it would be difficult to share my thoughts about this matter with her. Even she could not speak of him directly.

Thus, I began to guess at the kinds of things she had done in the early mornings—the times I thought I had been dreaming while my father was pacing back and forth in the house. Did it have anything to do with Mr Big? Back then I had simply thought it was my father's job, though I was still unhappy when he didn't join us for dinner for several days in a row. My mother hadn't seemed worried, as if she knew where he was, what he was doing and who was helping him.

Then, I went to England to study and became distant to that familiar home life.

And now, I had to recall every hazy memory and connect each fragmented image I had ever seen. Several faces seemed likely possibilities, but before I confronted them, I needed to know more about Mr Big. Who was he in real life? and what kind of relationship did he have with my father?

I could not yet answer those questions but felt no rush.

I had been told not to procrastinate with the golf course. Several sharks had begun to circle the waters around us. Many had come very close, anticipating the moment we dropped the bait so they could swallow it. *The same fish can't be eaten twice.*

First and foremost, I had to find time to visit the site where the new golf course would be built. When my father was alive, he had tantalized the local district officials with the many benefits that would come to the partners who agreed to collaborate. He made sure they knew it would be best if there was little administrative reorganization and these officials were still in their positions for the next five to ten years. Most of them lacked talent, which they replaced effusively with self-esteem. Fully aware of their tarnished reputations in the opinions of their subordinates and supervisors, they had long ago forsaken their dignity and instead focused entirely on their own individual welfare. More specifically, they wanted money. They had to be absolutely certain about the outcomes while they were still in power. And if the development plans took a long time to come to fruition, after their power went to someone else, they needed assurances that any new official would be legally required to fulfil the original agreement.

The chairman of the local district, whom I had met when I accompanied my father a few times as his assistant, walked with a stooped spine but reminded me of an experienced and cunning fox. Thanks to several consecutive promotions, he had risen from running a gristmill to being the chairman of the district. He climbed the ranks slowly but each step he made was sound. If necessary, he would crawl, or even slide like a snail, but he would always eventually reach his destination. Unfortunately, when we first started work on the plan for the golf course, he had only one-third of his term left as district chairman. That meant he had no time for delay. Evasive conversations would only waste minutes and cause misunderstandings. Whenever we requested his assistance, he would ask, 'How much will I get for doing this?' At first, such candour seemed to embarrass him, but then he got used to it. His life philosophy came to be: *Mind your own business.*

He knew he could deliver what my father needed. He could sell it wholesale or retail, however my father wished it. When I went to visit him, I passed a mansion that stood beside a pond and featured a curved driveway that allowed visitors to savour the lot's natural beauty. He had recently held a grand house-warming ceremony for its construction with my father's money—or to be more correct, the company's money, with my father in charge of doling it out. I hadn't been told outright about their arrangement. I simply overheard the district chairman complain to my father about what he needed—an agreed upon way for him to ask for what he wanted. The district chairman lived at the mansion when the weather was pleasant. Of course, someone from his staff always stayed there with him, too. It was well known that he slept with most of the women who worked for him, regardless of their age, but his favourite was a high-school physical-education teacher. Her husband was also a teacher, but because he had tuberculosis, he couldn't keep tabs on her. She had a healthy, tan complexion and they began their affair after meeting at a district celebration for a national holiday.

The district chairman always said he supported my father's project with all the sincere power of his office because he was a leader who prioritized the nation's well-being. He promised my father he would do his best to persuade his constituents to give up their land so the project would become a reality.

'My words are worth a truckload of your money,' he liked to say.

In front of me, the district chairman pretended he was joking, but anyone could tell what he meant. After he uttered those words, he looked at my father playfully, as if they could read each other's thoughts and shared the same hobbies.

My father nodded. 'I understand completely,' he said. But in the car on the way home, he said to me, 'That man can do only one thing well.' After a moment, he corrected himself and said, 'Actually no, maybe there are a few things …'

But money didn't grow on trees. I would not be generous like my father, especially with professional robbers. According to my father's reliable consultants, I wouldn't need to continue to deal with the district chairman, because he had already been taken care of—with money, cars and virgin girls, as it turned out—things I didn't know about until much later. I would, however, need to create a convincing display that we already had approval from a higher authority and then deal with the landowners whose property would be affected by the project.

The district chairman had once said, indirectly, that if the locals protested the project, he wouldn't have the public-relations skills to suppress them, and if a higher authority didn't approve the project, it wouldn't be his fault. Either way, he didn't want his cut to be affected. In other words, his office was just a front that mostly did nothing but stay quiet and take the money. The head of the project would have to take care of everything.

It was a very clever strategy for a gristmill man.

Chapter II

According to the planning map, two starfish-shaped ponds located between low hills would be the twin jewels of the golf course. Currently, two brothers cultivated fish in the ponds under a lease from the district. They had completed a lot of work by hand to enlarge them to nearly twice their original size and had made them both beautiful and productive. The project's landscape architects had incorporated the ponds' distinctive shape into their design—in fact, had made them the heart and soul of the course. Without them, the project would be worth far less.

I arranged to spend an entire day visiting the proposed development zone. Half-mountain, half-grassland, the landscape was beautiful and pristine. The grassland remained fertile thanks to the mineral-rich runoff from the surrounding hills when it rained. The great variety of produce found at the market revealed how productive this countryside was. Its residents never expected they'd have to resettle elsewhere. I understood completely.

My father's former assistants and I skipped visiting the district chairman's office and went straight to the commune officials to establish a close relationship with their chairman. I knew the proverb by heart, *The emperor's rule ends at the village gate*. It was the cornerstone of my father's business philosophy. When we entered the commune headquarters, several of the officials were gathered around a table playing cards—a common way to kill time they never seemed to tire of. Other low-ranking officials lounged on the sofas, chatting about sex, taking turns sharing how to seduce women and boasting about the number of their affairs. Married and unmarried women alike got naked in their vulgar conversation, and they cackled like hyenas with each half-witted obscenity. They seemed nearly indifferent to our arrival. Eventually, we were able to meet the commune chairman—the most important leader in Đồng Village. His residents were the ones we would have to relocate. His clothes appeared dishevelled, as if he had just rushed there from somewhere else. He peered at each of us over his spectacles for a moment and then signalled to his staff to get back to work. I could feel the power he held. He led us into his office and gestured for us to sit down on a bench across from his desk. He said nothing as he prepared tea while gazing out the window.

After a long while, he asked, 'Did you come here directly, or have you already visited the district headquarters?'

'We came here directly,' I said. 'Our most important task is to hear your concerns about the project that's about to get underway.'

The commune chairman rubbed his chin. 'Please have some tea,' he said as he poured out several cups. 'I had heard from the district that the government wants to build a golf course here. Goddamn! Why do you need to build so many golf courses? Are you trying to evict us?'

'We have only the best intentions toward the residents,' a member of my delegation replied quickly.

'What kind of intentions?' the commune chairman asked in a flat tone. 'Would it be *best* to steal our land, dry the rice paddies to grow grass, pour sand and chemicals to make the soil infertile and then make our displaced citizens your groundskeepers and garbage diggers?'

With a manic look in his eye, he let rip an overly forced and sarcastic laugh, as if sick of listening to nonsense but too uncomfortable to continue to speak so straightforwardly. 'Of course not!' I said. Several scars twisted his face and I realized I didn't know him well enough to know whether they were caused by having fought in the war or some kind of accident. 'Citizens who want to work will be able to find many new and exciting careers,' I explained. 'We just need to replace a few things, and everything will be different. For example, rice, vegetables and fish will be converted into money. And with money, everyone can buy things of much greater value.'

'Ah . . . ha,' the chairman said, in a kind of laugh with no spirit. 'That sounds nice. But when will all this happen, Mr Capitalist?' He stared straight into my eyes. 'Next century, or just after we're dead? You, of course, will live longer than me to enjoy it, but all the people my age will be dead by then. I would be glad if what you just said came true one day, but . . . honestly speaking, we're all quite sick of honeyed words. Let me ask you something: did anyone tell you about the things the big bosses have done to this commune? They've done horrible things. You'll know all about them eventually, so I won't say anything now. I'll just say, simply, that for years, we've been living quite well without a golf course. Now please get the hell out of here and leave us alone. This is our citizens' collective wish.'

'We can't do that. It's too late now,' I said. I had learnt how to talk like a totalitarian and I was determined. 'You know what *policy* means, don't you? The commune has little to say about this business.' I pointed my finger into the air and added, 'The policy comes from above.'

But I miscalculated.

The chairman was not like what I expected.

A fierce anger clouded his face and he jerked up his chin. 'What are you talking about?' he said. 'Don't threaten us.

No one would side with a bunch of thieves. The colonizers and the imperialists couldn't intimidate us, and you and your cronies are nobodies—just mosquitoes. A few days ago, in the office of the district chairman, I explained to him that we don't need a golf course, and we don't want our children to become whores. That under your plan, with a golf course built here, the grass will become poisonous, and our children, deformed beggars. The district chairman just scoffed and then threatened us like you just did. I'll tell you what I told him. I pointed to these scars like this and said, "Look at me, goddamn it! During the war I was lucky that bullet didn't hit me directly, or my brain would have been blown all over the Trường Sơn Mountains. I survived that, and if I've made it this far, I'm not scared of death, and I sure as hell am not scared of you.'"

'What are you trying to say?' I asked.

'Don't even think about trying to kill us,' he growled, 'because it would be a waste of money to hire murderers. We know the consequences. You want to take away our land and sell it to other investors when the price goes up, right? We know everything. We're not gullible.'

'No one wants to murder you,' I said. 'In fact, we're discussing ways to improve the quality of your life.'

'That's enough,' he said, cutting the air with his hand. 'We're doing just fine. We know how to make our lives better ourselves.' He continued to stare at my face. 'Who are you, anyway? You look familiar.'

I introduced myself, reminded him that he had met my father, and explained that after his death, I took over the family business.

The commune chairman swallowed back a look of surprise. Then he said, 'Lucky me! I won't have to meet him again.' He retrieved a small parcel from one of his drawers and set it on top of his desk. I recognized the package instantly. It was the same as those I had seen my mother place so many times into my father's briefcase. 'Please take this with you. I have never had this much money in my life, but even so it's not enough to remove the scars from my face.'

This meeting with the commune chairman was proving more difficult than I imagined. My father had once told me, *If you can buy something with money, it's cheap.* And he made me learn another proverb by heart: *If something can't be bought with money, it can be bought with more money.* I took three additional parcels from my briefcase and placed them next to the first. I spoke in a friendly voice to the chairman.

'Unfortunately, my father died because of a terrible illness.'

The chairman blinked.

'But before he passed away, he told me he wanted to give you these. As a good and faithful son, I must follow my father's wishes. Please accept them and help me to fulfil his request.'

'I am sorry to hear about his death.' Now the chairman seemed a little regretful. He lowered his head and said, 'When he came here last, he looked so healthy. How could he get sick and die so suddenly?'

He looked up, right into my eyes, and let the question go unanswered.

'Your father's wishes did not end with giving me these parcels,' he murmured. 'And as I said, your compensation is nothing compared to what we stand to lose. Don't drop your cash and call it benevolence, Mr Young-and-Handsome Man! I know your father was essentially a good guy and I like you, but I cannot allow you to turn our children into alley cats. I know a lot of people who spend all their time trying to deflower virgin girls so they can brag about it later. I also know an equal number who spread syphilis, HIV and many other filthy things. People like that would flock here. We'd have to build fences just to stop them from entering our villages. It would be horrible! So, please, take back these "gifts" from your father.'

'Perhaps you misunderstand,' I said. 'Whether we build a golf course or something else, it will benefit all of you. See the lake over there? How many tons of fish do you harvest per year? How many tons of rice from the land around it? It's chickenfeed. Would a hundred more ducks make your life any better? Would the children be able to enjoy the best education? I visited a few families before coming here and noticed most of their gardens had been abandoned. They had no cows or chickens. I saw only dog shit and weeds.'

I paused to observe the chairman's reaction, though it was hard to read. Then I continued, 'If we build a golf course here, there'll be a lot of well-paying jobs. Your people will be able to wear nice clothes. The whole commune's infrastructure will be improved, and everyone will enjoy the numerous benefits generated by the golf course. There'll be restaurants, hotels, gear and clothing shops, spas and massage parlours, gift shops and more. You can all make a lot of money from wealthy golfers. They may be capitalists, but they're still human! They're not tigers. You don't have to be frightened of them. Just take them to the cleaners! And the biggest benefit isn't even the money ...'

'Oh!' the chairman interjected. 'You're making me cry.'

I admit, his sarcasm rankled, and made me want to show him my true power.

But then he added, 'Let me tell you—if we follow your plan, a few thousand of our people will be trapped like monkeys in a cage. You developers don't care what they'll have to do to feed themselves, because to you they are just ignorant peasants. And they won't be able to blame anyone but themselves because they'll fall for your sugary words. Hundreds of hectares of land and water will be poisoned so not a single tree will grow. The lucky ones among us will become servants, whores and gigolos for your wealthy degenerates. The rest will be garbage diggers, gangsters and drug addicts. Even worse, and please pardon my language, there'll be nothing but shit, not the fairy dreamland you say. Our people will die gradually of disease after you've exploited everything. Let me reiterate the reality: the whole ecosystem where birds, fish, people and other organisms all live in harmony will turn into a wasteland. Nothing will be able to survive. Humans will devolve into wild animals. This has been our land for generations, but if we want to set foot on your golf course, we'll have to beg and clean our mud-stained shoes. We will only have whatever you deign to give us. Let me ask you this: if money is not the greatest benefit, why are you trying so hard to convince us to give up our land? I'm sure it has nothing to do with ethics, or morality, or anything but money. My apologies for being so direct.'

'All right,' I said. 'That's fine. I hope you will eventually understand our good intentions. There's no use arguing about it now. We still need to discuss everything thoroughly, and nothing will happen right away. This is just the plan that has been decided upon from up above, and we wanted to give you plenty of time to prepare. Please keep those parcels, and if you want to return them, you can do it next time.'

'Don't you understand this is our last time meeting as friends?' he asked. 'If you come here again to talk about the golf course, we'll receive you as our enemy. I'm not joking. All you low-ranking and high-ranking officials are bastards. You only know how to exploit people. I don't want your money because I am not a bastard. If you don't believe what I'm saying, just try me.'

Leaving the chairman's office, I felt rattled. I needed to investigate who this guy really was and figure out a way around him to keep the project moving forward. Moreover, his comments stung like bees. I couldn't ignore such a passionate speech. The meeting confirmed two things, however: my father had been an excellent businessman with good vision, and he had known the right time to get things going. How had he alone been able to envision a modern, luxury golf course in this hilly, desolate area? It would certainly be the perfect place for a golf course thanks to its geography and picturesque scenery, yet several years ago, if you had told people here you were buying land for their dogs to shit on, nobody would have raised an eyebrow. But now, it had become so desirable that every developer in the country had begun to circle it like a school of money-grubbing sharks. My father had taken the risk to get the project started when he did because he knew how the market would behave.

In the past, when I joined my father on his business trips, I had noticed how interested he was in the potential of golf courses. On the other hand, he had not paid much attention to the commune chairman's resistance, since peasant heroes like him had tried to stand in my father's way before. And there was no single way to deal with them—one had to learn from each experience. I wished I had my father's courage. He rarely grew frustrated or lost his temper. He always acted respectfully, as if it were just a matter of doing his duty. And so, he never seemed too concerned about how people's lives might change after a golf course had been built, simply because it was not his business. His sole duty had been to contribute to the development of a project, and it seemed to me he didn't care much who would be affected, who would benefit, or how the benefits would be shared.

I would have to present the project's difficulties in a meeting with the partners the following week. But first, I needed to sit down and think seriously about what the commune chairman had said because I had not yet ever considered the issues he raised. Even so, my primary obstacle, in fact, would come from another direction.

Chapter III

I would have to visit the district chairman again—my second official meeting with him after I took over my father's position. In the past, I had been my father's assistant, so, in the district chairman's eyes, I was still an outsider, the son of a capitalist and probably a spoiled brat. Although I had a PhD in finance from a country famous for higher education and political power, he couldn't care less about what I said, probably because he thought he could learn nothing from me. His arrogant demeanour suggested he felt he didn't have to listen to anyone.

To my face he said, 'You're just a kid. You know nothing about adult business. Regardless of your education in England or America, you're worthless here.'

The week before that second meeting with the district chairman, I had suffered through a heated conversation with my colleagues, most of whom were board members. I still hadn't met all of them due to vaguely explained sensitivities. Only a few ever came to the meetings, but they convincingly claimed to represent the wishes of the whole board. Nonetheless, despite being out of sight, those secret partners were actual human beings who could always interfere with important decisions at any time. To them, the golf course was such a lucrative project that they demanded to be involved, even if secretly. My father had ridden a tiger, and now I sat atop the beast. Even if I wanted

to give up after hearing the commune chairman's logical
objections, it was too late. To get rich, one must be heartless.

With the board members present, I talked about my meeting
with the commune chairman, emphasizing his concerns
regarding the thousands of people in his care. I told them,
'He's an unusual leader. He knows very well that he himself is
a nobody, a mote of dust, and that he can't fight against the
decisions made above him. He must support them. But he also
considers himself a hero whose ethics demand that he ensure his
people's welfare by sacrificing himself through confrontation.
His arguments have led me to wonder whether it's necessary for
us to go through with this project at all costs. I mean, shouldn't
we listen to the wishes of thousands of people?'

At first, my question was not immediately answered, as if
everyone thought I was still giving a long speech that shouldn't
be interrupted.

'There's no room for sympathy here!' exclaimed one of the
godfathers at last, as if he were the one running the meeting and
what I had just said was irrelevant. 'We are here to discuss how
to best develop the project.'

'Let's stick to business,' said another.

I observed my mother, who remained silent. She wanted
me to learn to manage these difficult confrontations and she
was there to determine whether it came to me naturally now
that I was in charge. Or at least that's what I thought.

I repeated myself. 'Everyone, please just consider what I'm
saying. Do we really need to force this golf course project through
despite the bad reputation it will give us? Especially when we
don't have a magic wand to wave all these problems away?'

'Surely, you're joking, Mr New Chairman!' blurted another
of the godfather board members before covering his mouth
as he laughed. 'Now is not the time for us to discuss that
insignificant commune chairman's nonsense. If needed, he can

be thrown in jail, just as we've done with inconvenient people at other projects. After that, he'll no longer be in our way. There are things we cannot give up or we'll be dead in the water.' He had started out laughing, but by the end of his speech, his tone was intimidating.

Other members of the board joined in.

'Who does the commune chairman think he is? He's a frog squatting in a well who thinks he understands the world. Show him how a frog is skinned and fried. The only issue here is whether it's worth the effort to skin the bastard alive!'

'If we didn't want his people to have a better life, we wouldn't go to the trouble of obtaining an investment licence for the golf course. Let us remind you, New Chairman, that your father put a lot of effort into this project. The company's money is our money and other people's money too. And, money is blood! I went to meetings like those before with your father and I know we're riding a tiger. It could kill us if we fall off its back, and now many people are beating the tiger with sticks to make sure that happens.'

'In a situation like this, we either go all the way or die trying.'

'The bottom line is that if the project is canned, a huge amount of our money—everything paid under the table so far—will be wasted and gone. The new chairman must be aware of this. And it's not just us. Our shareholders will not accept such a loss. Besides, if we pull out, others will jump in, so you can forget about all these so-called ethics.'

'With enough money, we actually do have a magic wand. What we need is a leader with courage.'

'Let's continue the discussion of how to proceed,' said the board member who had spoken first. 'We don't need to waste any more time on this nonsense.'

Their comments had made a mockery of my concerns and left me feeling utterly humiliated. At midnight, when I got up to drink tea to soothe my emotions, I found my mother sitting at my father's desk with a photo of her and my father in her hand. I smelled incense. She must have been thinking about him. She often burned incense on the family altar when we, her children, could not fill the emptiness in her heart.

When she noticed me standing there, she said, 'I lit some incense and asked your father to help you.'

I thanked her.

She said, 'Go back to bed, son. You have a busy day tomorrow. Honestly, I wish you'd resign and stop doing your father's work. Can't you just give it all up? We have enough money to live comfortably for the rest of our lives. There's no need to earn more. Your father was thinking this exact same thing on his deathbed. He had wanted to tell you. But I don't have the right to speak for him now. He invested his whole life into the company, and now many people want to take it away from his family—I don't think he would like that either. Plus, to give something up is not so simple. You must be strong, and if you want peace, you must fight until your last breath.'

I understood my mother's contradictions and sympathized with her because of her unspeakable sorrow. I have a younger sister, and my mother didn't need to spell out that, if I gave up, it was possible that she might not have everything she wanted or needed. My mother wanted me to act strong and confident as an example for my sister as she approached adulthood. I also think, perhaps most importantly, that as long as our business was running, my mother could, in a way, still feel as if she were by my father's side.

***

When I walked into the meeting at the district chairman's office, his lips curved into a smile, and he looked me over from head to toe as if appraising how much I was worth and whether he should cooperate.

'Your father, Mr Nam, was a generous man,' he said meaningfully. 'I hope his son has inherited his genes.'

'Sir, I wish I could be half the man my father was.'

'Like father, like son. You're so tactful. I know what you want to say. I'm ready! You should remember that before you sit in that chair, I had to keep it clean for your father and others like your father to sit in for many years. It disgusted me.' He looked away for a moment, a nasty expression flickering across his face. 'Imagine that you're a servant, but your boss is a repulsive, stupid bastard. You wish he would die in an accident, but he lives on, forever polluting the environment. And so, you must continue to kneel before him, clean his chair meticulously, tell him what he wants to hear and give him gifts that make him happy and his family proud—nothing is more shameful. But that's life. Life is shitty, but if you know the way, you can enjoy its sweetness. I'm aware of the price I have to pay.'

The district chairman now smiled and shook my hand, a gesture to indicate our mutual understanding. Then he continued, 'I know you're not comfortable with the commune chairman. He is stubborn and eccentric, but he's good at his job and well-liked by his people, who aren't easy to deal with. It would be easier if we could just make him step down, but I can't find anything he's done wrong publicly to justify it. He's the only one who can deal with those ignorant, stubborn bumpkins, who act like they might revolt at any moment. Remember that the French failed to suppress that area. They kept finding people they thought were in charge, but the insurrection continued. Later, they discovered that the true leader orchestrating all the French assassinations from the shadows was a shaman with rheumy eyes. That was the commune chairman's father. Like father, like son—fearless. Thousands of households cherished the commune chairman's father, so you cannot play games with them. Damn it! If they all came here one day and occupied the district headquarters, you and I would be in serious trouble. You just have to endure him as long as you can.'

'I was hoping you actually had a plan,' I said, 'not just vague advice.'

'Well, this is our only option. Put up with him for now and wait for an opportunity. Watch those wild peasants carefully and postpone your plans as necessary to find the best way forward. Be patient as long as you can. Then, do what your father did many times—he never failed.' The district chairman blinked his eyes and shrugged.

I had to think about what he said.

'We've tried—' I began.

'Keep trying,' he said. 'One time, two times, three—that's not enough. Let me tell you a story, and don't misunderstand it. Once upon a time, there was a not-very-high-ranking mandarin, just like me, who was known for his righteousness. A trader wanted to do business in his territory, just like you want to build a golf course.' He pointed at me. 'Again, don't misconstrue my story. I don't deal in insinuations. The trader wanted to bribe the mandarin, and the first bribe was ten taels of gold. The mandarin refused, saying, "A state official must take care of his people and treat them like his aging parents. He can't take bribes to do them harm. I would rather be a dog than take your money." The second time, the trader offered him fifty taels of gold, but the mandarin refused again, saying, "A state official must not be a greedy dog." The trader was patient, and came back again and offered him one hundred taels of gold. Can you guess if the third offer changed the situation? The mandarin remained firm and refused a third time. So, the trader returned one more time to offer five hundred taels of gold. You're a businessman—you know the value of five hundred taels of gold back then—it was a lot! But the trader was wrong. The mandarin told him not to try to bribe him again. If he did, the mandarin would put the trader in jail. The trader still didn't lose his patience. This time, he loaded one thousand taels of gold wrapped in cloth on to his wagon and went to meet the mandarin. Seeing the wagon filled with gold, the mandarin told his servants to tell the trader that he would accept the offer just this once, but the trader must never do it again.'

The district chairman burst into laughter, his saliva scattering in all directions.

'Later, a close friend asked him why he had declined four times but accepted the fifth offer. The mandarin replied that even a saint would not refuse such an enormous amount of money. I repeat, I am implying nothing here because we know each other quite well. I just want you to learn something from the anecdote. Honestly, you're very lucky to have me on your side, because I'm not like the commune chairman at all.'

I thought to myself that the district chairman was truly a gristmill man, through and through. So disgusting. Concerning the district chairman's background before becoming chairman, the original version of *The Termite Queen* also says the same thing. However, the way the author portrayed him was somewhat unreliable. It says he only finished the fifth grade and used fake degrees, which I don't believe because most people who only finish grade school can't quote morals from classic books the way he did to prove how smart he was. Still, he was no better than a common thief! In fact, most thieves looked more trustworthy than he did.

Still, I had to coddle him. I smiled and said, 'Such an insightful and practical story!'

Listening to the district chairman prattle on so cheerfully, I felt sorry for my father. As usual, when I left, I placed on his desk one of the parcels my mother had prepared. Just before I passed the gate, the district chairman sent someone to ask me to come back inside. I thought maybe I had done something wrong. But he smiled and whispered into my ear, 'Thank you. Now I know who I am working with, just like when your father was alive. I also have a gift for you. If you can meet this person, everything will run smoothly. The commune chairman won't be able to resist and will have to give up. Everything will be more interesting from then on.'

I asked the district chairman who that person was.

He looked around as if the information was confidential. Then he whispered, 'Mr Big. Listen carefully, because it's risky for me even to mention his name. Don't criticize my stubbornness. I may be a nobody, but I'm the son of a man whose noble deeds have been recognized by the government. I've been through life-and-death moments. I've been bent and broken. So now I'm not afraid of anyone. The commune chairman can never beat me. But we shouldn't force him, like a wild dog, into a corner, because he might bite us. At any rate, I wish you luck.'

'Have you ever met Mr Big?' I asked.

'No way! I'm a nobody. But when your father had too much to drink one time, he told me about Mr Big. As I prepared a room for your father to sleep it off, he mumbled, "Mr Big, do you know how much I am suffering? My life lies in your hands. Whether the golf course becomes a reality or not completely depends on you." I asked, "Who are you talking about?" Your father probably thought I didn't hear him mutter the name of the person, so he just said, "A very important and powerful man. He's a godfather. You and I? Nobodies." He uttered those words without opening his eyes. I guess Mr Big is a god seated on his throne somewhere up there.' The district chairman pointed upwards and looked up into the air.

'When you father woke, he panicked and asked if he had revealed anything. I asked him, "Don't you remember what you said? Did you speak with anyone else?" Your father said, "I was so drunk, I slept like the dead. How could I have even talked with you?" I said nothing to save him from worry. At home, I realized Mr Big had to be your father's secret trump card, and he didn't want to reveal Mr Big's identity. But I didn't begrudge your father for not trusting me. He was a businessman, so he had his own strategy. Now that he's dead, I'm telling you about this guy so you can . . . you can find out whether you're as blessed as he was.'

I thanked the district chairman and said goodbye, but as I left the building, he caught up to me again.

'Our job is to welcome you at the gate, but the person who orders us to open the gate lives elsewhere. Let's agree on this: I'll take care of the land-clearance paperwork—the agreement based on the affected residents' reactions, which is a difficult task—and you hurry and get the investment licence, which will be your lucky charm. It'll be huge to have it in hand. As soon as you've got it, anyone who causes trouble will be a criminal because it's against the law to oppose the government's policy— or its administrators, or its people, or its progress—and they can be thrown in jail for sedition. But until you have the licence, you have to be tactful. You have to beg people the same time you're threatening them. That's a revolutionary tactic the capitalists call *the carrot and the stick*. Remember that solving a problem with money is always the cheapest way. Goodbye for now! I have to run to a meeting.'

He got into a waiting car and sped off. Damn it! He was a poisonous snake, worse than a common thief!

I stood motionless outside my car, at a loss. The district chairman's long, horsey face and his story about my father swirled through my mind.

Chapter IV

A passage from the chapter, 'Rumours of Mr Big', from the original *Termite Queen*:

> Mr Big—a name subordinates always said in hushed voices, according to the rumours—often organized entertaining performances at his house, sometimes three or four times a month. A real-life experience was not just about going to parties and having sex. Mr Big liked very much the word *real*, which was also favoured by the performers, because the adjective expressed fully and exactly the level of luxury and satisfaction he desired, such as *real* value, *real* happiness, *real* talent, etc. The word *real* needed no further explanation.
>
> A high-class, elegant person must live a *real* life.

I knew I needed to meet Mr Big as soon as possible. He held the miracle key to my success. The problem was I knew nothing about him except that he'd sent that congratulatory note when I took over my father's position. I didn't even know how he had sent it.

Based on what the district chairman said, I was certain Mr Big must be very powerful. He never appeared in person thanks to some important reason I couldn't fathom.

My father had believed in Mr Big's power as well and had also tried to find ways to meet him, according to Mr Tâm, my father's chauffeur. But he died before he had the chance. Now I was in his shoes. Whatever my mother had done to help my father, she now did for me. I used the same chauffeur and the same car. I decided to keep them because I needed my father's blessing, spiritually speaking. And I also wanted more information about my father from Mr Tâm.

According to the district chairman, Mr Big never met with strangers, so, in order to meet him, I would first need to meet one of his trusted associates. I had to find out who the associate might be and I hoped Mr Tâm could help. He had told me that whenever he took my father to meet someone, he always knew how important the person was based on my father's expression. One day, he said, my father had wanted to meet a very powerful person, and the meeting had to be arranged through an intermediary. My father had Mr Tâm take him to a mansion protected by high courtyard walls near the city centre. When he returned to the car after meeting the intermediary, he said, 'This guy was just a toady, but he tried to act like he was my father.' Mr Tâm told me, 'I wished I could help him, but what could I do? I was just his driver.' Still, he assumed the toady was in fact an important intermediary.

Based on the information provided by the chauffeur and his description of my father's facial expressions, I had a hunch that the intermediary was, in fact, Mr Big himself. The story was so mysterious and intriguing that I felt compelled to go to the same mansion. At the very least, I might learn something.

Mr Tâm said he remembered the address, but when we got there, he wasn't sure if it was the right place. Located in the centre of the city's busiest district, the mansion was an old colonial building on a tree-lined street, surrounded by an imposing, stone wall. The courtyard teemed with all kinds of plants, young and old, including unfamiliar climbing vines, which probably came from abroad. Life clamoured from the city outside the mansion, but inside the courtyard walls, it was nearly silent. When I rang the bell, a woman wearing an apron came to the gate and spoke to me without opening it.

'How can I help you?'

'I would like to meet the owner of this mansion.'

'Do you have an appointment?'

'No. Your boss doesn't know me, but I am sure he knows my father.'

'Unfortunately, he's not home, and besides, he doesn't meet anyone without an appointment.'

'Are you sure he's not home? It looks like his car is in the driveway.'

The woman parted her lips slightly in a mysterious, incredulous way, but then replied politely, 'You don't know much about my boss. He owns twelve cars and there are, in fact, four of them in the garage and driveway right now. My boss loves cars.'

She was about to go back inside, but I pleaded, 'Your boss must have an assistant. May I meet him?'

'He has no assistant. Please leave your name, and I'll tell him you were here.'

'Honestly, I don't even know your boss's name,' I said as I gave her my business card, 'because I just took over my father's position. He and your boss have a few unfinished tasks, and I'm responsible for completing them. That's why I'm here today.'

'I understand. But I'm just a maid. I don't know anything about my boss's business.'

'Any idea how I can meet him?'

'Why are you asking me?' she said. 'Now you'll have to excuse me, I need to go inside and feed the dogs.'

The woman walked away from the gate and disappeared behind the yard's large plants. The mansion's quietness reminded me of a building in the Forbidden City where concubines would be imprisoned for the slightest mistake. I imagined all the difficulties I would have to overcome. A regular person's family status gives them some amount of power, but the owner of this mansion was so powerful that he couldn't even be approached.

I asked Mr Tâm to return us home.

The next day, I visited the mansion again, and the same maid said the same thing. Her boss wasn't home.

I felt so tired and confused. Why did I have to meet someone I didn't know? Why was he so important? What if he wasn't Mr Big or even his trusted associate and just some nobody? It would be a waste of my time. What if my father had come here for some other business and met someone else? What if Mr Tâm had a bad memory? Everything was so puzzling. I felt weak and vulnerable because I knew nothing for certain. Everything was just an assumption.

Exhausted, I wanted to erase Mr Big's name from my mind completely.

But then Mr Tâm advised me not to give up. He said my father had knocked on the door ten times in order to meet someone who wasn't even the boss. And my father had shown neither anger nor anxiety, saying that they needed him, and not the other way around. That was a matter of fact. I had to learn to be as patient as my father.

Suddenly, I realized that even though I had studied abroad for nearly ten years, I knew virtually nothing about my father's company or how to run it. I had studied very hard, but that kind of knowledge was useless here. I learnt skills and information that would be helpful only in a country that played by those rules. While overseas, I called home only when I needed money transferred from my mother's bank account. She always sent three times what I asked for. Everything had been so peaceful back then, except for the freezing winter winds. With my family's wealth, I never worried about money. That made it easy for me to live a life quite detached from my parents and thus to know absolutely nothing about their business affairs. History can be made in ten years. In those years, I read online about various scandals back home, but I paid very little attention to them. Now, I had to investigate to see if my parents had been involved.

On the internet, I searched for *land-grabbing, corrupt state officials, cemetery relocation, fraudulent development projects, golf courses, coercing land rights, resettlement protests, abandoned development projects, reactionary farmer arrests, commune H., district K.,* my father's name and company, and the names of a few other people in the company. I printed everything relevant to the time I had been at school in case someone deleted the websites. It was more than a thousand pages.

At first, the sheer size of the stack made the notion of finding anything useful seem impossible. Just as I was about to put it aside, the title of the first article caught my attention: '400+ Graves Disappear Overnight'. Apparently, one morning, a group of villagers woke to find all their ancestors' graves had vanished. A mountain of sand and mud covered the centuries-old cemetery. The bewildered villagers excavated immediately to rescue the spirits of their suffocating ancestors but found no bodies, no graves, nothing. The suspect, Company X, had been given rights to the cemetery land despite the villagers' refusal to relocate the graves. The article writer insisted the authorities must intervene and investigate to get answers for the village.

But all the authorities said was, 'We've found some clues that will probably lead to evidence. We're hunting for the criminals and will have an answer very soon.'

One thing my European education taught me was how to read bad news for the silver lining. What I'd just read was horrible but, with no follow-up information, the public lost interest. What mattered to me, though, was that it read like a blueprint for what my company needed to do to clear the land for the construction of the golf course. Several articles I read detailed scandals worse than the 400 vanished graves. They involved land clearance, coercing villagers, and swindling farmers' land for development projects that resold the same land at dizzyingly high prices. The land of the people was being plundered by those in power. But the media focused almost exclusively on the unfair compensation the developers offered the farmers. Some people were even put in jail for protesting the government's coercion.

What I had hoped not to find finally appeared: a legal case directly related to my father. A long time ago, my father's company had been the primary contractor for the construction of a steel factory. Thousands of farmers protested the project because they knew the steel factory would pollute the environment and ruin their lives. There had been violent confrontations, some people died, many were beaten, several farmers faced trial and were imprisoned, and then suddenly the media stopped talking about it, as if someone powerful had intervened to silence them. Could it have been my father? Could the politics of the steel factory project have gotten so hot that the government stepped in to muzzle the public?

While I was lost in guesses, I received a call from an unknown number. In a soft, deep and confident voice, the caller said he wanted to speak with me. He said he had seen me standing at his gate and knew who I was after reading my business card. I asked him his name, and he replied, 'I am the person who can help you find what you need.'

How did he already know what I needed? Was this Mr Big?

We scheduled a meeting for the next day. I arrived fifteen minutes early at the small coffee shop by the lake he had chosen. The café was not for commoners. Everything on the menu was extremely expensive, and anyone who would have to check how much cash was in their wallet before ordering was out of place. I didn't care much about the prices. A beautiful waitress came and took my order for a cup of coffee, and I sat back and enjoyed the view of the lake and surrounding park. After a few minutes, a man wearing a Chinese-style tunic suit and holding a newspaper sat down beside me.

'Please order the same thing for me,' he requested.

'Are you the person who called?' I asked.

'You are not calm like your father,' he said. 'In the country, there's a popular saying: *Be patient, and everything will be fine*. But I don't blame you—you're still young and energetic. You've been influenced by European culture, and you want everything to be transparent. Here's my advice: some things are too clear and obvious to see.'

'Who are you?' I asked.

'I should have asked that question myself. You've been looking for me, so you must already know who I am. Of course, you don't want to meet a devil. But that's irrelevant. The important thing is why we need each other.'

He talked and smiled like a philosopher, but he looked like a scoundrel, a professional middleman or a lobbyist. In Europe, it's legal to act as an intermediary, as long as you don't violate the law. But the person in front of me looked like someone who remained in the shadows. I had no idea how powerful and important he was for the work I needed done.

'I know what you need,' he said. 'I can help you. So, let's be clear. I'm Đào Kiến Sinh, and you can call me Mr Connection, because I make everything come together. Tell me what else you need my help with, besides meeting Mr Big.'

'Sounds like you already know what I need.'

'Who else do you need to meet?' he asked. 'Except for the devil, whether alive or dead, I can arrange a meeting with anybody. I can ask them to help you, bribe them, or even get rid of them if they're your competitors. I know more about sales than a Harvard marketing grad. But if I remember right, you studied in England, not America.'

He revealed his conniving talents without embarrassment. While I stirred my coffee and tried to think of what to ask, he held his cup close to his mouth and looked at me through the steam.

'You can't possibly just want coffee. Why do you keep stirring? There's hardly anything left.'

Something clicked and I said, 'Are you trying to blackmail me? I'm not used to working with people I know nothing about.'

'Well, finish your coffee and leave then,' he said, sounding insulted. 'Never mind what I said, and we end our conversation here. But let me tell you this—you should know how much money you have before talking with me.'

He snapped his fingers to call the waitress. She came and waited respectfully for his request.

'I'll pay for the coffee,' he said to her. 'You'd better take good care of him—he needs it.' He put his unfinished coffee on the table and stood up.

'Wait a minute,' I said. 'Please forgive me if I offended you, but what would you do in my place?'

He clapped his hands gently and with a big, beaming smile said, 'You should've said that sooner!' He dismissed the waitress and sat back down. 'I'll try to put myself in your situation. You see how close I get. To begin, I—meaning you, of course—have succeeded my father's chairmanship after his unexpected death. (Very sorry to hear about your loss, by the way, but let me continue.) My father passed away before I was ready to live independently. He left me a gigantic business I can't manage with my limited experience. Everything is very complicated. Honestly, with the money I inherited, I could live very well in Europe, America, or Singapore. I could buy a luxury house in

Beverly Hills, enjoy a peaceful life, and have whatever I want. I could fly to Dubai to screw prostitutes who cover their faces but spread their legs. I could travel anywhere and do anything without ever having to worry about money. I don't actually need to burden myself with this job. But it's not just about me, because I have to live for other people too, and some of them want to skin me alive. I've gone too far to retreat anyway. The problem is my father established a system that relies on and rewards not just him, but a host of others, including some who are sadistic white sharks that would swallow a sandbag to satisfy their hunger. They'll kill me, kidnap my sister and do harm to my mother if their money is lost. I'm having difficulty with the golf course project. I don't want to pursue it because I'll have to do cruel things, like evict people and risk their children turning into whores or gangsters . . . but, if I'm soft-hearted, the sharks will eat me alive. Therefore, I must not give up. But I can't move forward without a certain someone's help, and I'm looking for that person but he refuses to be seen. He sent a subordinate to meet with me, but I don't trust the guy.'

He stopped, looked at me coyly, and asked, 'How'd I do?'

I did not want to give him the satisfaction of answering, but I was surprised he knew so much about me. I tried to understand what he meant at the end of his little speech. He seemed like the sort of malicious person who'd know how to exploit my fear and desperation to squeeze me for every penny.

'Let's get to work,' I said. 'Just tell me how much you want for your service.'

'Absolutely! Everything must be transparent. I must be paid for the work I do. In a professional society, services deserve to be paid for fairly and properly. This way we'll owe each other nothing after you receive the service you need. Book a flight for us to X City on this day next week. First class—I don't want to sit with chatty, economy passengers. They know so much, and yet have no idea how to make real money. When we get there, we'll visit Y Beach and you'll get what you need to do, what needs to be done.'

I waited until he left before I examined his business card. His name made an impression on me, though I couldn't say to what effect—Đào Kiến Sinh.

Could he really arrange a meeting with Mr Big? Who was Mr Big anyway? Concerning this detail, I completely agree with the author's portrayal of the character in the original *Termite Queen*. In my imagination then, Mr Big was a corpulent man who wore baggy clothes, but carried himself, controlled his expressions and even walked in a way that said he was the very pinnacle of elite society. He had servants around him at all times who showed their utmost deference while satisfying his every demand. In his dining room, everything was gold and silver and studded with gems. His wine cabinet held only the most expensive bottles. On the walls hung the kind of Renaissance-period reproductions favoured by the wealthy. The sterling-silver plates put his status right under the guests' noses at every meal. But, in his bedroom, the valuables weren't the furniture or décor. Instead, it was what people brought into the room every night. I had heard about a high-end sex industry that catered to old and impotent but extremely affluent men. Their exquisitely trained prostitutes were so young and beautiful they could make a corpse rise. I had also heard that the fluid they emitted when aroused would rejuvenate an old man. Maybe I was becoming obsessed.

In truth, I was both nervous and afraid. I worried if I wasn't tactful, I'd ruin everything. I still had time before the flight with Sinh to learn more and build some confidence. I went back to the stack of documents I had collected online. I read several additional articles about the steel factory, the people who protested losing their land, and the pollution caused by the factory. My father's company had been the contractor, but who knows who actually owned the factory. The name of that company was half English and half Vietnamese, which meant absolutely nothing because anyone could make up a name and hire a board of directors to make a company look like anything they wanted. If it all went smoothly, no one would know who got the profits. Everything was so opaque, only God would know.

I paid close attention to a letter to the editor I found on a newspaper's website. Written by a man named Bích, the real addressee was my father. It read:

To the editor,

This is an open letter to Mr Nam, chairman of the development corporation, V.

I'd like to introduce myself: I am a disabled veteran and a full-time farmer. I am writing to you before irreparable damages are done by the steel factory currently under construction. I know that your company is only one of many involved in this project and from its role, has only so much say in this matter.

It is necessary to again raise the question: Why are they building such a factory at the centre of a fertile and peaceful countryside—a place that supplies fresh air and water, and rice and vegetables and fish to the whole region? Please excuse my improper language, but we farmers are fully aware that, for the sake of profits, people will do anything, even step on the most sacred object, and they don't give a shit about morality or self-respect.

I remain hopeful that you are not on their side—the people who do whatever is needed, including mass murder, just to make money. I don't mean to exaggerate the problem, but if we don't stop the steel factory's construction, the countryside will be ravaged by smoke, chemicals and toxic wastewater. Our trees, plants, animals and lives will be destroyed, and we will gradually perish. People will suffer tragic deaths every day, but neither you nor the factory owners will take responsibility; you will be off enjoying a guilt-free life of luxury at the finest resorts. You will not be haunted by your participation in the mass murder. You will probably even be proud of what you have done, thinking that you have helped a few people have a better life. That could be partly true, but it is nothing compared to what we farmers and our future generations will have lost. You should not destroy our future for your own immediate profit. These are our most urgent concerns. You will ask what we need from you. As a friend, here is my suggestion before we become enemies: give up the small profit you currently have in your hands for the sake of righteousness, and help us stop the project. You should not do something that benefits a very small group of people when it costs many other people their lives. You can afford to help us, because, even without this project, your company will survive. Like me, you also have children. Both of us would do anything to protect them.

A few months ago, a close friend of mine and former soldier died of cancer. His family sold almost everything they had to pay for his treatment. I was at his deathbed and witnessed the terrible pain that tormented him. I don't want another person to die like him because of a toxic environment. Please think seriously about what I've said before you and I both become characters in a tragedy.

Sincerely,
Bích

PS: I protect irreplaceable values. I will die for justice.

I read each word as if they had been addressed to me. I tried to imagine the writer's face, appearance and personality. He sounded strong-willed and sensitive. He cared about other people, so he must be thoughtful and mature. I was most impressed with how firmly and concisely he wrote. He had the qualities of a leader. Any community would need to rely on someone like him. Suddenly, I felt a great urge to discover the end of the story, but feared I wasn't strong enough to face the reality I'd uncover. I admired the writer of the letter so much I wished I could meet him. I wanted to meet him even more than I wanted to meet Mr Big.

Early the next morning, the district chairman phoned to urge me to take care of the licence paperwork so he couldn't be accused of betraying his people. He begged me to drop to my knees and lower my head if needed, to finish the deal, as my father had done so many times.

'It's wise to kneel in front of a single person so you can trample thousands,' the district chairman lectured over the phone. 'Not just anyone can do this. Learn from great Chinese men: sometimes you have to crawl on your belly, cut off your own hand, eat shit, or even sacrifice a lover.'

I knew the residents where the golf course was to be built had confronted him in his office the night before. I could imagine him trembling with fear during such an encounter. People who accept bribes want to keep everything quiet, at all costs.

The district chairman continued, 'The commune chairman has become the biggest obstacle. Forcing him to step down might seem like the easiest way. All I'd have to do is sign the pink slip to dismiss him from office. But please understand that, with the way things are right now, if I did that, everything would get much worse. You should learn from your father, who solved problems like this very effectively.'

Why did he always have to speak so vaguely? 'What do you mean?' I asked.

'Don't make me tell you what to do. You yourself should know what to do. You're a part of this system. Stop pretending to be naïve.'

I laughed good naturedly to comfort him. I promised I would hurry to do the two things he'd requested: obtain the investment licence and learn from my father.

Sitting alone, I asked myself: How *did* my father solve problems? More specifically, how did he respond to Mr Bích's letter? He must have done something to make sure the construction of the factory continued smoothly. This led me to wonder how Mr Bích was doing now. What did he do after writing that threatening letter, and what did he accomplish? Strangely, no one seemed to care much about the letter he wrote. I could find no published responses, as if the letter had fallen into an abyss and vanished forever. All I knew for certain was that my father's company got the factory built.

Everything was so complicated and confusing. I needed to find out what had happened, but then another concern crossed my mind: would investigating the steel factory just make things worse?

On the drive to work, my chauffeur, Mr Tâm, noticed how exhausted and confused I seemed. He had driven a supply truck in the Trường Sơn Mountains during the war. When the war ended, he accidentally lost all his identification papers when his truck was commandeered by another unit, so he couldn't prove that he had served. Some people even suspected he had deserted. After that, wherever he went, his job applications were turned down and people ridiculed him behind his back. He spiralled into depression and even considered suicide. But then he met my father—I don't know in what situation.

My father encouraged Mr Tâm and renewed his hope for a beautiful future. They belonged to two different social classes, so how they became friends remained a mystery to me. Mr Tâm was his chauffeur through it all, though, right up to the day my father died, and I knew I needed to keep him in the family. At first, he said he would just retire, reasoning that no one other than my father could understand him, and that his service had been wholeheartedly devoted to my father alone. But my mother intervened and managed to persuade him to stay on. In no time, he became as dedicated to me as he had been to my father. He may have been my chauffeur, but deep in my heart, I considered him like a father.

Normally he only asked me where to go or whether I needed anything, but on that morning Mr Tâm offered me some advice.

'I know you're in a labyrinth,' he said. 'You have to cope with too many things at the same time. But I have something to say. May I?'

'Please tell me. I need your advice.'

'I don't dare advise you because I know nothing about your business. When your father was alive—you make me miss him very much, by the way—we talked a lot, but I never gave him advice. I know where I stand.'

'It's all right. Speak freely.'

'You should learn your father's patience,' Mr Tâm said in a sombre tone. 'I've never known anyone so patient.'

At any mention of my father, Mr Tâm always became quite serious. He said many times that if he hadn't met my father, his life would've been over a long time ago. Naturally, Mr Tâm felt very grateful. After a few quiet minutes, he continued:

'One time, your father needed to meet a person who, I think, was very influential in the business world. The gate at that person's house was truly impressive, much bigger than the gate of the house you recently visited. Marble columns with

dragons and tigers framed either side. The high walls kept
everyone outside from seeing in. Your father said the owner
had many live-in maids, and big German shepherds patrolled
the grounds, which had many enormous old trees that made
the place look like a forest. I would've had a heart attack if
I had to step into that house. But your father had to meet the
owner for business. I later learned the owner was a powerful
intermediary—a wizard who sat behind a curtain and ran
everything, I guess. Your father eventually met him after going
through many channels. Each channel was like a rainbow in
a fairy tale. Beneath the slippery rainbow lived fierce animals,
snakes and scorpions, ready to devour anything that fell to the
ground. When I drove in the Trường Sơn Mountains, I was
known for being literary. Everybody loved my stories.'
     Mr Tâm laughed. He rarely did that.
     'If you fall from the rainbow,' he continued, 'the fierce
beasts will eat you alive. I remember your father sat on a bench
and waited outside that gate all day on at least ten occasions—
and you want to give up after just a few? Every morning, your
mother told me to remind him to eat ginseng if he had to wait
overnight. There were days when he asked me only to bring
him a bottle of water and some rice wrapped in banana leaves.
I didn't dare ask anything. I'd hand him the water and rice
and go back to the car. I'd return to pick him up as soon as
office hours had ended. He never complained. A few other
people waited there too. He'd stay for hours but get nothing.
Then he'd tell me to drive him home. And he would have me
come and pick him up at the same time the next morning.
I'd get up at four and drop him off at that house by six. Your
father would arrive just as the sun was rising, and everything
was beautiful. He waited ten times, and when they finally let
him inside, he only got six or seven minutes. He told me he
befriended the maids, who had no power but were arrogant,

nonetheless. He kept all kinds of envelopes in his pocket. He told me wherever he went, he had to bribe people so they wouldn't make things difficult. On other visits to other godfathers' mansions, if he was lucky, he'd get an appointment within an hour. If the person he wanted to meet didn't have time, he'd have to leave and come back another time. He said the hardest part was when the servants said they would inquire for him, and he would just have to sit there and wait. What I learned from your father is that you have to be patient. That's your real business, after all.

'Once, I asked him why he was willing to wait so long, and he said: "In a society where power gives birth to money, you must know how to network. There are a lot of smart people. But not everyone knows the king's face and name. Therefore, experience matters and patience is the key, even if one has to suck honeyed ginseng to keep from fainting."

'Now I know every pebble on the path outside that person's house. I can still recall the fierce faces of his German shepherds.'

The chauffeur spoke haltingly, as if he had to think about what he should and shouldn't say.

'Even those dogs wanted to be respected because they knew how good they had it. If you want to get the work done, you have to make even the dogs happy. Your father once told me he was sick of the whole thing and wanted to give it all up and go live in the mountains. He said he would be happier there with nature. But I knew he was a persevering man who would not give up so easily. He only said that because he was tired and the next day he would be ready to go through it all over again. I loved your father dearly.'

Mr Tâm's story reminded me of the time my father took me to a forest far away from the city. This was just before I left the country to study abroad. He shared his thoughts with me—the same kinds of things the chauffeur had told me. I didn't pay much attention to what my father said then because I simply felt so happy and so lucky to have such an intelligent and wealthy father. Now when I recall that day, I can see the wrinkles and the sadness on his face and feel his suppressed feelings. He perked up only when I told him about my plans for the future. I had thought I might become an environmental scientist, but he suggested I study business. He probably didn't really want me to study that, but felt he had no choice.

Revisiting this memory and listening to the chauffeur, I realized it wasn't the right time for me to give up. I had to face reality.

***

We had first-class seats on the airplane, but I didn't feel comfortable sitting beside Đào Kiến Sinh as he savoured the luxuries of the flight. Sinh reclined his seat and pressed the service button the way the elite do. He held a glass of red wine and spun it slowly between his palms. He tasted the wine, bit his lip, and flicked his tongue.

'Don't you want any?' Sinh asked.

'Honestly, in times like this, I prefer to watch people drink.'

'I didn't say you were dishonest. You're in the air and drinking a glass of wine gives you such a wonderful feeling. Give it a try. Damn! Without the Europeans and their wines and technologies, we'd never have a chance like this to live like kings above the clouds.'

I looked into his eyes and got the impression that all his sophistication was just a sham. Sinh knew he was just a middleman and he disgusted me. He was opportunistic and undignified. I asked myself: who is he? and what does he want from this trip? I could feel myself succumbing to his temptations, like a sap who drowns in the ocean because someone says there's a diamond beneath the waves.

'You must already be too familiar with this wonderful feeling,' Sinh said. He twirled his glass again, not looking at me. I ignored him so I could concentrate on my business. While he tried to show off his knowledge about red wines and wine culture—pieces of information he had probably gleaned from other people—I was thinking about Mr Big. What did he look like? Short or tall? In my imagination, Mr Big, like any mysterious man, would have a large face, beady eyes and hooked eyebrows. He'd have the look of a spirit medium who could communicate with the dead, but also that of a rich and powerful land baron who wore gaudy, silk clothes.

I would use the letter he had written to me when I succeeded my father as chairman to ask him for help because he and my father must have had a good relationship. I hoped he would regard me as an inexperienced son in need of his protection.

I was not used to kowtowing to influential and powerful people, but I would learn. In fact, meeting Mr Big on a holiday was not a bad thing, because I wouldn't have to worry about unnecessary formalities. Normally, meeting at a romantic place on a holiday where people are enjoying good wine, delicious food and the best cigars, made them friendlier and less demanding.

I turned my head to glance at my companion. He looked very satisfied—not a single sign of worry on his smooth face. Suddenly, I wanted to burst into laughter just to assure myself that he was in fact a middleman taking me to a gold mine. He would do what was necessary to get his share. He was a typical intermediary—a screech owl, a sewer rat, a vampire.

'You look so meditative!' Sinh exclaimed.

I flushed as if caught doing something naughty, but quickly regained my composure.

'Do you regret taking this trip with me?' Sinh asked. 'I completely understand if you do, but you should know that if you don't listen to me, you'll regret it for the rest of your life. You'll lose it all.'

I turned my shoulder away from him to show I didn't care for his assumptions about me.

'So, what do you think?' Sinh said, knowing how to reel me back in. 'Do you really want to meet Mr Big? Do you believe I can help you?'

'Of course, I want to meet Mr Big. That's why I'm here.' I forced a smile to cover my true feelings. 'I'm curious. What is Mr Big like? Will he be comfortable meeting me?'

'You're just like your father,' Sinh leaned toward me and spoke in a flattering tone. 'But it'll take years to become as experienced and savvy a gentleman as *my* Mr Nam. You can't possibly think you can know Mr Big from a few second-hand comments.'

Sinh finished his wine, pressed the service button and handed the flight attendant his empty glass. Then he reclined further in his chair and asked, 'Are you worried we haven't spent enough time getting to know each other?'

'We will meet Mr Big soon, and it seems better if I know something about him in advance. I assume you're close with him.'

'You're right—we'll meet Mr Big eventually. But you're mistaken to assume I'm his close friend. You underestimate him. In fact, we are both just like his dogs. Fortunately, I've never had to meet him in person.'

'What are you trying to say?'

'To be honest, I'm as nervous as you are. This will be my first time seeing him in person. I want to meet him even more than you do.'

'What? I thought you knew him.'

'Relax. Just because I haven't met Mr Big in person yet doesn't mean I can't meet him or that what I'm doing is pointless. Just enjoy the flight and have some wine. You're at 11,000 metres. Everything is beneath you—trivial.'

Sinh pressed the service button again and asked for another glass of wine. This time, he wanted to clink his glass with mine. After smacking his lips to savour the wine's bitter taste, he explained, 'Eventually, you'll learn the kind of relaxed preparedness your father was very good at. Here's the plan. We'll rest after we arrive, and you can do whatever you want. But you have to be ready to meet Mr Big when I tell you, even if it's short notice for an even shorter meeting.'

I had to acquiesce. What he wanted from me was not as much as I had imagined. He requested a standard hotel room with massage service. He didn't hide the fact that whenever he visited someplace new, he wanted to screw local women. I stayed in my room the whole day, just waiting for his call from the next room. Nothing happened. Two long-legged prostitutes came to his room, one at a time, and I was sure I'd end up having to pay for them as well as his other expenses, though we had no agreement on this matter.

All through the next day, I imagined the powerless face of the district chairman as he stood in front of the angry protestors, the stony faces of the godfathers on the board and how quickly the circling sharks would attack if I failed. I imagined my mother's worried face.

By the third day, still nothing had happened. Sinh disappeared at some point and I had no idea where he went, whom he met, or what arrangements he made. He only told me he knew several people who had the right connections. I didn't care whether it was true or not. Whatever happened, happened.

That evening, he appeared at my room door wearing one of the hotel's thick robes. He licked his lips, looking satisfied. He told me I should follow his lead. I asked what he wanted me to do. He winked—a signal all men understand. I told him I was tired, but all he really wanted was to share how excited he was about his sexual conquests over the past two days.

'You're still young, so there's no hurry,' he said. 'But soon you'll need to get comfortable acting on your desires with women. Everyone associates a successful career with the beautiful women you have around you. Conquering women might just be the most important step.'

I didn't even have to pretend I was listening. He didn't care. He was shallow and small-minded. He considered himself above everyone else, so he didn't need to look up to see who or what was above him. He talked endlessly and passionately about sex. I pitied him for his pathetic perversions.

Fortunately, at some point his cell phone rang. His face went rigid, his demeanour turned professional, that of the obsequious servant. Over the phone, he said, 'Sir' and 'Yes, sir,' repeatedly among other shallow, flattering words.

'That was Mr Big's assistant,' he said after the call ended. 'We'll meet him tomorrow. Everything's been taken care of. I'll sleep well tonight. I know what you're thinking, but just remember, I am Mr Connection. I know all the shortcuts and keep all my promises.'

That night, Sinh may have slept well, but I did not. My mind kept spinning from one disparate thought to the next. I tried to figure out where everything started, and when I'd gotten lost in this maze. I asked myself: is the golf course worth compromising my ethics? I recalled my father's eyes as he was dying. They held secrets I was now close to uncovering. I wished he had told me, for example, not to take over his position. Everything would be much simpler. Though my mother had told me his wishes, I needed to hear them directly from him.

I resolved to be strong and firm. When dealing with sharks, I had to be more aggressive than them to survive. I'd have to show them that swallowing me would bring them more bad luck than good. If I quit now, everything my father had established would collapse, and likely bring about a host of unexpected misfortunes. Our company's future depended on making good decisions under pressure. I had to destroy my rivals. I could not let myself get emotional when deciding to bury 400 graves under a mountain of sand. I had to force myself to not be affected by pleading words and the heart-wrenching testimony of homeless people and farmers who lost their land and whose children and wives lived miserable lives or people who were dying from illness and hatred.

I'd have to get used to seeing bony bodies and deformed children because their parents were poisoned by mercury, cyanide and other toxic chemicals.

If I was determined to pursue my father's career, I would have to become emotionless. What Mr Tâm had said made me love and admire my father even more. I would not let his business be destroyed.

Chapter V

In order to have a more complete understanding of what my father went through, readers should note the following excerpt from the original *Termite Queen*, which provides additional context to the details I provided earlier. They're told from a broader perspective, and to the best of my knowledge, the author does not seem to fabricate any details, as some people might think, though he does exaggerate a bit in places. Please be reminded that Mr N. is my father in the original.

Mr N. and the Gatekeepers (chapter from the original *Termite Queen*)
Mr N. was familiar with having to wait half a day or more to meet a very important person. It wasn't a matter of time lost; rather, patience. Success does not come easily. Moreover, a person with something to gain appreciates it more if they know the thing gained could have been someone else's if only the other hadn't given up earlier.

As an experienced businessman, Mr N. was patient and knew what he had to do. He was fully aware of his position. If he wanted to rule above thousands of people, he had to accept being ruled by a few. Thus, he was never irritable if he grew hungry while waiting, or if his bottom and legs became sore from sitting for too long. He accepted the reality unconditionally. In order to meet one particular important person, Mr N. relied on bribed servants to navigate him through a twisting and turning tunnel that led to a courtyard where many other people sat waiting for their name to be called. If the navigator had not yet arrived, because he was fully booked, or because he had more important clients, Mr N. had to bide his time. He could neither ask the navigator a question nor make a request. He had to be humble. He had to say flattering words to please other people, but most importantly, he had to not underestimate even an ant, knowing very well that it could become the obstacle to prevent a tank from moving forward and thus ruining everything.

During the first few days of this particular vigil, he befriended the VIP's gatekeepers. The security guards working as gatekeepers were hired because they could be impervious to other people's feelings. They had no sympathy for the countless people who came and went because they knew the visitors were all there for some personal gain. The gatekeepers were tall muscular men. They wore cruel expressions and were always accompanied by fierce dogs. Every day, Mr N. gave each of the gatekeepers an envelope as a friendly greeting. An envelope filled with money was the best form of non-verbal communication because it could touch the heart of even the most callous, cold-blooded person. Eventually the gatekeepers began to accept him. A challenge remained, however. The dogs—apparently they wanted for nothing and could not be bribed.

From the very first day, Mr N. felt like the dogs were watching him. He felt unsafe, although they didn't threaten him outright. Every now and then, the lead dog would yawn, as if bored from having to rest in one position for so long. The other dogs were hot-tempered and disliked the people who waited for hours day after day. One dog looked at another and then at Mr N. and snarled, as if to suggest, 'Why don't we bite that bastard's pants to scare him away? He would piss himself, for sure. He thinks our boss has a lot of time to waste.' Of course, this was only Mr N.'s imagination, but he felt intimidated by the way the dogs glared at him. He knew he would have to establish a close friendship with them, or he might find himself in trouble someday. On one occasion when he happened to be the only person waiting, he came up with an idea to find out what they wanted.

The dogs had taken over the patrolling duties of the gatekeepers, who had started a card game in the garage. Mr N. cautiously approached the lead dog, which was lying down but had its eyes partially open.

'Woof . . . woof . . . woof,' said Mr N.

All the dogs raised their heads and stood, quivering in wait for an order to attack him. They growled and barked. Mr N. was terrified. One of the gatekeepers ran out and commanded the dogs to shut up.

'You're provoking them,' said Mr Gatekeeper to Mr N. 'If they get mad, you'll be sorry.'

'Oh,' said Mr N. 'I thought I was just showing them my respect by imitating their bark. I wanted to tell them we could be friends. When you are in another country, you try to speak the native language, and usually the locals don't get mad at you for doing so.'

Mr Gatekeeper laughed. 'Of course not, if you say nothing offensive. But do you know the canine language? What if what you just said was a curse? Like, "Hey dogs, fuck you!"'

'I see what you mean,' said Mr N. nodding appreciatively. 'My fault, my fault! I won't do it again.'

'The problem is the dogs recognized you wanted to say something, but then you barked and said nothing important. They would have to assume then that you don't respect them. They may be dogs, but they have their own hierarchy and sense of manners. When you refer to someone as Mr Security Guard, Mr Labourer, Mr Housekeeper, etc., for example, it's impolite, and they're not pleased. A lot of people think of themselves as highly educated and holders of important positions in society, so they become arrogant. They think they have the right to put their noses into others' business, but they are, in fact, just servants. Of course, you cannot call them Mr Servant. If I were in the dogs' situation, I would hate you and want revenge. Because I'm human, I'd use words to teach you a lesson. But the dogs can't speak to you, so they'll use the means they do have to teach you. Even we have to be careful with them. My boss would rather see any one of us die than one of those dogs. Why do you need to see my boss, anyway? I never see him do anything to help others.'

'What do I need to do to make the dogs happy?' Mr N. asked, avoiding the guard's question. 'I don't want them to hate me and take revenge. I just want to be their friend. Why is that so difficult?'

Mr Gatekeeper took on a haughty look, like he knew everything this well-dressed man before him did not. 'You should have asked me about this earlier,' he said. 'The dogs think they're important, so they're aggressive, but like anyone else, they just want to be flattered. Find a way to show them how highly respected they are. The dogs are well fed—you know that—and they live in a luxurious, air-conditioned mansion. They have their own massage service and wear expensive cologne, but still, they suffer. They are powerful, muscular beasts at the peak of their youth. Just like all young people, they're perpetually horny. But because of their duties, their sexual desires go unfulfilled. Of course, it's unbearable. Even worse, when these well-fed dogs lie down inside the mansion, their long wieners touch the floor, and they have to watch humans leading pleasure-filled, decadent lives, so naturally they become jealous. But that's life. They can't do anything about it. Our boss raises these dogs for security. If they were allowed to fuck, they wouldn't focus on their work. So, in short, what they really need is sex. But you can't bring in a female dog in here. The boss forbids it. And if somehow it did happen, the female dog would probably get fucked to death. Solve their blue balls problem and the dogs will love you forever.'

Immediately Mr N. phoned one of his assistants and asked him to order a high-quality, canine sex-doll from Japan. The robot dog had been designed to look frisky, with silky, white fur and a heart-shaped patch of brown fur on her chest. She had some internal mechanics that allowed her to move somewhat realistically. Apparently Japanese dogs were much luckier than Vietnamese dogs, except for this pack of guard dogs under Mr N.'s provenance. One morning, a few days later, he carried the toy into the courtyard and then pressed a hidden button on her belly. She immediately came to life, stretched and whined suggestively, wagged her tail and circled as if in heat. Immediately, the security dogs all trembled and stood up. They wondered where such an unusual canine specimen came from. They ran over and drooled as they sniffed her all over, especially the rear end where the silicone vulva had been musked by the manufacturer. The lead dog, in a disciplinary tone, told the other dogs to be careful, but their instincts were stronger than their obedience. The toy was flirty but reserved, as if testing their patience. Then she leaned her haunch toward the lead dog lasciviously. One drooling male dog barked, 'She wants it!' And another barked, 'Wants it bad!' And another, 'Me first!'

Then they all jumped on her. The quickest one immediately mounted from behind. The slower ones bit at her shoulders and belly. Within a single minute, the toy vanished amidst the scrapping, horny dogs. They growled, moaned and drooled as they ejaculated. After the male dogs dispersed, all that remained of the canine sex-doll was a slobber-stained scattering of fur and plastic parts.

Watching the chaotic scene, Mr N. and the guards laughed and shouted encouragement. As soon as the dogs settled back down, they became docile and kind, with big panting smiles on their faces. They seemed grateful to Mr N. for his generous gift.

From that day on, the dogs considered Mr N. their friend. They looked forward to seeing him every day. Any time he sat and waited on the familiar bench, they came over and begged for his attention, which, after that first episode, involved sharing some bones or other meaty dog-treats with them. Thanks to the friendship with the dogs, Mr N. felt at home, even when he sat and waited an entire week to be called inside.

Chapter VI

Apparently, the author of the original *Termite Queen* wrote the chapter, 'People Coming from Somewhere Far Away', after someone else told him the story, which he then supplemented with additional details he managed to uncover about the steel factory my father's company built. I can see myself in the character Việt, though he is not completely me. My father and the chauffeur, Mr Tâm, are described as they were in real life. I've asked myself if such an accurate portrayal reflects the miraculous power of literature to provide universally identifiable characters, or whether the author secretly spied on us? Regardless of how he did it, I admit that what he wrote was true.

People Coming from Somewhere Far Away (from the original *Termite Queen*)

Việt, Mr N.'s son, planned to do two things. First, he would take over his father's company and the leadership of the golf course project, starting with meeting the district chairman again to receive updates and discuss next steps. This was for the well-being of the company. Second, he would visit the steel factory for which the company had been the construction contractor several years ago. Even if plenty of shocking information related to the factory could be found on the internet, he had to see the place in person. Ostensibly, Việt needed to learn how his father had solved thorny development problems, but truthfully it was his conscience that demanded he find out more.

Việt decided to let the district chairman stew for the time being. He wanted him to suffer the same discomfort he and other people experienced while desperately waiting for something day after day. Việt knew the chairman had been clamouring to see him to learn how the meeting with Mr Big had gone. The chairman had never had the honour of meeting the mysterious Mr Big. He only knew of him from the respectful way other people spoke of him. Anytime someone mentioned Mr Big's name, the chairman lowered his voice to a whisper so no one else could hear. He repeatedly asked when the investment licence would be issued because it held the key to his grasp on power and the financial gains he might make from the project. The licence would legitimate the bribe money he had already received, protect him from threats made by higher authorities and reel in the district's violent, disaffected residents.

Việt shared his plans with no one. He wanted to know the truth about what his father had done to resolve the issues surrounding the building of the steel factory because the golf course project faced similar problems. Mr N. had been an experienced businessman and must have had some genius strategies to quell the rebellious farmers after they lost their land and were forced to live with all the factory pollution. Strangely, the news never reported on the affected farmers once they had been pacified. It was as if the protests had never happened.

Việt went to the steel factory, believing he would be able to find the key to his father's involvement in its construction. Contrary to what he had imagined, the factory didn't manufacture products for industrial use. But Việt didn't care much for the particulars of its operation. He just wanted to enjoy the peaceful countryside and pristine natural beauty,

see its rustic houses, tall trees, grazing cattle and birds flying
in the sky before the factory's pollution caused them to vanish
for good. As they reached the factory gate, Việt excitedly told
the driver to stop. He got out of the car. White clouds drifted
in the impeccably blue sky. Gentle breezes carried the scent of
rice ready for harvest. On the road to the rice paddies, farmers
were riding their motorbikes to work. Việt came very close to
the factory, but he didn't pay it much attention. He was afraid
he'd get entangled in its problems too. More of the same kind
of problems he already had.

'That's it,' the driver said. 'That's the place you're
looking for.'

Việt said nothing. He stared at the factory in silence. After
a long while, he asked, 'You know the place, and know how to
get here, so why did you make me look at the map and give you
directions?'

The driver pulled a face. 'Honestly, I thought you'd get us
lost and give up trying to come here. I didn't want to come back
to this place, especially now with you.'

'Why not? What happened here?'

'You'll find out. I'm not a good storyteller. Besides, focusing
on the road to avoid potholes makes me forget everything else.'

Việt said nothing. He decided to visit a few families in the
nearby villages. They greeted him with unfriendly expressions,
especially when they noticed he dressed like a young
businessman. But the graciousness Việt had picked up abroad
came in handy. He made small talk with the locals easily and
played with the children. Gradually, they warmed up to him.

Việt struck up a conversation with an artist, Mr Quang,
who used to be a motorcycle tour guide. He could play several
traditional instruments and sing *quan họ* folk songs very well.
When Việt and the driver stood outside his house, Mr Quang

was singing and playing a *đàn bầu*[3] along with a recording and
did not invite them on to the porch.

After Mr Quang finished the song, Việt clapped his hands
and said, 'Wonderful!'

'How can I help you?' Mr Quang said, looking at the men.

'Can't you see I'm practising?'

'We're sorry. You sing so well, I wanted to stop here and get
to know you. I love quan họ Bắc Ninh folk songs.'

'Really? That's unusual—not many young people these days
care for the old music. Please have a seat. Be my guests now. Do
you really think I sing well?' Mr Quang's face grew brighter. 'Do
you know much about quan họ Bắc Ninh? Can you sing it well?'

'No, I can't sing it myself, and only know enough to
recognize it when I hear it and that I like it.'

'Let me tell you about it, then.'

The artist introduced himself as Hào Quang, which means
halo, but his face looked dark and miserable. He was originally
from Bắc Ninh but had been stationed nearby, along the river,
during the war. Instead of describing quan họ Bắc Ninh, he told
Việt about his time in the military and bragged of his popularity
with the local girls. He fell in love with the one who became
his wife after she demanded point blank to see his penis, which
apparently passed her inspection. He said this region was a
great place to live—it had fertile land and girls with beautiful
bodies. 'I'm in my seventies,' he added, 'but I'm still addicted to
sex. I want to fuck all the time.'

Việt listened attentively and at the appropriate time,
applauded the old man's virility. Excited by his own bragging,
Mr Quang launched into several more songs before Việt could
ask another question. When he paused after the third one, Việt

---

[3] A Vietnamese, single-stringed instrument whose tension can be
manipulated to change pitch.

complimented the village's natural beauty, assuming that Mr Quang was proud of his home and would be pleased to hear it praised. But instead, Mr Quang just looked contemplative.

'Nothing is beautiful here now,' he said. 'Ten years ago, you would've been amazed. Now there's only trash and hatred.'

'What do you mean?' Việt asked, feigning surprise.

'I'm just telling the truth,' said Mr Quang. 'No big deal. By the way, who are you, where are you from, and why are you here?'

Mr Quang didn't wait for Việt's reply. He adjusted the string of the đàn bầu, and then sang a song incoherently, as if sobbing. Right in the middle, he stopped singing abruptly and pointed toward the steel factory.

'Everything's gone to shit since that goddamned thing appeared.'

Việt held a neutral expression to keep from revealing his real reason for coming. He looked at the factory and pretended to be surprised. 'What do you mean?'

'Can't you see it?' Mr Quang sneered. 'That monster's been polluting the air here for many years now. The land's been trashed. Children are being born deformed. All the jobs there are demeaning.'

Việt nodded, as if listening to an interesting story, but deep in his heart, he needed to know more. 'How can the factory be a monster? It's modern industry.'

'Modern industry, my ass!' Mr Quang spat. 'That factory's even worse than a monster. It's made our lives miserable.'

Just to see how Quang would react, Việt used the company's stock responses to convince villages to do their bidding. 'The factory's right in the middle of some terrific farmland and so it's great that it creates jobs for people when they aren't farming. Right? I bet the youngsters who work there are learning how to be professional and punctual too, like good industrial workers.'

'Ha!' spat Mr Quang again. 'You talk like a textbook, repeating the same things we were first told. I'm sure the ones who approved the factory project quoted the same book. They sold us on the same bright future. Good jobs for everyone! Even a person like me could at least become a security guard, wear a uniform and have health insurance and a pension. The factory would transform this sleepy backwater into a booming industrial zone. They promised all sorts of secondary industries would pop up. There'd be a car-manufacturing plant, a cellphone factory, a supermarket. They promised electricity for everyone, new roads, a port, a hospital and on and on. The man who made these promises had the face of an owl and a heavy, regional accent. He said there would be an airport and even tourists. Our countryside would become bright twenty-four hours a day, like a city. Roosters wouldn't know if it was day or night. He said we'd be able to open restaurants, offer services and sell our farm produce and handicrafts to make lots of money.'

Mr Quang played a single mournful, quivering note on the đàn bầu. When it finally died, he continued, 'But there isn't shit. The only thing they did successfully was take our land. It was once so rich and fertile, and now it's ruined. An oil spill destroyed that whole area over there,' he said, pointing. 'Tailings have leeched into the water and soil. Coal dust covers everything. They released a plume of toxic chemicals into the river and killed all the fish up and down the coast. And now I hear the factory will close down anyway because it loses money. The equipment they purchased from China worked only for a few years but then broke. Now it's just more industrial waste. The people who were forced to resettle are now homeless. A whole generation of children are either unemployed or work as prostitutes, gravediggers, or garbage-pickers. So many people have died because of disease and resentment.'

Việt was shocked to hear the factory would soon close down. How much had his father been involved? Did other mysteries surround that monstrous factory? Việt wanted to ask so many questions, but at the same time, didn't really want to face the answers. They would be too much for him to handle.

Việt and his driver gave Mr Quang some gifts—a bag of tea, a box of European cookies and some money. Then they left.

In the village, Việt asked to be directed to the house of an elderly teacher. He had read that the best way to learn about an area was to find a respectful and educated local person such as a doctor or a teacher.

At the teacher's house, Việt introduced himself, and explained his presence by saying that he had just come back from studying abroad and felt the urge to visit the countryside of his homeland.

The grey-haired teacher looked at Việt and his driver without judgment. 'Please come in,' he said. 'I'm sorry our house is not as neat as a home in the city.'

'Actually, I like the way you've arranged things here,' said Việt.

The elderly teacher looked at Việt with a hint of surprise. He invited them to sit and then prepared hot tea for them.

'Please have some,' he said, filling three cups. 'Have you visited many families in the village?'

'Only Mr Quang, but he didn't seem pleased with my questions.'

'I understand. Even I sometimes make him angry. Since the steel factory was built, the villagers' personalities have changed completely. We've become more aggressive. Whenever I hear someone raise their voice, I feel unsettled because it's all too easy to imagine the bloody scenes that might follow. In the past, we were gentle and polite. Now everything's different. I don't know who to blame.'

Việt nodded and asked, 'How long have you been retired?'

'Many years. I am now in my seventies. What do you think about our countryside so far?'

'It's beautiful. I like that, even though things have changed, most people still seem kind and sincere.'

'I'm glad to hear that.'

Việt felt he could dig a little deeper. 'I'm curious about your mention of the steel factory. Have things changed since it was built?'

'Oh yes,' said the teacher. 'I'd have to use the word *disaster* to describe the damage it has caused.'

'Mr Quang said so too. He was very angry.'

'Of course, he's angry. It's a real nightmare. I think I know what you're thinking, and if you want, I'll tell you the truth, which probably isn't what you expect.'

'What do I expect?'

'I know you've come here with some purpose. I'm sure you're involved with some kind of plan to do something, but that's not my business. Why do you want to know about what happened?'

'Because I'm interested in the truth,' said Việt, his tone serious.

'All right, then. Let me begin with how I first got involved in the whole thing.'

The teacher's story
It was a beautiful Saturday in the village. People had erected several colourful wedding tents to celebrate the fact that the road had recently been graded and paved to cut down on the dust as it ran through the poor, crowded neighbourhoods. The village was changing.

Out of the blue, a convoy of ten unfamiliar cars came flying into the district up the dirt road from the city. In the villager's eyes, the cars resembled shiny monsters. Some looked like boxes, some like whales, some like scorpions. No one knew where the vehicles had come from or at which village in the district they would stop. The cars kicked up a terrible mess as their wheels stirred up dirt and straw. People cursed and yelled at them, but they didn't slow down. Eventually, people's anger turned to curiosity: who were in these cars, where were they going, and what were they doing here? They seemed to have come from somewhere far away.

To my surprise, they ended up stopping at my house as I sat out front cutting bamboo.

Since I retired, I had taken up making bamboo baskets to sell to the fishermen. Our waters were filled with fish and shrimp back then, enough to feed everyone in the region. A young and confident man with a thoughtful face sat down next to a stack of my baskets and looked through them, praising my work.

'Will you sell the whole stack to me?' he asked. 'Name your price.'

I couldn't imagine him using one of my baskets, let alone all of them, so I said, 'Why don't you come in for some tea first?'

But he wouldn't be put off. 'I'm not joking,' he said. 'Each of your baskets is a masterpiece. I'll hang them up so they can be seen, as they deserve to be. Anyone who wants to admire them will have to pay for the privilege. I'd hate to see them ruined by using them to fish in the river.'

My young guest sat down and introduced himself. 'My name is Dung, and I run a development company. These people are my colleagues. I hope this might be the beginning of a mutually beneficial collaboration. We have a small gift for you.'

A woman in the group placed a square parcel on the table. Another person put another one on top of the first while I politely looked away.

'These are just small gifts. This one is a box of Korean ginseng. They say it was grown on a rocky mountain in the cool and pure air. They had to wait ten years before harvesting it. And here is some wine money for you, which is nothing compared with what you must make from such a giant property. You're a teacher and lead such a humble life. But you don't have to live so frugally.'

I pushed the gifts back toward the guests and said, 'I've done nothing to deserve these gifts. It would be unethical to accept them.'

Dung smiled cheerfully. 'I like you very much, especially your gentle appearance and personality. You must have studied Confucius to uphold such moral values. Please accept our gifts as tokens of our appreciation.'

'I'm sorry, but no.'

'We don't want to make you feel uncomfortable. Maybe you can just hold on to the gifts for us. We're visiting today because we've heard that your voice has influence in the village, so I hope you will help us.'

'I'll be glad to help if I can.'

'Your generation defended our nation against foreign invaders,' said Dung, respectfully. 'Our generation must be responsible for making it prosperous and beautiful. Therefore, we are comrades. When I first arrived here, I felt so ashamed. I drive a luxury car while farmers struggle through hard, impoverished lives. That is unfair. We must change it. Very soon, there'll be a steel factory here, with a million-tonne annual capacity. This region is the perfect place to build it. The river will make it convenient to transport goods to the port and to other regions. The national highway passes nearby and has four lanes, which is very good for ground transportation. And there is space to build an airport if it becomes needed. Coal, oil and ore will be shipped here from the North and the finished steel will be loaded on to boats and exported to other countries. Our country has plenty of natural resources, and we can all become rich by exploiting them. The factory's profits will enrich the nation, but first, they will benefit the village.

'I know you're wondering, "If we, farmers, rely on the land for survival, how can we survive without it?" The answer is this: you're poor because your farms don't use the land to its full potential. How much rice can you harvest per hectare? When you total the cost of seed, labour, fertilizers, pesticides, taxes and fees, how much do you actually earn? I don't want to mention the specific figures because they would wrench our hearts. Nobody can get rich farming. We must do something else. The steel factory will industrialize the countryside. A hectare of land will increase in value ten-fold, even a hundred-fold. Can you imagine that? But it's true. Instead of toiling in the rice paddy to earn a mere pittance, the farmers can become factory workers or have jobs in the surrounding industries and services. There'll be hundreds of kinds of extremely well-paying jobs. That's our goal for this development.'

Dung talked non-stop while his colleagues looked on approvingly. I listened without understanding much. I was anxious, whereas my guests were excited. Every now and then they nodded and clapped their hands. Seeing me wanting to raise a concern, Dung waved his hand and continued:

'Let me finish. That's just the beginning. The future is even more important. What will the children do when they grow up? After the steel factory is constructed, other industries will invest here, too. There'll be lots of workers with all sorts of needs. There'll be retail stores, offices, restaurants, supermarkets and hotels, which will create all kinds of jobs: chefs, drivers, waiters, janitors, massage therapists, multilingual interpreters, office workers, etc. When the capitalist sharks come here to feed, they'll bring lots of money, so your new businesses will be able to charge them high prices without feeling guilty.'

Dụng was so articulate. But I was sweating all over, continually wiping drops of perspiration from my wrinkled face. The more earnestly he spoke, the more sceptical I became. If he told the truth and I took the villager's side against the project, I would be a fool. But if Dụng was being deceptive, supporting the project would betray my fellow villagers. Already by then, villagers had heard about the factory proposal and blocked the road so the construction crews couldn't enter. The protest had attracted attention from the media. People had also set up tents and took turns guarding the land around the site. I had not yet determined what we should do.

Another member of Dụng's entourage now spoke. He told me he was a state official and the investors' spokesperson, and he gave me a thorough explanation of the situation. But I still didn't know what to do. If the government had already made a decision, it must have considered all the pros and cons. The villagers protested because they were afraid of losing their land and suffering from pollution.

As I looked at the gifts Dụng had brought, I realized something didn't make sense. I said, 'I'm old and won't live much longer but, if what you described comes true, I'll be very happy. One thing I don't understand is whether this project is the government's policy, or just the work of a small group of people with private interests?'

Dụng laughed. 'Of course, it's the government's policy!' he said. 'No one else would dare make such an important decision. It's a government of the people, by the people, for the people. It wants everyone to live a happy, comfortable life, but it can't always make public statements about every little thing. Building a huge project like this costs trillions of *đồng*, so the decision must come from the highest authority.'

'If it truly comes from the government, then we can't oppose it. We'll do as we're told.'

'Please don't say that. You and the farmers have rights, too. No one can take away your land, your river, your lakes, forests, fields, etc. Not even an army equipped with the most powerful weapons would dare rob you of your property if the villagers were not content.'

'So,' I asked in a trembling voice, 'what do you need from me?'

'We're visiting you first and foremost because we respect you as a senior member of the community,' said Dụng. 'You have a good reputation and have always set a fine example for the younger people to emulate. As we move forward with the construction of the steel factory, we'd like to see you support the project. A single word from you is more powerful than an entire army. In the meantime, just relax, and we will keep you updated. In fact, not us, but the project's big bosses will inform you of all progress. Excuse us, but we must go now and report to them that you've agreed to help us. We'll come back soon.'

The guests stood up respectfully. I did, too, and hurriedly tried to hand the gifts back to Dụng, but he smiled and would not take them from me. Then he bought all the baskets he said he would when he arrived. Dụng and his team took the baskets to their cars and were thrilled, as if they had just signed a big business contract.

After they left, I sat in my house alone. My mind nearly exploded. I paced back and forth. If it was government policy, I had to comply. If I didn't, I'd be labelled a reactionary. I put the unopened gifts in a drawer, as if hiding some kind of contraband.

The villager leading the protests against the steel factory was a veteran named Bích. He had a teenage daughter named Diệu. Bích was an upstanding and outspoken farmer-hero who defied tyranny. The commune officials, who all supported the project, were annoyed by Bích's behaviour but could do nothing about it. I planned to invite Bích to my house to discuss what Dụng had told me, which was that the construction was a matter of government policy, and to tell him about the gifts. But before I could do that, Bích came to see me.

Straightaway, he asked, 'Did those land robbers bribe you to get your support?'

I showed him the unopened parcels. Bích glanced at them and asked me to put them away.

'Did they bribe you so you'd agree to sell us out and turn us into beggars? Bastards! As long as I'm alive, they won't get what they want.'

Bích asked me to stay out of it. He and the villagers would take care of everything. I didn't know what to say.

Within the month, the farmers, under Bích's leadership, were protesting the construction around the clock. They put up more tents, and each household sent someone to help protect the village. Commune officials who came to persuade the villagers to calm down were chased off. The district sent representatives to negotiate with us but they were all turned away too. The villagers argued they must protect their land because it was all they had. The factory should be built someplace else, where the soil was infertile. Everyone listened to Bích and would not yield. Finally, the state officials asked someone named Mr N. for help.

***

The elderly teacher was so absorbed in telling his story that he didn't see Việt's agitation. Mr N. was Việt's father. Việt had to stay calm if he wanted to get more information from the elderly teacher. If he discovered that Việt was Mr N.'s son, he probably wouldn't continue the story.

'What do you know about this Mr N.?' Việt asked calmly.

'He also paid me a visit,' the teacher replied, 'just to hear my opinions. I told him the same—I would comply with the higher authority's policy. Mr N. was not verbally deceptive like Dụng. Mr N. was polite, knowledgeable and calm. What he said was brief, but clear and logical. He was reluctant to do things that could not be undone. You can ask Bích for more specific details, but please don't mention my name. He and the villagers consider me a traitor. Honestly, I don't want to think about that awful factory again.'

The teacher wiped a tear from his eye with a handkerchief.

It may have been the last teardrop of a kind and gentle man. A few months later, he hanged himself, having written in his suicide note: 'I only wish I had found a way to protest sooner. Please, forgive me.'

Chapter VII

After a restless night of no sleep, the day to meet Mr Big had finally come. Sinh met secretly with his agents that morning, and then, later that afternoon, they took us both to a mansion overlooking central Việt Nam's most beautiful beach. Along the way, Sinh told me the mysterious and intimidating home could only be visited by the most select guests.

Arriving was like entering a pantomime. Everyone seemed to move without making a sound. The ones who greeted us at the gate showed absolutely no emotion, so I couldn't tell what they were thinking, though they treated us with deference and respect. The staff took excellent care of each guest, performing each act of service meticulously, but never smiling or even saying a single word.

The person Sinh and I were supposed to meet certainly had to be very wealthy and powerful. I didn't dare ask Sinh how he got us invited to the home or even if it belonged to Mr Big, mainly because I suspected his answers would disappoint me. Following everyone else's lead, I referred to the host as 'His Excellency'.

The day before, Sinh had been so arrogantly confident, but when he mingled among the large, intimidating men here, he acted just like me, deferential to a fault. From the gate, we strolled a long, winding path before arriving at a white, picket fence. Perhaps Mr Big, the king, was seated on his throne in the mansion behind the fence.

The owner must have loved Gothic architecture. Everything had been elaborately sculptured and artistically lit with accent lighting. At one end of the massive portico stood a white, marble statue of a naked woman with a voile scarf draped across her body. Water bubbled in a fountain somewhere. Clearly the mansion had been designed for important meetings and social events. With all its many varieties of rare and exotic trees, plants and flowers, the garden out front seemed fit for royalty. There was a crescent-moon pond, a low hedge labyrinth and a small menagerie. Off to the side, a patio facing the ocean allowed visitors to sit and look at the moon, the thousands of stars that shimmered on the horizon, and the far-off little boats, all just like in a fairy tale. There was an outdoor wine cellar. I wouldn't have been surprised if all this belonged to Mr Big. As rumour had it, he entertained all kinds of guests—singers and celebrities, high-class prostitutes, bank owners, government officials, and so on. Members of the powerful elite were at the top of the social ladder, and directly below them stood their children and relatives. One level down from them were the wealthy businessmen. Truly, not just anyone could set foot on Mr Big's estate. But of course, these were just rumours, as I myself had never even seen a photo of him, let alone observed him in person to know what company he kept, and of course, I had no idea who really owned that house.

It was said that money to Mr Big was as plentiful as leaves in a forest. If he needed cash for something, he could just clap his hands and his servants would bring him a truckload. If he wanted to be pleasured, he just picked up the phone. Any number of gorgeous, sexy women would come please him, and be immediately discarded once he was satisfied. People said he also invited singers and writers, because, despite their low social standing, they reaffirmed his philosophy about how to live a *real* life.

After going through security, Sinh and I were taken inside and seated beside a group of singers and writers who had achieved some small fame. I knew none of them. I saw a few bearded men who acted important and several young women wearing short skirts and elaborate make-up. They were loudly discussing politics and social issues with some arrogance. Then they argued about something, a poem, a book, or an award. They cursed its writer for his lack of talent, praised a different young poet, talked about a conference that a high-ranking state leader had attended, and gossiped about how certain writers had plagiarized and paid bribes to win awards.

'Does His Excellency, Mr Big, have an appointment with us?' I asked Sinh in a whisper.

'Who do you think you are?' Sinh whispered back. 'Even your dad wouldn't have dared ask such a question. I had to go through a lot of agents and use all my connections to get us here. Even if we cannot meet Mr Big one on one, what we are doing won't be useless. Don't be so anxious. Think about what you'll accomplish from this trip and be patient. I'll tell you what to do. In the meantime, just focus on what you're responsible for.'

I knew what Sinh was reminding me of. I put my hand in my pocket to make sure the wrapped stack of twenty-dollar bills I had prepared was still there. Guests kept arriving and acted as if they knew His Excellency very well. But when they looked for a place to sit, they became shy.

As the servants busily prepared food and beverages, Mr Big, I assumed, suddenly appeared. Sinh probably hoped it was him as well. He didn't quite have the look of the important, powerful person I had imagined, even though he did wear wrinkled, baggy, silk pyjamas. As he scanned the room indifferently, I noticed his thick, up-curved eyebrows. Then he stepped behind a thin curtain. When he came back out, he puffed on an ivory pipe while pacing back and forth as if concerned about something.

I made some assumptions based on the information I had. There were plenty of rumours about him—that he had an eccentric lifestyle and mannerisms, that his mouth was as large as a giant python's. People said his most favourite pastime was to bathe with a naked girl in a bathtub filled with expensive Italian and French wines. He believed that the wine could rejuvenate his aging skin and return him to his youthful years. It was rumoured that before he became His Excellency, he had deflowered an eighteen-year-old girl in a bathtub. She bled and he used the mixture of wine and blood to wash his face. He had loved the smell of it and continued to try to experience it again. Whether this rumour was true or not, it was generally agreed he bathed in red wine frequently.

The man I assumed was Mr Big had appeared only after the nearly sixty guests had taken their seats in this large hall inside the mansion. They all looked very cheerful. Sinh and I sat in the last row, far from the centre, and mimicked the other guests' behaviour. Our host occasionally spoke with a guest who sat near him in the front row. The rest of the guests talked amongst themselves in low voices. Common topics of these hushed conversations were the various rumours, as well as trying to figure out what the host was thinking when he glanced at them.

Throughout the reception and entertainment, Sinh and I just held our wine glasses and sat quietly. Every now and then we sipped a little bit. We smiled whenever someone gave the host a compliment, but no one cared. Mostly he didn't say much. Then suddenly he pointed his finger at a guest and asked in a powerful tone, 'Are you a poet? A member of the Writers' Association? Do you know T., Kh., D. and Ng.? If I wish it, they will have to come see me. If you see them, tell them I said hello and to come and have a drink with me. Have you written anything? Read me a good, sentimental poem you've written.'

The host didn't even wait for the poem or anything else. He pointed his finger at another guest. 'Are you a professor? What do you teach? Political science? That's good—it's a hot field nowadays. Anyone who wants to be a state official must fawn over you because you issue the certificate their career requires. Mã Xôm and Liệt Trọc come to drink with me all the time. Do you know them? If you see them, tell them I said hello.'

'And you, where do you work? You're a CEO—that's a big position! Don't forget to please your wife in bed. What do you think about the reception today?'

'And you, Miss, you should be in a beauty contest. Your breasts are so beautiful! Pull up your shirt so I can see them. No, no, just kidding. Why don't you sing a song? Can you pole-dance?'

Each person the host pointed to was elated. They enjoyed having the host's attention, and especially the attention of everyone watching them get the host's attention, and they laughed, told jokes and shared their opinions on the best ways to have sex, eat snails and do other things. The assumed Mr Big sat like a king on his throne, surrounded by appointed mandarins who waited for their turn to offer him their gratitude.

A group of beautiful, young women wearing sexy, revealing clothes came out and danced on the platform at the front of the room. The most beautiful one wore super-thin, transparent panties. She knelt before the host and placed his hands on her breasts before singing a song to him. He slid a handful of US dollars into her see-through bra.

Next the poets took turns giving emotional readings of their odes to the host. 'Your eyes are bright as stars, your hair soft as a cloud, your face is the sun, your smiles are the light.'

A poet read a poem lauding the host's friendliness, humility, leadership and ineffable love for all people, ending it with the lines: 'I want to kneel down so I can look up at you / hold your face in my eyes.'

After listening to the poem, the host clapped his hands and said, 'Very good! Very good! Send your poem to the literary committee and ask them to give you an award immediately. Then ask a musician to turn it into a song.'

The party began to wind down, and the host hadn't even glanced at us seated in the back. We felt really out of place, but we couldn't leave. Sinh worried that this golden opportunity might slip away, so he took a deep breath, raised his wine glass and said very loudly, 'Everyone, please, may I have your attention.'

Everyone turned toward Sinh and stared at him as if he were a wild beast. Only then did they probably realize that he was one of the guests, and not a housekeeper or a dog trainer.

The host, His Excellency, looked at Sinh with astonishment. His tired, bloodshot eyes rested atop plump bags of skin. He seemed irritated at first, but then appeared to recognize Sinh, and kept his calm to listen to what Sinh had to say.

'Sir, it's my great honour to be here today. I've heard so much about you over the years. You look so different from what I remember.'

'What was your name again?' the host asked. 'Is it …?'

'Of course, you might not remember me because I am a nobody. But I live to be your loyal servant. Today, I have seen something very bright surrounding your face, like a halo. I have seen the same kind of aura around the face of only one other person, but please don't ask me to reveal his identity.'

'No need to equivocate,' said the host. 'I can even invite God to come here anytime.' The host laughed heartily, taken with his own sense of humour. 'I respect your request, but did you really see a halo around my face? Tell me more about it.'

'The halo indicates one of two things. Either you are about to marry a beautiful woman who'll take good care of you, or you will soon be promoted to a very high position.'

He laughed. 'I'm old—no woman would want me. But explain what you mean about the second. What are you saying?'

'That's all I know. But I feel everything will come to you very easily.'

'I trust your feelings because I'm very happy today.' He then directed a servant to pour Sinh a glass of rare wine as a reward.

I was certain the host was Mr Big. After Sinh emptied his glass, the host sat lost in contemplation for a few seconds. Then, he looked at Sinh, who was acting demurely, and asked, 'Tell me, where did I first meet you?'

'At Mr V.'s house.'

'Ah, yes. I remember now. Are you his son's friend?'

'Yes, sir.'

'Why do you consider me a patron? Have I helped you with something?'

'You don't need to help me, sir. You are, in fact, already offering me something that's more valuable than gold.'

'Tell me what you need,' said the host, generously.

In the dead silence that followed, Sinh slowly turned his head and looked at me. It felt like an electric shock had surged through my head. Several days later, I still couldn't explain the strange feeling when Sinh looked at me—his eyes resembled sharp knives ready to slit my throat.

Then the host's cell phone rang.

His face turned pale, as if, indeed, God Himself had called from above.

Up until that moment, I was still thinking our host was Mr Big. But then, whose phone call could make him so nervous? In a heartbeat, he transformed from the powerful man he had seemed into a subservient child. He shoved his wine glass into the hands of a waiter and mumbled something unintelligible before clumsily shuffling behind the curtain. We could all hear him speaking in a respectful, obedient and fearful tone, 'Yes, sir . . . yes, sir . . . I am your faithful dog. Command me, please. I am honoured to be at your service.'

Sinh stood there waiting patiently for the host to come back. The other guests clearly both admired and envied Sinh. When the host finally re-emerged, he looked like a completely different person, nervous and horrified, as if something terrible was about to happen. He looked like a robot whose battery was about to die. Seeing Sinh, the host waved his hand and said, 'Everyone, good night. Now go!' And then he told his servants, 'Get the car ready for me.'

The guests, except for Sinh and me, were probably familiar with what had just happened because they didn't seem surprised at all. Some guests finished their wine and others ate one last morsel before standing up to leave. Sinh and I were the last people to exit through the back gate. I wondered: Who had just called him? Who could make him so nervous? Was he really Mr Big? Or was there a Mr Bigger?

Back in our car, Sinh was no longer excited, as he had been earlier. He remained still and silent for most of the ride back to the hotel, except for the drumming of his fingers.

'Damn it!' he exclaimed at last. 'That guy was just one of Mr Big's lackeys.' Sinh sighed. 'It was a waste of time after all.'

***

I told no one about the trip when I returned. Instead, I pored over the documents related to my father's past, especially the mysterious condolence letter signed by Mr Big. I couldn't figure out how it had gotten on to my desk. What kind of power did the guy that both Sinh and I had assumed to be Mr Big have over his staff and all those guests? Was he really one of Mr Big's close

subordinates, or something else? These and other questions
caught my mind in a matrix of doubt and confusion. To keep
the situation from overwhelming me, I decided to occupy
myself with something else.

That was why I took the first trip to visit the steel factory, as
described in the original *Termite Queen* chapter, 'People Coming
from Somewhere Far Away'. All the major events described by
the author were accurate. The author depicted the character
Việt's trip rather vividly, though he left out some details about
Việt's feelings, or rather my feelings, because I was, after all, the
real Việt. The author made assumptions about the old teacher
and Bích. For instance, he depicted Bích's attitude in such a way
that made the character not seem very calm. In reality, when
Bích met with the elderly teacher, he was extremely polite and
sympathetic. Bích never spoke to him with the kind of scathing
tone the book employed.

By that time, I had grown quite confused about my famous
father, so I decided to return to the village to find out more
about Bích, and hopefully my father too.

When I first visited the village, the elderly teacher told me
something not included in the original *Termite Queen*. Bích had
been paralysed for over ten years. When I returned, I went back
to Mr Quang's house, and he had not forgotten the gift that
I (Việt in the excerpt) had given him. He welcomed me warmly.

'Haven't you finished your work in my village yet?' asked
Quang. 'Pardon me if I'm being rude, but what are you actually
doing here? I hope you're not planning any more harm.'

'I am a freelance journalist,' I said. 'I want to learn more
about how the steel factory has changed the village.'

'Journalist? Why didn't you say so last time? I wouldn't
have wasted my time. Get out of here, you bastard. You've got a
lot of enemies in this village.'

Clearly, I had made a mistake choosing my cover. 'What
did I do wrong?'

'You personally have probably done nothing wrong, but others like you have made our lives miserable. I'm warning you—we don't welcome reporters here.'

'There are good and bad people everywhere,' I said. 'If you think I'm evil, I'll leave immediately.'

'Okay, I trust you,' he said after some consideration. 'But don't tell the other villagers you're a reporter. They won't trust you as easily as I do. Please sit down and have some tea.'

Quang sang a folk song that featured horrendously sad lyrics. He closed his eyes. His voice was clear and vibrant. (In the original *Termite Queen*, the author didn't pay enough attention to Quang's deep emotions while he sang, focusing instead only on the character's appearance.)

I asked him to tell me what happened just before the construction of the steel factory began.

Quang immediately got excited, as if I'd given him just the right, rare opportunity to vent his anger. He promised to tell me everything.

He disappeared into the back of his house, and when he returned, he plopped on to the table a stack of official documents, reports and governmental summons, all of which he said were related to the agreed-upon compensation. It was kind of funny when he raised his hand and said in a serious, formal voice: 'I am Quang, a veteran. I swear to tell the truth, the whole truth and nothing but the truth.'

I almost laughed.

With a wild look in his eyes, he said, 'Listen carefully!'

Quang's story

When we were informed of the steel factory project and the impending loss of hundreds of hectares of land we used for rice cultivation, we opposed it. We held several meetings at the neighbourhood, village, commune and district levels. We wanted to know why the factory was to be built in the middle of a peaceful countryside that supplied rice to the entire region, and why not in a place where it wouldn't damage the environment. Instead of giving us answers and a clear explanation, the investors only said that they had been issued a construction licence, and whoever protested would be considered in direct opposition to the government. We emphasized that we were not against the government. We were only against wrongdoings. All the villagers declined the monetary compensations and guarded their land so that no one could take it from them.

The tension lasted for ten days. We thought we had won because the investors finally left. We started to live our lives as normal again. We were grateful to our ancestors for leaving us fertile rice paddies and a river. The river provided fish for the entire village, and if the factory were constructed, it would become a busy port occupied by cargo ships loaded with coal, ore and oil. No fish could survive all that. The river would no longer be a place for young couples to enjoy each other's company. Thank God, we thought, the government had finally listened to our concerns.

But we were wrong. One dark night, while everyone slept, hundreds of people wearing black outfits and black masks that looked like skulls stormed into our homes and dragged the adults outside. Silently they bludgeoned us in the faces and chests. They didn't beat the women, but they tore off their clothes, stuffed rags in their mouths and threatened them with their clubs. They tortured everybody at the same time, so no one could run to anyone else to ask for help. Then the masked, ghostly men disappeared into the dark. The following morning, the victims talked about what had happened, each hoping they had just had an awful nightmare. They were terrified and bewildered.

We sent a representative to report the incident to the commune the next day. The commune said it would report it to the district and then on to the higher authorities. But the way the state officials talked with us was very strange. It was as if they already knew what we were going to say. A few of them even helped us remember what had happened.

'Was it a whole bunch of black ghosts,' asked one government official, 'masked men who emerged from nowhere and then disappeared into the dark? It's a typical ghost story, but we'll work with the higher authorities to solve the problem.'

After that, a few officials came to our village to investigate. Instead of listening to us seriously, they laughed at us and repeatedly said, 'We know,' while we had no clue what they actually knew. The media wrote stories that claimed we made up the ghostly attack to get attention. One newspaper reported that a person in village X was mentally ill and imagined the ghosts and the whole attack, and that the entire village just repeated his story.

We became miserable victims ridiculed by outsiders. But who would dare fabricate such a horrifying story? No state official answered our questions seriously, and this confused us more. We looked at each other, asking ourselves what had happened. It was impossible to say we had all hallucinated the same thing.

There was another strange thing. A few weeks before that horrible night, we had heard strange noises, as if a giant army was marching towards the village. The ground trembled. The noises were clear and real, but we couldn't tell where they came from. We also heard whispering sounds and couldn't say whether they were human or ghost. We also heard the sound of motorboats on the river. It came again a few minutes after the masked men left our houses on that terrible night.

The district officials held a meeting, and invited other state organizations and some select members of the press to attend. They tried to reassure us, cautioning that a group of individuals had taken advantage of the situation and fabricated the entire superstitious story not only to terrify us but also to stain the reputation of the government and state officials. They said this group wanted to divide our country. That was truly horrifying!

To prove nothing suspicious was happening, the land clearance for the construction of the factory was delayed. The contractor, the uniformed guards with their walkie-talkies and the noisy bulldozers left. At that point, we had nothing to protest and the public lost interest. But the delay was just a game they played while their true strategy was legalized. But we believed we'd won, so we went home and prepared for the next harvest.

A few weeks later, on another dark night, the ghosts appeared again out of nowhere. This time, no one heard a motorboat on the river. It was a nearly moonless night—or rather the moon looked like a surreal, bloodstained sickle that quickly sank into the Thiên Lôi Mountains. The masked men did the same things they had done before. They stormed into our homes, dragged out the people and tortured them. And as before, at the end, they vanished into the dark. We were too terrified to utter a word.

The representative of the commune sent an incident report to the higher authorities. They held well-attended meetings. They investigated and had witnesses verify the information shared. But they came to the same conclusion: some of the villagers had made up the story and the rest fell into a trap set by individuals with bad intentions. The media started to lose patience.

To prove our story had been fabricated, the higher authority sent a group of officials and scientists to our village to investigate. News reporters hid in a few of our homes and installed hidden cameras in others, but now the ghosts seemed to know about the plan to catch them and didn't show up.

'So where are the ghosts?' an investigator asked sarcastically during a village meeting.

No one could answer his question.

'We told you what we saw,' a villager said. 'We don't know where they are now.'

'We're on to you,' said the head of the delegation, mocking us. 'Before making up another story, bear in mind there will be consequences. Stop trying to scare people.'

Disappointed by the conclusion drawn by the higher authority, we relied even more heavily on Bích. He was calm, brave and fair. He wrote all our reports. I heard that one of the project's managers came to his house several times, trying to negotiate something in secret with him, as he had done with the elderly teacher. But Bích remained firm. He told us to believe in justice and not to give up. We trusted him and asked him to be in charge of everything on our behalf. Bích came up with a secret plan to expose the truth.

Then, all of a sudden, Bích disappeared. No one knew where he went. The commune said they were not privy to his affairs—he was a private citizen. Maybe that was just how he did things. Impatiently we waited for his return.

The whole time he was missing, the villagers lived in fear. The ghosts didn't come back, but the noises of motorboats and clanking iron chains disturbed each night. We also heard shrieking voices and women screaming. Later we learned these women had come from the city, and while waiting for the factory's promised jobs, they'd turned tricks with the labourers who had also showed up and with the many boatmen now anchored along the river. Some of these people were stabbed, their legs and arms cut off and their bodies thrown into the river. But none of the survivors gave any details, apparently to protect themselves and their relatives. People started drifting away, to the cities or who knows where.

The next thing we knew, Bích reappeared, a large parcel of land had been cleared, and the factory was built. That's the complete story. We lost our land and had to find other ways to survive. Young people left and went to the big cities. They couldn't attend their parents' funerals. Many of them went to jail or became gangsters and prostitutes. Those who came back shaved their heads, sang all day and acted crazy. Many of them now waste all their money on drugs and booze.

***

I asked Mr Quang, 'What about Bích? Where had he gone?'

'If you have time, go to his house and ask him directly. But he probably won't tell you much. He signed a non-disclosure agreement with the contractor, so he hasn't said a word since he returned. And then, of course, after his wife died of cancer, he has been paralysed with grief.'

Quang wiped a tear from his eye and continued, 'After everything was said and done, the higher authority sent a representative to the village and released an official statement that what we claimed we witnessed and experienced was true after all. He concluded that the masked ghosts were members of a terrorist group from abroad and that they must have been completely wiped out. But, by whom or what, they never said.'

Forcing a bitter smile, he said, 'That's the story. And that's life. Very shitty!'

After listening to Quang's story, I resolved to meet Bích immediately. I left Quang's house and saw that I'd gotten a text from Sinh: *Wait for me at home. You must show up immediately when I call tomorrow. Mr Big is now very close.*

The district chairman had also called and left a voicemail: 'They're going to kill me soon. I can't wait for you any longer. I must live.'

Chapter VIII

An Unholy Army (chapter from the original *Termite Queen*)
Kim Village[4], an agrarian community known for its classic architecture and civilized culture, was located near the coast north of the delta. Most of the villagers were kind, hospitable and polite, and frequently did charity work. They lived primarily by rice farming. They also grew sweet potatoes, corn and peanuts, and raised goats. The river behind the village provided most of their food. It was at its widest where it ran through the village and looked like a bow beneath the Thiên Lôi Mountains. The villagers called this part of the river the Vòng Gulf. Fortune-tellers and *feng-shui* experts had long ago divined that Kim Village would be home to many talented people. Before the steel factory was built, flocks of pheasants had danced at the foot of the mountains at dawn. One villager said he had once seen a giant white snake curling on a rock. A rooster comb the size of a star fruit grew on its head and sparkled like a ruby.

The legend of the giant snake didn't frighten anyone, however, and no one was scared to go out at night. The villagers believed the serpent was a god who had taken the form of a snake to protect them. For several years, there hadn't been a single fight in the village. A horrible scandal soon changed everything.

---

[4] Mr Quang's village in the real *Termite Queen*

One night, the Kim villagers heard many heavy footsteps outside their homes. At first, they weren't sure what was making the noise. But it kept coming back night after night and people started to pay attention.

The villagers decided to determine the source. To some, it seemed as if it came from the other side of the mountains. Others thought the noise was echoing from somewhere very deep underground. No one knew what to think, but the oldest man in the village observed Saturn moving west. He also saw a duck with cloudy eyes, which was very unusual. The whole village wondered if these were omens.

A righteous and heroic man named Bích was village chairman at the time. He despised sycophants and didn't believe in ghosts. He had wanted to be a teacher, but had dropped out of college to join the army. Years later, after being honourably discharged, he returned to the village and devoted himself to farming and helping the poor. He was well-liked, so the villagers elected him chairman for several terms in a row. Bích had been paying close attention to the unusual incidents occurring at the foot of the Thiên Lôi Mountains.

One night, he discovered a training camp that had recently been established. The property used to be a tree nursery but had been abandoned years ago. Now it was fenced in with tall sheets of corrugated metal—the kind used for construction projects—and no one could see what was inside. But Bích climbed to a perch on the mountain above the compound and through binoculars observed hundreds of large men in black uniforms practising martial arts and combat techniques. The men in black trained hard but didn't utter a single word. Only on the occasional break did they make even the slightest noise. Were these men mercenaries? Gangsters? Bích wasn't sure.

He told no one about what he'd discovered. He wanted to find out exactly what these men were doing first. He was frustrated that he couldn't get closer to see the faces of the men in the camp clearly. But even from a distance he could tell they were meticulously well-disciplined and professional in everything they did. Their training sessions often lasted far into the night. Watching them reminded Bích of his time spent in the military. He could tell that the men in the camp were skilful, strong and very disciplined.

One moonlit night, from his mountainside perch, Bích watched as the little army assembled into three long lines. They wore hoods that covered their faces. When they marched, they looked like a moving wall. Each step remained perfectly in sync. Their commander raised an arm and within seconds, the entire army dropped to the ground and vanished into the grass and trees around them like ghosts.

Who could defeat such an unholy army?

Chapter IX

Instead of jumping right back into work after my visit with Quang, I spent a quiet day thinking about my father. Whenever I felt depressed, I always thought about him.

Because of his busy schedule, he didn't usually spend much time with my sister and me. My mother took care of us. When I went away to college, he called me every now and then and we would talk briefly. I remember once he joked, 'I want to have a grandchild, but don't bring home a European wife. Your mother won't be able to communicate with her.'

I realized a lot of my memories of him were at home in the early mornings when he had a worried look on his face. As a rich and famous businessman, he rarely revealed weakness. He had to show people he was strong and had control over any situation. When living among sharks, showing weakness would get a man swallowed alive. The sharks were cold-blooded, heartless and greedy. My mother said he sometimes went to a nearby Buddhist temple and stood reverentially in front of the statues. No one knew what he prayed for. He had a lot of things going on in his head because his company competed with so many other companies to win contracts, and it had projects everywhere. He had often said, 'In business, being sympathetic means self-destruction. You should only have sympathy for the defeated.'

When I returned to Việt Nam from England the spring before my graduation exam, I stayed longer than usual. At that time, my father's company had no rivals. He won all the contracts he aimed for and thus became so well known that the media and many celebrities wanted to befriend him. Instead of feeling proud of himself, he became more introspective. Sometimes he stayed in his office after work, closed the door and met with no one. He smoked constantly and sometimes got drunk once he got home. My mother was in her forties and very lonely. She often slept alone because he was frequently away on business trips. She told me that even when he lay next to her in bed, she often felt empty.

As we returned home one day that summer from a spontaneous picnic, my father told me a story that took place before he was born. The story was narrated in detail in the original *Termite Queen* chapter presented below.

A Tragic Love Story

In a rural village a long time ago, there was a wealthy mandarin who had several wives and many servants. Even his provincial superior deferred to him. But due to the universal law of impermanence, the mandarin eventually lost everything and became a nobody himself.

Before then, though, the polygamous mandarin tried to commit suicide after his spoiled and ungrateful children insulted him and chased him out of his home. He mixed arsenic with rice wine and told his favourite maid to prepare the bed on which he would die. He had ordered his wives to take their children and the rest of the servants to Hà Nội, and then to go to the South where he owned another estate. He remained alone at home with his trusted maid. At midnight, the mandarin decided the time had come to end his life. He would drink the poisoned wine and die quickly.

And yet, he was still alive after drinking the entire bottle of poisoned wine. Instead, in fact, he got an erection that wouldn't go away. He called the maid into his bedroom.

'Did you give me the wrong wine by mistake?'

'I did it on purpose,' she said. 'I gave you the herbal wine you often drink before sleeping with Mrs Ba instead. I thought maybe you'd lost your mind. Why would you want to give up so soon? Suicide would ruin your family's reputation.'

'How dare you!' he fumed. 'You're illiterate and you have the nerve to lecture me on moral philosophy? That's not how a servant talks to her master. Who do you think you are?'

'I am your servant, sir.'

'I don't believe it. You're a devil. What are you trying to do? You've ruined everything!'

'I'm not done yet. I am forever a woman.'

'Be quiet! Get out of my sight!'

The mandarin snatched up the bottle and was about to throw it at her but lowered his arm when he looked into her big, bright eyes. She didn't look frightened. Rather, sympathy for him radiated from her face. He realized suddenly that she was more beautiful than any of his wives. 'My God!' he said, and then threw the bottle into the corner and beat his chest. He moaned as if in terrible pain.

The maid remained calm and quietly left the room. He had always been kind and generous to her and his life was her most important concern. Though he had berated her, she felt content knowing that no man could think about suicide in a situation like this. In fact, he must instead at that moment be imagining how to enjoy life. The truth was she loved him dearly. As a woman, like his wives, she wanted to be with him. But she was his servant. She could not cross that line. When the mandarin ordered his wives to leave, she knew her opportunity had arrived. Understanding that he wanted to commit suicide, she had switched the bottles, believing he would not hate her for making such an ethical decision. Thus, even while he was scolding her, she covered her mouth to hide her satisfied smile.

But then she realized her actions did not help herself so much as it did his wives. The thick-headed, old mandarin was obsessed with money and power and wanted to die just to save face. He was by no means a hero. She would be a fool if she didn't take advantage of him. He didn't deserve her. She went back to her own bedroom.

Just as she lay down to sleep, the mandarin entered the room and stood at the foot of her bed. His erection was plainly visible beneath his silk pyjamas. Her whole body began to tremble. She did not dare to ask what he needed. She assumed she was in for the kind of cruelty she had witnessed when he found out about Mrs Hai's infidelity with one of his nephews.

'Get up and come with me,' he ordered. 'Now.'

Hesitantly she trailed behind his heavy steps, following him into his room.

He sat on the bed and told her to close the door behind her. 'Take off those pyjamas,' he said. She trembled but did as he commanded. In front of him was a beautiful body the likes of which he had never seen. Now he trembled as he stared at her pink nipples, her navel, her groin. Demurely, she covered herself with one hand and crossed the other arm over her breasts. The gesture nearly drove him crazy with desire.

'I had decided to die so I wouldn't have to live miserably and to protect my dignity. Oh God! I wanted to die,' he sobbed. Then he looked at her again. 'But you ruined my plan. Do you want me to live, or do you want to take revenge on me? Why did you do that?'

'I don't know. I just knew it was what I should do.' She looked at him as if half begging for mercy, half ridiculing him. She remained naked, still as a statue.

'This is our fate,' he said at last, taking her hand. 'You have been my servant, but in fact you are a goddess. From now on, you are no longer a servant. You are my precious Mrs Năm, my fifth wife.'

'Sir, please don't say that. I don't deserve it.'

'It is the will of heaven. I can do nothing about it.'

He lit another candle to see her more clearly. She trembled, whether from fear or excitement or both he could not tell. But then she gave herself to him, and he felt extremely satisfied. It was the best sex he had ever had. He kissed her all over.

They made love five times that night, each time better than the one before. She moaned in ecstasy. It was the same the next two nights, five times each.

On the morning of the fourth day, the mandarin died. Even in death, his skin had a healthy, rosy glow.

The maid, now the mandarin's fifth wife, buried the mandarin and disappeared. Most people who know the story consider her a *femme fatale*. She gave birth to a son, to whom her only close relative later told this story.

***

My father's version of the story differed slightly from the one told in the original *Termite Queen*. At the end, he whispered to me, 'The maid who became Mrs Năm—she is your grandmother.'

Unsurprised, I asked, 'Where is she now?'

'Up there,' he said as he looked up into the sky where a white cloud was floating past.

On our way home, my father seemed a different person. He said he would try to go on picnics with my mother, my sister and me like this more often because most of the rest of his life was meaningless.

Noticing my look of bewilderment, he added, 'I want to go to a place where I don't know who I am. I want to find out more about my mother and my birthplace. I want to buy my father's house back. It was seized, and five or six households live in it now. I want to get out of—'

He didn't complete the last sentence, as if hiding something.

I remained quiet, not wanting to share my thoughts with him. Did he resent his status so strongly that he was determined to be rich so no one could look down on him? Did he inherit his father's perseverance and bravery, or his willingness to give up so suddenly? His mother's inventive mind? I had so many questions I dared not ask.

'It should be easy for you to do what you want,' I said, finally, trying to sound mature.

'Honestly, I don't know why I need to earn so much money. Building such a huge fortune means hundreds of other people cannot live comfortable lives. That's the reality. There are many things you don't understand. I have always carefully omitted your real grandfather's name from our documents to protect us. The pictures of the people on the altar to whom you bow every day deserve our respect, but they are not biologically related to us.' He shook his head and blew air from his lips. 'Just forget what I just said. Focus on your studies, graduate and come back to help me here.'

The past was a mystery. Did some invisible power control everything my father had done? I had been drawn into playing an endless game, haunted by the sorrowful and repentant look on my father's face when he drew his last breath.

***

At the district chairman's request, I came to his office to discuss how to negotiate with the residents protesting the golf course. While I had been away, some people had put up banners on the streets of the villages where the citizens were required to relocate. They had submitted a formal complaint to the district, and he didn't know how to deal with it. In fact, the district chairman wanted to avoid all responsibility and placed the blame on our company.

As soon as the district chairman saw me, he said, 'You can shoot yourself in the foot if you like, but don't drag me into it. I have lots of things to do and I love my life. I don't want to die like a rat.'

'I'm sorry for worrying you,' I said. 'I'll meet with the villagers today. Please send some officials to accompany me in case something happens.'

'If I could, I'd close my office and send all my employees to help you. But I still don't see how any of that will persuade those stupid peasants.'

'I know how. I'll start by explaining all the positives and negatives of the situation. I think they'll understand.' I had no idea.

When we arrived, the farmers had already gathered in the commune's meeting hall. I suspected I would fail because I had no interest in the discussions. But I also knew the godfathers were watching me from afar with their cold eyes—I'd be in real trouble if we lost the money they had invested. My mother was nervous. Suddenly, I thought of my father and felt resentment toward him for placing such a heavy burden on my shoulders, a burden that he himself had struggled with until his last breath.

In front of me stood about three hundred families whose land would be affected by the project. They looked angry and uncooperative. I didn't see the brothers who rented the pond for fish farming, however. Persuading them to give it up to make way for the golf course would be my most difficult task. The district chairman promised me that, if they refused to cooperate, the district would force them, violently if need be. But it was not as simple as he said. If the brothers lost the pond, they would lose everything. They had devoted their lives to it, so of course they would fight until the very end.

I took a deep breath and said, 'Good morning, ladies and gentlemen! Hello, everyone! I'm here today to express my gratitude for your cooperation.'

Some members of the audience shouted:

'No one wants to cooperate with you!'

'It's not cooperation. It's robbery.'

'Bullshit! You're lying. Don't bullshit us.'

'You already have tons of money. Isn't it enough?'

And then finally, a reprieve: 'Let's hear what he has to say.'

I remained calm and continued my speech. 'On behalf of the investors of this project, I'd like to discuss with you how we can all become rich together. Please take advantage of this opportunity to build a better future for the Đồng Village, the Hoàng Commune and the Chương District as well. Trust me. This region deserves to benefit from the nation's policy of reform. You don't want to be impoverished forever. We'll transform this place into one of the most beautiful, sustainable cities in the region. Besides a golf course, there will be large roads, high-rise buildings, shops, sports arenas, restaurants and resorts to meet the demands of the wealthy people who will come here to stay or visit. We'll use their money to build hospitals, schools, gyms and nursing homes for the poor. This planning document here in my hands details everything I just mentioned. And our top priority is to ensure your rights, benefits and happiness. Our goal is to make your dreams come true, and to make the impossible possible. All we need is your signature. It's simply a formality. Your bright future and a better new life depend on your cooperation.

'And to you, the young generation,' I continued, making obvious eye contact with the young people in attendance, 'we know your life isn't just about having enough food to eat and clothes to wear. You need good educations, good schools and places to relax after long days at work. You deserve to enjoy the benefits of a civilized life. You should become global citizens with every opportunity to discover the world. Please join us in making these dreams come true. Together, we'll change everything for the better. We may all become rich. But your happiness is our primary concern.

'We have intensely researched the geology and geography of this region, as well as your cultivation methods and harvest yields, and I can assure you that a development project like our modern, five-star golf course is the only way to propel it from poverty to prosperity. You might be surprised to hear this, but it's the truth. You'll get used to the new life. Every one of you can become a restaurant owner, or the manager of a swimming pool, park, or gym. You can have whatever business you like and make a lot of money. Those infertile rice paddies will no longer haunt you with poverty. You will no longer have to suffer the stench of cow manure. You won't be hungry. You won't be forced to sell your rice at pitiful prices. Together we'll make Đồng Village better. We're here today to help you build a new life.'

I paused to observe my audience's reactions. The room was quiet. I could see many of the families had been moved by my speech.

'We are here today,' I continued, 'as your friends. We will be allies working together in harmony and solidarity. We'll solve problems through fair exchange, discussion and negotiation. You can bargain if you wish. Let me repeat: money is not the most important thing that we're pursuing with this project. Instead, the project is an expression of our responsibility to the community and to our country. Together we will discover the most effective way to use our natural resources for our children's long-term benefit. I have been inspired by the words of Martin Luther King Jr., and similarly we must make our world a place where your dreams can come true. Please let me know if you have any questions.'

I felt exhausted as I ended my speech. I had run out of energy. I knew I was lying to them. I had plagiarized ideas from famous speeches and added a few fancy, academic words to make it sound more 'global'. But my speech didn't make much sense for this situation. I knew I was deceiving them and asking them to side with the greedy, cruel sharks. What I said was exactly like what Dung had said to the elderly teacher regarding the steel factory in the original *Termite Queen*.

As they sat thinking, some members of the audience remained sceptical. One middle-aged man spat at what I had said. He asked, 'If the golf course is built, can I apply for a security job?'

'Definitely. Please remind me when you do.'

I was surprised at myself for telling such a blatant lie. By the time they started building the golf course, I would be long gone, so how would I keep my promise to him? My father had done the same things. I had no choice.

'And you, please.' I pointed at a raised hand in the audience.

'Who set the policy for this project?' he asked.

'The government, of course. No one but the government has the power to set policy for your land. The government has carefully considered the large, long-term benefits for all of you.'

'According to you, we're going to live in a paradise very soon. We don't know if we'll live long enough to see the golf course, but we do know our land can't make more land, so please tell the government that if they take our land, we'll have to live in the mountains like monkeys.'

'I'll certainly pass your concern on to the government. May I know your name?'

'Doan,' he replied.

'Top economists and development experts have already discussed this issue at a conference,' I lied. 'I assure you they've considered everything carefully. Our government is perfect and run by brilliant leaders who love the people, especially the poor. Our leaders are intelligent, talented, honest and incorruptible. Trust them. Their only duty is to work for everyone's happiness and ensure each citizen has a comfortable life. According to a recent survey, less than one per cent of state officials are slacking off in their duties. I have studied and worked in England, one of the five most powerful countries in the world, and they don't even dream of such a near-perfect percentage. Obviously, our government is the best in the world. You should have complete faith in it. Don't believe people who are upset with the government and distort the truth in order to divide the country. You might not live long enough to take care of your children, but our government will last forever and take great care of them and even your grandchildren.'

'Stop lying!' a young man shouted. 'That's enough. We're not gullible. There's no government here, just a group of greedy people trying to fill their pockets with more money. As long as I'm alive, they'll never take our land.'

Several audience members shouted loudly in support as he finished. I thanked him for expressing his thoughts, not wanting to confront him. It was time to bring this conversation to an end. But then, suddenly, the commune chairman appeared. He looked defiant and told the crowd to stay put. He wanted to say a few words to the investors.

'Hopefully, now you see,' the commune chairman said as he stepped up to the podium and pointed his finger at me. 'You cannot deceive us. We'll put up fences to protect our village. You can't win. Consider our friendship over right here and right now. By coming here again you've revealed yourself as an enemy, so you can forget about cooperation! You—all of you—are nothing but disgusting liars!' Then he turned toward the audience and said, 'If you have young daughters, keep them inside the house, otherwise these bastards will carry them off.' He turned back to me. 'Keep your filthy hands off our land, our rice paddies, our gardens, our lakes. Stop sticking your nose into how we live our lives. On behalf of our people, I'm telling you what we need is our land, not a golf course. Do you get it, finally? I'm warning you, land robbers, get out of here before we beat the shit out of you. Get lost!'

The crowd cheered and began to chant, 'Get lost! Get lost!' and 'Let's kick their arses!'

I knew I couldn't stay there any longer. As I left the building, I told myself to simply wait and see. Every problem has a solution. My father had always said so. If a problem couldn't be solved peaceably through negotiation, we'd use money, power and coercion.

I told myself I would not give up. Now I knew why my father felt he had to win, even though his victories had brought him endless sorrows.

Mostly, I regretted I had not yet been able to meet Mr Big.

Chapter X

The original *Termite Queen* included several passages from a memoir written by Bích, the leader of the resistance to the steel factory. It quoted this passage at length:

Bích's Memoir
After the unholy army captured me, they tied my hands and blindfolded me so I wouldn't know where I was being taken, but I could feel the car turn several times before it came to a road full of potholes. I felt that the kidnappers were probably taking me to a desolate area in a canyon northwest of the village. The large men sitting on either side of me said nothing as they locked their arms with mine so that I could not move. I asked who they were and whether they were the ghosts who had terrorized the village. Silence. I knew the villagers were relying on me, and that my resolve would help them fight against these terrorists. I knew my responsibility as a leader.

But in fact, I didn't think much about myself. Rather, I was most worried for my wife and daughter, who had to have been panicking. My daughter was too young to understand what was going on. And my wife was very sick. I worried she wouldn't be able to withstand the fact that I had been abducted. I hoped she would stay quiet to protect herself. I could deal with these so-called ghosts because I knew what they wanted. They dared not kill me. If they did, they would lose everything.

I started to put some things together. My abduction had to be related to the steel factory because they knew the role I played in the protests against the land grabs. The farmers were on my side and protested because they trusted me. The investors would play their final cards. Everything had become worse since some of their people secretly visited teacher Trương, who then remained silent. I didn't blame anyone, but I needed to escape and return to the village.

Suddenly the car stopped, and they pushed me out. I was still blindfolded tightly and could see nothing as they led me forward. I slipped and nearly fell several times until they again locked their arms through mine.

I heard a door open, and then they threw me down on to a brick floor. The door was slammed shut and locked. Everything dead quiet. Never before had I experienced such a terrifying silence. I could feel that I was surrounded by a very thick wall.

Where was this place?

***

After the debacle of my failed speech to the farmers, I had run out of ideas and felt exhausted. I decided I'd have to return to the steel factory town to try to learn some new strategies, but this time, I would go directly to Bích's home. The house had a bright and airy design with an open floor plan for the living and dining spaces as well as a small home office right by the windows opening on to the wide front porch where we sat.

I pretended to be a scientist doing research on the negative environmental impacts of industrial projects on the countryside. Bích was paralysed, but his mind was still sharp. Although he used a wheelchair, he didn't look ill. He seemed like he needed someone to talk to.

'I don't care who you are,' Bích said. 'If you've come here, we're friends. Since I've been stuck in this wheelchair, I've just been reading and thinking by myself a lot.'

'I love reading, too,' I said. 'May I ask how you were paralysed?'

'It's a long story,' he said with a wry smile.

'Did it have anything to do with the steel factory?'

'It happened before the factory was built.'

'I'm sorry if my questions make you uncomfortable.'

'It's fine. I just don't want to remember it. I have forgiven them.'

'Who were they?'

Bích urged me to drink the tea he had poured for us. While I took in the simple furniture in his home, my eyes fell on a stack of papers on the desk just inside the window. He must be writing something, I thought. In England, I was taught that it was impolite to read someone else's personal papers without permission. Therefore, I pretended not to have seen them, but he had noticed. He called a woman's name, and within a few moments a young woman came from one of the back rooms through the house and stood in the doorway. I was completely stunned by how beautiful she was. She greeted me, and at Bích's request, quickly gathered the pages of the manuscript from the desk and put them into a drawer. I was holding my cup of tea, but my mind followed the woman even after she disappeared again into the back room.

'My daughter, Diệu,' Bích said. 'I am alive only because of her. My wife gave birth to her when we were no longer young. I wanted her to become a teacher. In her second year at university, she changed her major from education to law. Now she's a senior and will graduate very soon. Before I became paralysed, and before my wife died, my daughter had been so innocent and so happy. Now, as you can see, she always looks concerned and pensive. I worry for her. Because of me she has not given a single thought to getting married.'

My heart suddenly beat faster, but I forced myself to remember why I was there.

'All parents worry for their children,' I said. 'My mother is no exception.'

'True but my daughter grew up in an unusual situation. Anyway, let me change the subject—why did you choose me to ask about the steel factory? Might we have met before?'

'I don't think so,' I said. 'Do you?'

'Well, I'm not sure. I can't remember anything these days. But you seem familiar.'

'Interesting! Sometimes, I have the same feeling. I meet a complete stranger but I feel I know them already.'

'Exactly.'

A gentle noise caught my attention. My eyes met Diệu's as she stood in the doorway to one of the back rooms, apparently listening to our conversation. I thought maybe she wanted me to know she was there, but I later realized I had been wrong. Probably the conversation with Bích was going too far, and she felt an instinctual need to be on alert to protect her father. Naturally she would want to know the real motivation behind my interviewing him. Bích remained contemplative, as if trying to recall when or where we'd met. I believed many residents of this village would remember the image of my father, but I couldn't be certain what kind of impression he had left. My father and Bích must have met many times. My father had managed to come up with a solution that got the villagers to agree to give up their land, and I needed to know how he'd done it.

But I had no idea where to start. Of course, I couldn't reveal my true identity to him. Bích might forgive me, but I doubted Diệu would. I didn't know why I was so obsessed with her eyes.

She was beautiful and elegant. I could tell just by looking at her that her mind was sharp. Her face made me think of light—her skin was as pale as fresh snow, her eyes resembled two copper ponds, her lips were full. She looked resilient and strong. This woman was the opposite of deception, I thought. Had she switched her major because of the injustices her father and the villagers had suffered?

I was surprised when Bích invited me to stay for lunch. On the one hand, I thought I should decline out of respect. On the other, I knew I would regret it if I missed an opportunity, even though I wasn't completely sure what that opportunity was. Was it Diệu's bright face and beautiful eyes that made me stay, or did I just want to learn more from Bích?

Noticing my hesitation, Bích asked Diệu to go to the market and buy some food—already acting on the assumption I would stay, and so making the decision for me. Diệu responded to his request enthusiastically. As she prepared to leave for the market, gathering her purse and a vegetable basket, I stood and offered her some money, saying I wanted to help with the meal, but Bích told me, 'Please, be our guest. It's just a simple meal. You don't need to pay for anything. Besides, I really feel like I've met you somewhere before.'

'But I'm sure we haven't.'

'I don't know how to explain it. But since you arrived, I've felt like I've been transported back to my youth.'

'Thank you for the kind words, even if we don't really know each other that well. I hope everything will be fine.'

I didn't know what I meant would be fine, after saying that. Was it the steel factory, or my relationship with Bích, or my sudden secret infatuation with his daughter?

As I looked out at the village lane to conceal my confusing emotions, Bích rolled back and forth across the porch in his wheelchair. He went inside and rearranged the papers in his desk, searching for something, and then put them back in place. When Diệu returned from the market, I helped her prepare the food. Bích called my driver up to the porch to drink tea. Diệu seemed light and cheerful, but I felt nervous. She talked about her university, picnics and some of her friends. I told her briefly about the picnics I had when I lived in Europe. She seemed not to care much about my having studied abroad, but obviously didn't miss a word I said, especially when I mentioned my ex-girlfriend.

With the tray of food on the table before us, Bích no longer looked contemplative. And he became more talkative after a few cups of rice wine. He asked about my job, my family and my plans for the future. When I mentioned that I had been so busy with school and my new job that I was still single, he responded by playfully chastising Diệu for studying too hard and never introducing her boyfriends to him. Diệu said nothing, her face revealing nothing.

'She lost her mother,' Bích said. 'Only she and I live here now. If she had a boyfriend, he could drink rice wine with me.'

'I agree. But I imagine so many men want to date her, you have to chase them away.'

Diệu pouted her lips slightly and placed a fried frog leg in each of our bowls as if to say, Eat, and leave me alone.

Then, as if I had become his confidante, Bích started to tell me the story of the steel factory.

'If you really want to know everything about that factory, I'll lend you my memoir. But only if you promise not to show it to anyone and will return it to me as soon as you finish.'

I tried to suppress the complicated emotions rising in me. I wanted to know what he'd written, but I was afraid to confront the truth. I hoped my father had nothing to do with Bích's paralysis, with the villagers' illnesses and deaths and with people's awful memories of the factory. How could I have a relationship with Diệu if my father had somehow caused these tragedies and she knew who I really was?

Bích asked Diệu to retrieve the manuscript. He handed it to me and said, 'Please be careful with it. I still need to revise and edit before it can be published. But the changes will be minor. In general, the events are as written there. Do you think you could find me an experienced editor from the Writers' Association?'

As I received the memoir from him, my hands trembled. I looked at Bích and asked, 'Who did you write this memoir for? And why?'

'Take it home and read it, and you'll find out. Just don't forget to return it to me.'

When I said goodbye, I bowed to him as respectfully as a son bowing to his father-in-law. Diệu saw and turned away. I couldn't tell whether she was pouting or smiling. Maybe neither.

Diệu walked me out to the lane. We said goodbye to each other and I signalled to my driver to start the engine, but then turned back to the gate.

'Did you forget something?' she asked.

'I want to ask one more question. I hope you'll answer me honestly.'

'I will,' she said, nodding.

'When I come back, will you invite me to have lunch again?'

'It was my father who invited you for lunch today, but yes. Thank you for taking an interest and making him so happy!'

I was half sad, half elated without knowing why. I put aside the work that needed my attention and ignored all the urgent phone calls from the district chairman. The whole ride home, I devoured Bích's memoir.

***

The following excerpt from Bích's memoir was not included in the original *Termite Queen*.

A Previously Unpublished Chapter from Bích's Memoir
Blindfolded, bound and locked in a completely dark room, I at first lost my sense of time, but eventually, my stomach told me when the sun was about to rise.

Soon footsteps approached, and someone asked in a deep voice, 'How are you? All right?'

'Who are you? Why did you guys kidnap me? Where am I?'

'You're asking too many questions! Everything will be fine. For now, you should eat. Most villagers would love to have such a breakfast.'

I was blindfolded and saw nothing, but I could tell he had placed a tray of food next to me. As he untied my wrists, I contemplated sweeping the food on to the floor to show them I would not cooperate. But then I recalled something I had read in a book by Suzuki. It described a man hanging from a cliff. Above him, a hungry tiger waited for him to climb up so it could eat him. Below lay a pit of venomous snakes. He would die whether he climbed up or tumbled down. While he debated what he should do, he noticed a bunch of ripe grapes growing from vines along the cliff face. He was too scared to have noticed them before. In a heartbeat, he worked himself over to eat the grapes.

I had read the story many times without understanding its message. What would he do after eating the grapes? If he knew he would die anyway, why bother to eat them? It seemed foolish to think about eating in such a situation. I was obsessed with the story for years.

Now that I found myself in a similar situation, I began to admire the man's decision. Sometimes, if you keep asking questions about something, you'll never find an answer. Often the answer can only be instinctual.

I ate every bite of the food—stir-fried noodles with crab, ice cream, a piece of cake, chilled fruit and hot tea. There was a pack of cigarettes too, but I didn't smoke then, and still don't.

After eating, I lay on the brick floor, waiting for whatever would happen next. A little while later, someone came and apologized for the rough treatment I had received. In a gentle voice, he said, 'We couldn't have brought you here any other way.'

After a pause, he continued. 'Let me start to build our friendship with a gift that no one, I believe, would decline. If you stop protesting against the steel factory, you will receive a sum of money so large you'll be able to live on it for the rest of your life.' I heard the rustle of paper as he took out and unfolded a document that he went on to read in full, including each and every subclause and contingency, including the punctuation. 'This will be our compensation to you personally,' he said, repeating the astronomical number at the end. 'You deserve it. We guarantee this negotiation is completely confidential.'

'What if I say no?'

'No one has ever turned down such a generous offer from us, so we don't yet know the answer to your question. We hope everything will end here. You just need to sign the document we have prepared, and everything will be fine. After that, you'll soon realize how beautiful life is. Despite the present circumstances, we're not forcing you to do this, so take your time and think about it seriously.'

The man left. Everything was quiet again. Of course, I wouldn't sign the document. I wouldn't sell the villagers down the river because they were relying on me to represent them. The kidnappers must be setting a trap. During the first day, they left me alone so I could think about the offer. Still blindfolded, I saw nothing, but I knew there was a man standing in the room in case I needed anything. He brought me water, took me to the toilet and served me food. I tried to get him to talk with me, but he remained silent.

In the middle of the second night, I was woken up. The same man as before came and asked me politely, 'Did you enjoy the food? If you need anything, please let us know.'

I smirked and said I needed nothing but my freedom. He changed the subject.

'Have you thought about our offer carefully? You have plenty of time, but I don't. I would like an answer from you as soon as possible.'

I needed more information, and asked if he would answer my questions.

'Yes, definitely, but please get straight to the point.'

'Why didn't you ask the government to force the villagers to give up their land? Why waste your time on negotiations with the farmers? I know you've bribed the commune, the district and even the authorities above them. If you have an official document in hand and bring a hundred armed security guards and a few bulldozers to the village, we can't resist. If you really have control over everything, why play this wicked game with me?'

'You are a true leader. You don't want your reputation to be ruined, and neither do we. We prefer deals over coercion. We would be cursed if we had to destroy homes and arrest people. We want to make money, but we don't want to cause hatred and resentment.'

'Your reputation is already shit,' I said. 'Do you really believe cutting a few deals won't cause resentment?'

'I'm not sure about that, especially since the completed project will change everything for the better. Maybe at first, some people will still be resentful or upset because they don't trust us, but they do trust you. I hope you know that the young people are on our side because they want a brighter future than the one farming for subsistence will bring them. But I won't go into that now. I guarantee everything will change, and the villagers will thank us, not hate us.'

'What if things don't change for the better?'

'How can it not? We're just doing what America, Japan, South Korea, Hong Kong and the rest of the developed world have already done. Some of their people protested industrialization too, and resented resettlement, but their governments were firm and smart, and now look at how rich they've become.'

'What about the people whose health will be affected by the project?'

'Only a few people will suffer. Not everyone is lucky, and everything has risks. But think about this: just a few people might die of cancer while millions of others actually prosper—which option is better?'

'You scare me! I'm glad you're just a businessman. If you were a leader, life would be a disaster.'

'Are you sure? Do you think I can only make money but not do anything else?' His voice began to rise, but almost immediately he regained control over it. 'I am, in fact, a leader. One who's leading our nation to prosperity. I'll take my leave now. I don't have time for insults.'

He left the room as quietly as a cat. And yet, the man seemed more like a bull to me.

Still blindfolded, I was escorted to a car again. The same man who had brought me meals sat next to me. I didn't know where we were going, or whether they meant to leave me alive or dead. We drove all night, and at times I felt for sure I was in hell, surrounded by devils. But then I realized I had to still be alive because I could hear the men in the front seat whispering to each other. Maybe they just took me for the drive to confuse me, or to scare me into thinking they would kill me. At some point, they took me back to the same room with the brick floor.

On the fourth night, they squeezed me into a tiny, wire cage meant for taking pigs to slaughter. They locked me inside so I couldn't move my arms or legs and tossed me into the back of a truck. When the truck stopped, they rolled me out and dumped me onto the grass. I heard the wind blowing, insects chirring and fish splashing on water. I must have been close to a pond. Then they lifted the cage, swung me back and forth a couple times and threw me into the water. I sank immediately and started to drown. I thought my life was over. In the dark water, I thrashed violently, desperately, but the cage held me tight. I would soon drown so I stopped thrashing and tried to hold my breath. I clenched my lips to prevent water from rushing into my mouth. I sank deeper. My lungs were about to explode. Suddenly, they lifted the cage and I could breathe again.

I opened my mouth wide to suck in oxygen. I coughed brutally. When I smelled the stench of mud and rotten watercress, I knew I was alive.

Still in the cage, I still felt trapped and like I couldn't pull enough air into my lungs. It was a warm summer night, but I felt cold and scared.

'So how was your bath?' someone asked rudely. 'Did you like it?'

'You guys are devils,' I cursed feebly. 'Poisonous snakes. Just kill me, why don't you?'

'Unfortunately, you have to live,' the same man said. He laughed a big brutish laugh. 'But if you die, everything will be over. We paid experts to help us come up with this great idea. You were a hero in the war and what you did was admirable. But today, you won't be a hero because we're much stronger and more dangerous than any enemy you've ever fought. Speaking of which, let's try round number two!'

They drowned me repeatedly throughout the night. The torturers had perfect timing. Just when it became unbearable, and I was about to fill my lungs with water, they raised the cage and let me breathe again.

But they could not make me change my mind.

Until they threatened the safety of my daughter.

That's when I surrendered.

A week after I was kidnapped, I returned to the village by taxi. I looked fine, as if I had just returned from a vacation. The villagers asked me where I had gone, and I told them I had gone to visit a relative who needed my help. They sighed with relief because they could rely on me again to protest the factory. But if someone had looked closely, they would have seen that I was pale and my mental health had suffered. No one knew I had betrayed them. I had signed an agreement to accept the compensation for land clearance, to persuade the villagers not to protest and to keep everything confidential. The kidnappers gave me an offer that was three times larger than what was initially put on the table and assured me that they would do no harm to my daughter. One by one, after talking with me, the villagers accepted compensation, though many were bitter about it. Some asked why I had changed my mind so suddenly, but on that matter I remained silent. I became a rock and didn't care what people thought about me.

I don't want to hurt my daughter, but I have written this memoir to be published after my death to set the record straight. I don't want her to nurture hatred and resentment, but the truth must be known. She is my only hope. Her safety has to be my first concern, even above my beloved village, and those bastards knew it.

Since that terrifying week, I have lived in hell every night.

***

The later sections of Bích's long and detailed manuscript described what happened after the steel factory was built and went into operation. It also told the story of his paralysis from bacterial meningitis. The whole thing seemed dismal, desperate and painful. It said nothing else about Diệu—the only reason for his defeat.

Chapter XI

Every day we had to pay larger and larger bribes and the pressure had become overwhelming. I could no longer defer to the district chairman and decided to confront him.

It was too risky in the internet age to do what had been done to Bích and his village while my father led the steel factory project. During the discussion with the district chairman about my plans and strategies, he clasped his hands behind his back and paced the room, never taking his eyes from my face. He reminded me of a silverback gorilla during mating season. His bent back called to mind the familiar image of the stages of evolution that shows apes turning into humans. Every now and then, he'd raise a finger above his head and spin it around in the air as bellicose politicians often do. I wished I knew what he had in mind.

'You're very smart!' the district chairman said, nodding. 'If I tried to use your strategies, even I would be defeated. Please don't bribe my staff. They would bury me alive to prove their loyalty to you.'

You are such a clown, I thought, but my facial expression remained stern. 'We really need you right now,' I said. 'If you get thrown out of office, we'll all lose money. I'm not a fool.'

'Of course, you're not a fool. I know that. I just want to be prepared in case something bad happens.'

Both of us burst into laughter, like two friends who could read each other's minds.

My plan was to do everything possible to win over the young people dreaming of a new and extravagant urban life. I would tell them about all the many wonders of the metropolitan experience. Those rural kids had lived a hard life for a long time, and I was sure when they saw how rich people lived in the city, they would become envious and want to improve their places in the world. They would be the ones to pressure their parents into giving up their land to earn money so their children could achieve their dreams. Already, so many parents today borrow money at high interest rates, which their over-indulged children just gamble away before ending up in jail. They buy cars to show off to their neighbours but rarely use them. I could take advantage of the reality that these social ills had already taken over.

I would be able to defeat the obstinate commune chairman by strategically splurging on the spoiled youngsters. They would eat my sugar-coated words and once they became addicted, they would do whatever they were told.

To the godfathers, I proposed an idea to sponsor a motocross event in Đồng Village. The event would be organized totally legally and profess to have the noble intentions to promote sports and increase the knowledge of traffic laws to the rural youths. We'd invite reporters who would know how to give it positive coverage.

At first, I had also thought of having a small rowing race, but I couldn't persuade the brothers who rented the fishpond to cooperate. They were true hard-working and strong-spirited farmers. They made decent money but always dressed like slobs. I told myself to be patient with them because, eventually, their picturesque pond would belong to the golf course.

Everything went smoothly thanks to the support of the district chairman. Wherever money is spread like manure, paradise sprouts. I rented several fancy sports cars and hired trendy drivers who wore expensive jewellery and clothes to show the country folks what it meant to be rich. A week before the race, I sent the cars and drivers to visit all the villages in the area to attract the young people's attention. They distributed advertisements for the event that promised the giving of charity gifts, a pop-music concert and opportunities to take pictures with the celebrities. Hundreds of young Đồng Village residents and teens from nearby villages rushed out to take the flyers and welcome the participants.

The drivers and other participants also visited the elderly and the poor and offered them gifts. We sent jugglers and magicians and other street performers to pique the village children's curiosity. Another group helped indigent families repair their houses, and then used the opportunity to talk them into supporting the golf course. These people were quickly persuaded and accepted compensations. Many of these even volunteered to convince other villagers to support the project and ridiculed those who disagreed. At the end of the race-promotion visits, the participants and drivers made a big deal about heading back to the city in their fancy cars. The young villagers couldn't keep their envious eyes off the visitors. I knew then we would succeed.

On the day of the motocross race, excitement overwhelmed the entire village. The district chairman opened the event with a speech that all the commune and village officials were required to attend. His speech, which must've been written by his secretary, was long and tedious, but I'd had the foresight to ask to see it first and cut most of it, leaving in just the rousing parts about the race and the need for more economic development of the area. Then the excited audience gathered around the pond where the race would take place. At first, only the professional competitors and their colourful, eye-catching motorcycles were allowed on the course. As the race started, the young villagers were ecstatic, especially once they saw the mountain of prizes. Many of them decided to sign up for what I thought of as the real event—the amateur race—which was all part of the plan to let them win. The prize ceremony had plenty of flowers, applause and banners. The races lasted the entire day and strengthened the friendship between the farmers and the investors behind it all. The villagers started to look at us with more kindness and positivity.

As I had expected, almost all the young people fervently threw their support behind the golf course and pressured their parents to do so as well. Within a few weeks, well over half the households in the village had approached us to negotiate compensations. In life, the faster you are, the more you get. The more aggressive you are, the more you earn. The more you lie, the more you achieve. We spread the rumour that the first ones to negotiate would get the best deals, which sped up the process and put even more pressure on the holdouts. Eventually, only a few people continued to protest the project, including the commune chairman, a few families and the brothers who owned the fishpond. But we didn't care. Money was power.

When I met with the district chairman afterward, I was appalled to hear he still wasn't happy. He wanted more acknowledgement for his contribution to the success of the event and he had other complaints as well. 'I had to put aside mountains of work to help you with that whole day,' he blustered. 'Shit! It's such a relief to have it finished. Even so, you still need to deal with the commune chairman.'

Chapter XII

When the district chairman said that last bit to me, he was not only asking for more money, but also reminding me not to celebrate too soon—we still had work to do. Handling the commune chairman wouldn't be easy, and he knew I would need his help.

The district chairman issued an official document requesting the commune chairman and the brothers who rented the fishpond to name the price they'd accept as compensation, or to state their opinions on the matter. The commune chairman threw the request into a rubbish bin in front of his employees. When one of them informed the district chairman about this, he didn't get angry. He simply furrowed his eyebrows and asked, 'Did he really do that?'

What happened next surprised me. A crowd of young people gathered in front of the commune chairman's house and hurled garbage over the gate. They demanded he do what they thought was best for the village and support the golf course, which would obviously bring wonderful changes to Đồng Village and Hoàng Commune. They urged him to set an example for everyone to follow.

At first, the commune chairman was firm and raised his voice when offering his justifications. He called the young villagers foolish and shallow-minded.

'Haven't you ever asked yourselves what those greedy robbers really want from us?' he shouted to them from his courtyard. 'They'll turn this village and this commune into a garbage dump. They're tricking you with fancy words like *development* and *civilization*. What will your children live on after you've accepted their compensation?'

'We don't give a damn!' someone shouted back. 'Mind your own family's business. We know what to do with our lives.'

'What's this great plan of yours?' the commune chairman shot back. 'You'll have no work, get addicted to drugs and die of cancer. Is that what you want?'

Someone in the crowd threw a clump of cow manure wrapped in newspaper into the courtyard and yelled, 'Here's our answer to your questions—shit! Your argument is shit! Your morality is shit! The future you want us to have is shit. Your life is shit, too. If that's all you want, here's some more. What we need is money.'

Most of the adults in the village remained neutral. On the one hand, they didn't endorse the young people's inappropriate behaviour and vulgar language. On the other hand, they didn't want to see the commune chairman turn the village against the investors. After a while, the commune chairman retreated inside his house.

I called the district chairman and urged him to do something about the heated confrontation because I didn't want those kids to burn down the commune chairman's house or hurt him in any way. It worried me that the situation seemed to be getting worse. Before I could finish, he interrupted to say, 'Don't you see how the situation has changed? Don't forget all I've done for you.'

'Please wait,' I shouted over the phone. 'Listen—'

'Even I didn't expect this to go so well,' he said, interrupting again. 'Everything is perfect now, beyond our imagination. I've received several phone calls this morning. At first, the commune chairman was stubborn, but now he recognizes he has been defeated. We've won. Why aren't you here to wrap everything up?'

In my mind I cursed the district chairman—such a rotten, greedy bastard! But over the phone I pretended to be polite.

'Just listen. First, of course I recognize all you've done. You'll be paid generously. Don't worry. But in the meantime, please send some policemen immediately to disperse the crowd. The commune chairman must be protected.'

'Are you crazy? We wanted the crowd to attack him, and now you want them driven away? There'll be no murder. You can't kill someone with a cow pie. Don't be so afraid! I'd like to see them throw more shit at him and you want him protected? Ridiculous!'

'Please listen. What if they get out of hand? They might throw rocks, or start a fire. What then? Even if he's hurt only a little, everything will be over. Don't you understand?'

The district chairman finally fell silent for once. Then he said, 'You're right. I should've thought of that. We need peace, not war. If he dies, we'll end up in jail. You're such a cunning fox! I'll send some police over there right away.'

But the crowd broke up on their own before the police arrived. The rebellious mob had no leader. They were just a bunch of hot-headed teens hungry for money who had nothing to lose by pressuring the commune chairman. When the police finally did show up, all they had to do was check that he was safe. By the time the officers returned to the district headquarters, I had arrived there as well. A huge weight lifted from my shoulders when they reported everything was fine.

The land-clearance challenge was nearly resolved, and we accomplished more than I had originally thought possible. Only one obstacle remained. The fishponds. Because of their shape, we called them the Starfish Ponds. It wasn't easy to persuade the Đặng brothers, Miện and Mến, because they actually made pretty good money from farming fish. They asked their relatives to help oppose the project. I called a meeting with our company's board of directors to ask for their advice. When I stepped into the meeting room, each of them held a strange, almost mysterious look on their face, even though the faces themselves had by then become familiar. I knew then why my father had died so young. These vultures must have somehow been involved. It felt like these men were enemies from a previous life.

The present members of the board—the godfathers—suggested 'less talking, more walking'. They warned me again that if we delayed further, the circling sharks would snatch the project from us. The board members insisted the fishpond problem must be resolved as soon as possible, even if it cost us a bit extra. If the Đặng brothers refused to negotiate, we should ask the district chairman to use violence to coerce them. But whatever we did, we needed to avoid a scandal. We absolutely did not want to draw the public's attention.

They greenlighted me to do whatever I wanted to accomplish the goal. Unfortunately, a somewhat similar land reform fracas in Hải Phòng had recently attracted the media, which sided with the victims and those protesting the land expropriation. The prime minister had to get involved to placate the public. We did not want to make the same mistake. When I mentioned this at a meeting with the district chairman, he argued, 'These are two different things. What we're doing is more legal. You should think positively. We won't make the same mistakes they made in Hải Phòng.'

'I feel better now that you put it that way. Thank you.'

He laughed. 'Don't just thank me.'

I knew he wasn't joking. I told him about my plans.

He laughed again and said, 'You're so very smart! You already know how to abuse the system.'

'I'm not the only one.'

'Let me finish. I agree with your approach, but we have to follow protocol. The law is the law. We have to be smarter than the villagers to win. Remember that.' He sniffed meaningfully.

We shook hands and said goodbye and he seemed very pleased with the square parcel I left on the desk for him.

According to my company's research, the Starfish Ponds had initially been part of a nineteen-hectare marsh. The area had never been used until the government built a canal system for the entire region, including Đồng Village. The marsh then became a public asset to the whole village. Prior to the Lunar New Year, they harvested fish from its waters and distributed them equally to each household. The marsh also helped purify the water and the air and contributed to the village's natural beauty. White herons, egrets and all kinds of other birds and animals lived there.

After the agricultural co-operative model was eliminated, the Đặng brothers won the bid to lease the Starfish Ponds and raise fish. The two were veterans, and after the war had already proved themselves to be business-oriented, industrious and frugal. Their relatives helped them enlarge the ponds, dredge their bottoms and clear weeds from the shores. The commune and district governments approved of the brothers' work, in no small measure because the Starfish Ponds supplied tons of fish and shrimp for the region each year.

Since the brothers began their work on the ponds, they had contributed a sizable amount of rent to Đồng Village, which its leaders used to improve the local infrastructure. In turn, the brothers became the region's wealthiest residents. They created jobs for dozens of residents and built a paved road and a kindergarten. Every year, they donated large sums of money to maintain nearby temples and pagodas, and participated actively in charity work. The villagers respected and appreciated the brothers for their generosity. And because it had been the commune chairman's idea for renting the pond, everyone admired him for his vision.

I learned more of the Starfish Ponds' history after a few visits to Đồng Village. According to some rumours corroborated by the district chairman, the commune chairman secretly had shares in the Đặng's business. He affirmed, 'Nobody works for free, just like you and me,' and that was why the commune chairman was against the golf course. Moreover, it was widely known that the commune chairman also invested in a three-hectare farm near the ponds where he grew pomelos, lychees and longans. The crop he was about to harvest would also bring him a lot of money.

Despite these conflicts of interest, based on my observations, the commune chairman was the kind of leader who fought for the rights and benefits of the villagers more than for his own gain. Every day, he was in his office to make sure he'd know immediately if we tried to confiscate any land or made a move on the marsh.

My father knew confiscating land was a difficult task. He had met Miện and Mến a few times and offered them a very high price, which they always declined. My chauffeur told me that during a negotiation with my father, Miện pulled up his shirt and showed my father a scar across his belly caused by a piece of shrapnel from fighting in Quảng Trị.

'If you had been wounded like me,' Miện had said, 'you would know that death is nothing. The important thing is our children's and grandchildren's future. Why try to force me to betray them? I abhor the people who came up with this murderous project. Why not build a golf course somewhere else? We have poured blood, sweat, toil and tears into this land. If we lose it, we'll never get it back.'

Mr Tâm didn't tell me how my father responded. After a few conversations with him, however, I could tell that the brothers had come to respect my father, even though they remained firm.

There was a cavernous gap between us and the commune chairman. In the business world, the stronger, crueller and more cunning person wins. I was not always a big fan of this philosophy, but it forced me to be daring. On the one hand, I wanted to follow in my father's footsteps and win at all costs. On the other, I felt like I was committing a crime camouflaged in the name of progress and collective happiness. Life would be perfect if only the wolf and the sheep could balance each other out.

On my way to the district, the district chairman called me, saying he had something far more valuable than gold that I would definitely be interested in. He wanted me to hurry so he could show it to me. As usual, he sounded greedy and malicious. He ended the call abruptly as if he had many other things to do. I imagined his face, which looked like a salesman's, and knew what I would need to do so that he'd think it was impossible to wash his hands of us—his gold mine.

Chapter XIII

So many times, I tried to imagine who the mysterious, invisible, but omnipresent Mr Big might be. Throughout my adolescence, I had accompanied my father to many meetings with important, powerful people because he wanted me either to get to know them or to learn from them. And maybe he also wanted to show me off a little, and to use my presence to make his business with them more casual and cordial.

So, really, anyone I'd met with my father could have been Mr Big. When I was a kid, those guys impressed me with their dignified and authoritative appearances. They all had big ears and faces with rosy skin that suggested their affluence and influence. I wondered how they could have so much power over other people. I was curious about the way they all so easily commanded the room—a seemingly unteachable task they performed at will.

I remember feeling so small before them, even sometimes with my own father.

While anxiously waiting for news from Sinh, I wrote a few sketches from my memories of some of those people.

Mr A

I was in elementary school when I met Mr A at a party at his mansion to celebrate some successful event. I heard it wasn't easy to get an invitation, but my father and I were there among hundreds of other people. Strangely, after Mr A addressed the crowd, he stood for a long time with my father. He offered my father a glass of wine, and my father bowed to him. With the rest of the guests, after the ritual clinking of glasses, Mr A would continue to another table and give another toast. My father told me later that Mr A couldn't remember everyone at the party, and that he probably stayed with my father for so long because he mistook him for someone else. My father was surprised when Mr A asked a few questions and called a waiter to fill their glasses a second time. My father told him about me, and Mr A listened and nodded. Before he went to another table, he said, 'Bring him here to see me some time. You should have plans for his future.' My father couldn't believe what he had just heard. It wasn't a big deal if Mr A just said it flippantly and would immediately forget it. But if he really meant it and my father didn't follow through, he would be in big trouble.

Better safe than sorry, my father said, so he took me to meet Mr A.

Unlike what I had first imagined, Mr A was a sociable, friendly person. He tousled my hair before he asked a servant to show me the garden. When I came back into the house, I bowed to him respectfully. I was able to study him for fifteen minutes when my father asked him for an autographed photo. He pointed to a chair and told my father to sit down and wait for him. Mr A took a headshot out of a drawer of a huge desk and laid it on a big, thick book in front of him. He chose a pen from a gold cup, looked at it carefully and adjusted his posture. He looked nervous as he signed. Then he crumpled the photo and tossed it into the trash.

'Not good,' he said. 'I'll do it again.'

He autographed and threw away seven photographs before he was satisfied. When Mr A handed my father the autographed portrait, my father bowed to receive the precious gift. He praised Mr A for his beautiful and firm signature. Mr A explained he believed a signature both revealed someone's emotions and also indicated the fortune it might bring to the person who requested it. My father covertly glanced at Mr A's autograph. Then Mr A talked about calligraphy, something he knew just a little bit about, and how to decorate a room and how to properly select china for various dishes and drinks. He praised the Europeans for their good taste in architecture, décor, culinary arts, fashion, wine and music. He said the Chinese and the Japanese couldn't compete with the Europeans in architecture. He talked about his trips abroad and the perfectly decorated hotels. He said he could talk for an entire day about his experiences if he had an interested audience like my father and me.

Mr B

I can't recall the exact meeting in which I met Mr B, but it was strangely emotional. I'll never forget the blandness of his nondescript appearance and my thinking that I'd wish I looked like him if I ever became an infomercial host. His face was smooth and perfectly proportional like a mannequin's. Words failed me. Even now I cannot describe him accurately. It's like the words just slid off him. He was emotionless and well-groomed and he spoke as if reading effortlessly from a script. But then, the one moment when he became passionate, his words seared themselves into me. 'Our rivals are much more dangerous than they appear,' he said. 'They're cunning, too. If we want to win, and we must win, we must be utterly malicious.'

He blinked like a vacant-eyed doll. 'Do you understand?' he said.

I remember nothing else about Mr B.

Mr C

Unlike Mr B, Mr C had the most memorable face in the world. It was a square brick with a few bumps. He had a big beer belly, and short, chubby legs that looked like honeydew melons. He wore crimson Berluti shoes.

While I was still a university student, I met him at a New Year's party for top-tier, successful businessmen that was held in a five-star hotel's huge, luxurious ballroom. My father was a nobody among the guests, but I could tell he wasn't invisible by the way the hotel staff greeted and treated him. My father encouraged me to chat with whomever I wanted. I met a bright and pleasant young economics professor and as we discussed the structural-change theory I had learned the previous semester, a crowd gathered at the door. A moment later, a grotesquely enormous man appeared. Mr C. His neck was huge but still did not seem big enough to support his massive head and face. He wore suspenders because no belt could fit him. Too large to walk by himself, the four aides surrounding him just made him seem even bigger.

Like a black hole, his incredible mass seemed to pull in all the light around him. He drew the attention of every guest, though he said nothing and only waved his hand in greeting. Everyone in the room took a turn respectfully shaking hands with Mr C. My father brought me along when it was his turn and bowed slightly as he said, 'Please allow me to introduce my son.'

Mr C glared at me, appraising me as if he wanted to eat me alive.

I was scared to death.

'Such a nice young man,' Mr C said at last. The air that came from his throat as he spoke rumbled like thunder.

That was it. We left the party soon after that. I never met Mr C again, but his tremendous face and the way everything was drawn to him made a lasting impression.

Mr D

I have an interesting memory about Mr D, who looked to be mixed-race—half-Vietnamese, half-White. He was taller and larger than most Vietnamese men. He had an unusually long torso but short and sturdy legs. It was said that he had a strange birthmark on his back, and that was why he never went shirtless, even when alone. His impressively thick and bushy eyebrows curved like hooks. Whenever he expressed emotions, whether sad or happy, those eyebrows made them clear. He had been married seven times. It was rumoured he had over forty children, including those born out of wedlock, now all adults. Mr D himself had been born a bastard.

One year, when I was in middle school, my father had the honour to accompany Mr D when he vacationed at a beach in Central Việt Nam. Because it was a personal trip, Mr D allowed my father to bring my mother, my sister and me with him. Mr D loved to eat, and he made sure there was a robust variety of seafood at every meal along with every kind of drink. He liked to stab a lobster with a big fork and tear off big bites, and then wash it down with a French white wine or an Italian red. I'd never seen such expensive labels, even in Europe.

Mr D never swam in the sea, or even went into the water. He always wore bright, yellow, Chinese-style silk that billowed around him. And he never ate the same food twice in a day, except sometimes Japanese-style lobster. In the morning and late afternoon, he walked along the beach, seeming to relish the adoring way people gazed at him.

Mr D often tousled my hair and smiled kindly. Many times, he said to me, 'You must try to be like your father.'

Diamond rings sparkled on his chubby fingers, and he liked to show off the gifts that people had given him. My father told me that when Mr D had guests at his house, he'd spend hours showing off his considerable collection of invaluable antiques. His favourites included an Egyptian vase that had been buried inside a pyramid, a gargantuan ruby from the Ottoman empire and a wine bottle from the fourth century reputed to hold St Nicholas's fingerprints.

After touring the display cases, and talking about the value of his possessions, he would grow tired and just want to eat. Benevolent and kind, he always approved whatever my father requested. Not having to worry about a thing in life, he looked like the Laughing Buddha.

***

Among all these possibilities, I thought Mr D the likeliest candidate to be Mr Big.

Chapter XIV

As if telepathy were really a thing, as I contemplated who Mr Big might be and grew ever more anxious about meeting him, Sinh telephoned. In a firm voice, he told me to join him as soon as possible at the café by the lake where we had first met for coffee. It took me less than thirty minutes to get there.

Sinh seemed different that day. Not conceited like before, and I couldn't decipher the look on his face. I wanted to ask: Who the hell are you, anyway? Is it just money you're after? Or something else?

He didn't even acknowledge me when I approached, as if he'd forgotten he'd been the one to demand a meeting.

'I have some important news for you,' he said at last. 'I was so embarrassed the other day. After some investigation, I discovered that the fat, pompous man we met is a nobody. Not even fit to wash Mr Big's feet. Did you notice his expression when he received that phone call? He looked terrified. He's a low-class bastard, no different from any other ordinary bastard. He acts big and likes to intimidate anyone he thinks is weak or beneath him, but he's really just another kiss-arse. I was such a fool when I knelt down in front of him. Well, it was my mistake, and I'll make it up to you.'

'It's all right,' I said. 'Everyone makes mistakes. The most important thing is we still must meet Mr Big so we can ask for help with the investment licence.'

'I know I've cost you money. I'm an honourable guy, I promise to make it up to you.'

'No big deal! It's like buying a first-class ticket, and on the way to the airport, you get stuck in traffic and miss your flight. Just call it bad luck. No worries.'

'All right. Thank you. Then let's get down to business. After working with several intermediaries, I've finally found the quickest way to reach Mr Big. In fact, he's very close to us. I hope we get lucky this time. But he's surrounded by all kinds of people, so we might have to stick our necks out for him to see us. I now know what he likes, including his routines and habits. The problem is it's impossible to make an appointment to see him. But if we're patient and lucky, we'll be successful.'

'What's the plan?' I asked. 'What do we need to do, and what do you need from me?'

'First and foremost, I need to know more about the golf course, beyond the fact that you need the investment licence to persuade the farmers to give up. Tell me how much has been invested so far, the site's economic-development potential and your company's ultimate goal. Will you build the course and adjacent commercial spaces, and sell the finished properties to someone else, or do you just need the investment licence so you can sell the incomplete project to another investor? Based on what I can tell, you seem more interested in the latter scenario, where you get the farmers to sell their land at a low price and then use the plans and maps to exaggerate the value and sell the whole thing to another investor at a much higher price. I don't care which strategy you want to pursue. That's not my business. But I need to be able to give Mr Big an overview if we're lucky enough to meet him. He doesn't give anyone much time, so we'll have to be concise and informative, and of course, well-prepared.'

I glanced at Sinh's face and then turned away to hide my scepticism. I wondered what he really wanted. Was he actually helping to get the investment licence, or was he stealing the information to sell to another client? Or was there some other secret agenda? I knew enough to understand the kind of wicked tricks often played in this business, and my father had taught me a few tricks of my own to deal with them. I hoped Sinh was acting in good faith, but I suspected there was something fishy behind his questions.

The potential danger here unsettled me. It wouldn't be easy for me to handle this as well as my father would. He had preferred to listen rather than to speak, somewhat mysteriously even, but nothing escaped his gaze. The strategies he'd employed were surprising, shocking even, to his rivals.

'If you don't feel comfortable revealing these things to me, I'll have to think of another way,' Sinh said.

I decided to stall, and said, 'I just don't know how to explain it all.'

Sinh's face remained neutral. He told me to stay close for the next few days because if he called, I'd need to be able to meet him immediately.

***

The district chairman gave me some surprising news. Somehow, he'd overlooked that the Đặng brothers' lease of the Starfish Ponds was just about to end, and even though it was customary for such leases to be renewed automatically, this time the district wouldn't renew. Allowing the lease to expire was legal and simple, and no one could say a word about it.

The district chairman pretended to look sad when he said, 'They'll say I'm unethical. The brothers and their relatives have put a lot of work into the ponds to make them what they are now. It has created hundreds of jobs and supplied fish to the whole region. Now, it'll just be scenery for a golf course. Thanks to you, my reputation is ruined.'

'You'll be generously compensated.' I laughed because I didn't want his greed to rub off on me. 'People make promises but don't always keep their word. I don't know *when* I'll be compensated.'

Then the district chairman laughed as if he'd been joking. He asked, 'How about the investment licence? It's still absolutely crucial. Without it, confronting the last of the hold-out farmers is useless. I'll do what I can, but you have to commit to doing whatever's necessary. We have to work together. You know how these farmers are.'

'I'll get it very soon,' I said. 'Everything's going well. Now it's just a matter of time.' I smiled to give him some assurance, but I was thinking Sinh better not let me down.

'Great!' he said, beaming. 'I'll have no mercy on the Đặng brothers then. Here's the plan: my office will send a notice of the lease expiration date that also states that the district won't renew it because the pond is to be repurposed for greater economic returns. They'll have to vacate by the expiration date. And we'll offer a fair compensation for the improvements they made to shut them up.'

'Do you think they'll go quietly, even with the compensation? I doubt it.'

'I know them better than you do. They won't make it easy. They'll insist that the repurposing of the pond won't benefit the whole district or the country, but only a few individuals, myself included. Bluntly speaking between you and me, it's a robbery. We all know that. I won't be surprised if they fight.'

'Then what?'

'I've been thinking about this all week,' said the district chairman to emphasize his foresight. 'Money makes people smarter very quickly. The district will stand firm. Miện and

Mến will sue us for sure, but my office handles all disputes, and with the lease expiring and only custom, not the law, on their side, they don't stand a chance. As a formality, there'll be an investigation, verification and reconciliation. In the next three to four years, I'll still be the district chairman, and under my leadership, everything will be fine.'

'You're so confident! Are you sure the district will do as you say?'

'Your question suggests you're not suited to be a leader. Who would dare disobey the district chairman's orders?

'I see. That's good. Then what?'

'If there's a hearing, the court will have to follow the law, not custom. The district will terminate the contract legally and ethically and we'll appear generous by giving the brothers a little extra time to vacate the pond and a bit of financial assistance to harvest the fish.'

'What will happen if they take this to a court above the district?'

The district chairman burst into laughter. 'I thought I was the only cunning fox. Don't worry. The law is the law. No district-lease lawsuit has ever gone beyond the district level. They might try to appeal, but every court has to follow the law, and act in the best interest of the majority.'

'What do you mean?'

'Are you a slow thinker, or are you just forcing me to say it out loud? Even if they sue or appeal after they lose, the district will already have seized the property. Any public property has to be protected while a final decision is being made. If not, Miện and Mến could poison the ponds or otherwise cause harm. Let them sue and keep suing the district for the rest of their lives. As soon as the Starfish Ponds are no longer in their possession, we can do whatever we like with them. At some point, they'll realize they can't win.'

I said nothing to disturb the chairman's look of satisfaction. Abruptly, he stood and paced back and forth. Then, he opened a cupboard and took out some glasses and a bottle of foreign wine. Looking at me meaningfully, he said, 'You're my friend. I'm doing all of these terrible things for the greater good of the community.'

I nodded. 'I don't want to upset you, but I still have some doubts.'

'You're my good friend, my ally, my source of light. Don't be so formal. Speak.'

'What if people think the district is colluding with business groups against the farmers?'

'You worry too much. Don't be pessimistic. Everyone is happy.' Then he gave me a short lecture on leadership that boiled down to this: 'To convince people to walk down a path with you, frighten them. You can't be soft-hearted in politics. Stick with business—it's better for you.'

Chapter XV

Then something unexpected happened. The district chairman showed me a video clip his staff had found on the internet. He told me he planned to use it as evidence to accuse Bích's daughter, Diệu, of subverting the government. The video showed Diệu addressing hundreds of Đồng villagers. Standing next to her was a young man whose relationship to her I immediately wanted to know. I was so jealous I couldn't care less about what she actually said. My heart teetered toward exploding, especially when his handsome face came into focus.

I had never felt so uncomfortable. When I studied in England, I always prioritized school first. I enjoyed, but then ended, relationships with two girlfriends in that time but never felt any heartbreak. Knowing my mother wanted to have grandchildren, I was serious when it came to dating. The first break up was with An, the daughter of a respectable, intellectual family from Hà Nội. Her parents were polite and cultured, and An possessed nearly all the desirable characteristics of a woman. We rarely disagreed about anything. She loved to cook and was a master of the art of floral arrangement.

During a vacation to Greece, we met a Japanese man who spoke fluent English. I nearly came to blows with him, even though he was much bigger than me, because he insulted my national pride. The whole thing was kind of childish, but it started like this: as An and I arrived at our luxury hotel, he happened to be watching from the balcony of his standard hotel across the street. Curious about us, he came down to the porte-cochère when he saw us waiting for a taxi a few minutes later. He introduced himself, and we thought it would be interesting to befriend another Asian in Greece. We invited him to join us for dinner, and by that evening we had started what seemed to be a close friendship. He told us he would love to date a blond, blue-eyed Greek woman. I liked his honesty and energy, especially when we were deep in conversation.

At lunch the next day, I told him I admired the Japanese people for their discipline, cleanliness and courage. Rather than accept my compliment, he launched into a disquisition on all the ugly traits of the Japanese. He said the Japanese were cowards at heart—they always kept a pair of shoes at the foot of their bed so they could run if there was an earthquake. They were afraid of everything.

I argued that it was not cowardice, but pragmatism.

He said, 'Go live in Japan and you'll see.'

We drank another beer together, and I told him the Vietnamese loved to learn, and that our oldest university was built over ten centuries ago.

He showed no respect and told me about his unpleasant experiences in Việt Nam. He said he had visited the Imperial City in Huế and met many men who were prideful like me. 'But Japanese poetry is much better and more meaningful than Vietnamese poetry, and in the nineteenth century we were already building battleships so we could rule the Pacific.' He finished his beer and continued, 'There are many people in many countries who think too highly of themselves and love to be praised, but all they can really do is provide labour for other countries. People like that never grow up. Their descendants will be ashamed of them.'

I stood to punch him in the face, but An placed a hand on my arm to stop me. I ended the argument with a curse.

As we returned to our hotel, I felt tired and frustrated. An tried her best to make me forget about the Japanese man. She ordered coffee to our room and sang a Vietnamese love song while we waited, but I was still angry. After coffee, she seduced me. At first, I went along, thinking it would help me relax, but my mood didn't improve. We got into a heated argument about history, with her taking the side of the Japanese man.

That argument led to others about the culture, traditions and ugly habits of the Vietnamese. An strongly believed everything was rotten. She believed state officials did only one thing—bribe others and take bribes themselves to get projects approved. They lied, acted servile and got down on their knees to get promoted. Once they gained some power, they became corrupt, but even then, they would later be commended as innovative officials who had made great contributions to the country. According to An, that was why Việt Nam lagged so far behind. She also believed most Vietnamese valued wealth above morality and this money-oriented mindset had destroyed Vietnamese culture.

'If you did a survey,' she said, 'you would see that in our country most people get rich illegally. They embezzle public funds, steal national properties and abuse the system that they themselves maintain. They're thieves who go unpunished for their crimes. As long as we let them get away with such crimes, the Vietnamese will continue to just provide labour to other nations.'

An didn't normally speak so harshly. Although she didn't refer to my father directly, I felt under attack, almost as if she had called my father one of those deplorable criminals. We set aside the argument to get through the trip but, after we returned to school, we gradually grew apart and eventually broke up.

In the last year of my master's programme, I met a Vietnamese student on a ferry across the English Channel to France. Though she was not quite as beautiful as An, her friendly, open-minded attitude was very attractive. We shared an optimism for the future of Việt Nam's younger generation. She criticized Vietnamese education for making students passive and hesitant in their social interactions. Parents wanted their children to do exactly what they were told without question. They weren't taught to be creative or independent thinkers. Parents just wanted them to live safely within their comfort zone.

We agreed about this, but I was surprised at first by her opinion on the virtues of female virginity. She thought it was selfish and hypocritical to demand that a woman must maintain her virginity while a man was encouraged to be proud of taking a woman's virginity. She said straightaway that she was no longer a virgin and kept confusing different lovers in the stories she told.

She and I made love the first night we were in France. As she'd said, she was experienced, and she taught me several things about how to give and receive pleasure. Knowing how to arouse me, she took control. But I discovered I had my limits. Even though I thought of myself as a modern, liberated man, I learned I was actually still somewhat conservative. Her superior sexual experience and knowledge, as well as the various positions she suggested, made me uncomfortable. She broke up with me after six months. When I returned to Việt Nam, I thought seriously about finding myself a wife, but then my father passed away, and I had to postpone such considerations.

From the first moment I'd met Diệu at Bích's house, the idea of marrying her had seized my mind. Her precise, legal thinking and apparent indifference intimidated me. But it also enchanted me, as much so as her beautiful eyes.

While watching the district chairman's video, I realized just seeing her image on the screen represented a dangerous challenge for me. I wondered how she had wound up at a protest against the golf course with the commune chairman and Đồng villagers. What was she up to?

***

'Please listen to me,' Diệu said to the crowd in the video. Her rural accent rendered the tones nearly indistinct. 'I have no personal agenda here. I hope you'll believe me.'

A few people of the hundred or so in the audience drifted away from the crowd, apparently not interested or not willing to take her seriously because she was so young. But most stayed. The young people especially seemed excited, bobbing up and down, talking and laughing, trying to get Diệu's attention.

'First, I want to show you these photos.' She held up a big folder and continued, 'This is the evidence I want to show you. Please pass them around.'

She held up one photocopied photo at a time and then passed them into the crowd. The photos showed thousands of dead fish washed onshore, a river filled with trash, foul-looking wastewater, dead animals, dead rice paddies, a horizon blackened by factory smoke, mountains of coal, ore and heavy-metal tailings, bald children who looked near death, blind, featherless ducks and people who looked in terrible pain on what must have been their deathbeds. The last photo showed an abandoned factory with its collection of broken machinery. It all looked completely apocalyptic.

After the photos circulated through the audience, Diệu collected them and put them back into the folder. She was a different person—she looked like a young orator or politician.

'While the steel factory project remains on paper, they tell you that it'll bring you a happy, prosperous, better life.

That it will create high-paying jobs for your children and help the poor. The factory is part of the industrialization movement, they'll say. It's the best thing that can happen to a rural community.' Diệu paused to look out into the audience, holding the gaze of each person for a few seconds.

'But those are sugar-coated lies! The factory is, in fact, a monster that will bring you nothing but disaster. We are not against industrialization, but we oppose allowing it to destroy lives. Your land has been here for thousands of years, and they want to force you to trade it for the construction of a golf course because a small group of people can make a giant profit from it. They will buy your land for a pittance and resell it at a very high price. Even worse, their actions are made possible by a few powerful but extremely unethical individuals. These people should be damned to hell. Think about living in fear and misery. Think about the ugly realities that you'll soon have to face. You don't want the kind of *progress* and *development* these villains are promoting. They'll exploit your natural resources, abuse your gullibility and destroy your future. A few of them will become insanely wealthy from this project, while most of you will end up miserable. This project is nothing short of mass murder. We must say no to this kind of deadly development.'

Now the crowd was silent, listening raptly to Diệu's speech. She was articulate, attractive and bold. I felt such a powerful personality would intimidate me if she were to become my wife.

A young man in the crowd shouted, 'Who are you and who's paying you to say these things? We know what to do with our own lives.'

'I'd like to invite you to come up here and explain your argument,' Diệu responded. 'Have you been blinded by the lies of the cold-blooded developers? Have they promised you'll become rich overnight and enjoy a luxurious life if you let them destroy your ancestors' land? I am a victim of these lies myself. I'm speaking to you as a victim.'

'We don't care about your personal life,' the young man shouted.

Diệu ignored him and said, 'I'd like the commune chairman to come up here and speak to you.'

The commune chairman stepped on to the stage. In a strained voice, he said, 'To those of you who threw manure at my house, do you have the courage to explain to your fellow villagers why you support the golf course? Why do you act so recklessly? I forgive you because I don't think you intended to harm me. Bad people have stirred you up. They've encouraged you to have a shallow-minded and immature response. Look at this young, law student standing here. Listen to her and speak with her. She came here today because she doesn't want to see our farmers lose their land and become homeless like her neighbours. She is educated, knowledgeable and ethical. Let me add this: not only is she a victim of the steel factory but also a plaintiff who will take legal action against those who victimized her. In fact, the factory caused her mother's early death and her father's paralysis. She plans to become a lawyer and work for justice.'

The crowd began to cheer, and the clip ended.

I didn't want to become Diệu's enemy after seeing what happened to Bích's village. My feelings for her had only grown. Whether Diệu or I won this battle, I would lose.

Chapter XVI

As the district chairman had predicted, Miện and Mến vehemently opposed the non-renewal of their lease. They argued that the lease should not have been allowed to expire because the government had no urgent agenda for the marsh, while they were currently creating jobs, generating income and regularly paying taxes to the government. They also argued that the government should have encouraged and assisted them with modern technologies so they could raise more fish and increase productivity. In comparison, the golf course could never be an urgent project related to national security. They wanted the government to mediate between them and the investors according to commercial and civil law.

It was no surprise that Miện and Mến were not easily manipulated. They hired many lawyers to press their case.

But the district chairman was also cunning and disputed their argument. The district was a local entity of the government and therefore, the land belonged to them. Once the lease ended, it was up to the government to decide what to do with it. Without a lease, the brothers had to vacate the property and they had no right to question what the district would use it for.

The district gave the brothers no extra time for further negotiations and decided to repossess the marsh immediately. The Đặng brothers sued the district. The district court rejected their lawsuit. Everything happened exactly the way the district chairman had predicted.

The district chairman consulted with his staff and came up with another plan. Even though he was up against only two men, some women and their children, he sent armed policemen to Đồng Village. He wanted to kill two birds with one stone. The police would repossess the marsh and also send a warning to any other stubborn reactionaries.

Three special-purpose vehicles rolled into the village carrying forty armed policemen led by an experienced officer. Speedboats delivered ten marines down the Gốm River to occupy the pier used by the brothers. More officers on motorbikes rode to the rear of the marsh, in case Miện and Mến tried to escape.

It was a beautiful, sunny day. 'Perfect weather to launch an offensive,' according to the district chairman. After the repossession unit was deployed, he called me into his office, very satisfied with his strategy. 'I'm sure Miện and Mến won't fight back. If they do, they're fools.' He showed me a map of the district and explained the whole plan of attack.

'If I were you, I wouldn't send in so many armed officers,' I said.

'You're a businessman and only good at making money. We don't know how many people Miện and Mến have, so we have to be well prepared. If they resist, we have to wipe them out and intimidate anyone inspired to act like them. These reactionary peasants must be taught a lesson—that's leadership!'

The district chairman had one of the policemen livestream the raid to a private channel, so he and I sat in his office and watched the entire thing unfold on a computer screen. Several curious villagers had also gathered to watch.

The district chief of police, a short man with a heavily pockmarked face, announced through a bullhorn, 'This is the district police. The lease for Starfish Pond has expired.

Miện and Mến are required by law to vacate the property. They and anyone still on the property are trespassing. Those of you standing nearby to watch, please do not interfere, or you may also be disciplined by the law. I request the brothers and their relatives be aware of the consequences of refusing to comply with the government's mandate. Mr Đặng, I request your cooperation so we can do an inventory and agree on a time to harvest the fish. We'll grant leniency if you and your relatives leave the property now.'

There was no reply, except the sound of dogs barking from within the thick bushes. The experienced chief of police knew the Đặng brothers would plan to ambush them from the little processing building, so he ordered, 'Move forward! Engage and arrest them alive.'

'Ridiculous!' the district chairman exclaimed with a burst of laughter. 'Look at that hen-pecked dwarf. Without me, his wife would've castrated him already. You should meet his wife—she's a terrifying woman.'

Suddenly, an explosion erupted from the garden, followed by blue smoke. The officers dropped to the grass. Then came another explosion. The chief fired his gun into the air and shouted, 'Seize them!'

The police started firing, not directly at the building, but into the air above its roof. There were no more explosions. Cautiously, the officers entered the building and found pots and cans and other junk all over the ground. They searched the whole property but found no one, not even a dog. They kept searching and discovered straw men had been propped against poles here and there. They were disappointed. Finally, they found two dogs.

'Impossible!' the chief of police blurted. 'Where are they? Keep searching.'

'We're right here,' came a male voice from the tall grass nearby. The chief of police pointed his gun at the grass and ordered the officers forward. Mến but not Miện, and most of their relatives, all sat there on the ground, concealed by the tall grass. They had dressed in their best clothes, as if attending a play. They held their hands high and looked at the officers without fear or resentment. Immediately, the police stood them up and bustled them into the waiting trucks.

The live feed stopped, and the district chairman breathed a sigh of relief. The following day, the media reported the event very differently from what I had seen. According to some newspapers, the Đặng brothers had planted landmines and used shotguns, attacking and injuring several law-enforcement officers. The reports said the brothers intended to escape by boat and to continue fighting if needed but had been ambushed and arrested. The media praised the district chairman for his leadership.

But also, many other newspapers disputed this narrative and reported more or less what I had seen. While the national government hesitated to make a statement, people from around the country were using social media to support the Đặng brothers.

The district chairman promised that the land clearance wouldn't be a problem, but there was a slight delay as they waited for the court's final decision on the Đặng brothers' dispute. I had some extra time to finish the legal paperwork side of obtaining the investment licence. This was my most urgent business.

I phoned Sinh instead of waiting for him to call me. I implored him to arrange our meeting with Mr Big because I was running out of time.

'Don't you think I feel the pressure?' Sinh said. 'Remember I provide a service. I've just been a little unlucky, so give me time.'

I mentioned to him the names of the people I had sketched earlier.

'I'm not impressed with any of them,' he said. 'I've been looking for Mr Big for the last ten years. I don't think any of them could be him. He's a person who springs spontaneously from one's imagination.'

'Well, I mentioned them just in case. Whoever he is, he's still a human being.'

'Let me tell you this: I've been investigating every lead. I haven't been sitting here doing nothing these past few weeks. And I'm exhausted.' Sinh blew out a long breath and continued, 'Through a friend of mine who knows a lot of VIPs, we settled on one person who fit all the criteria. My friend was able to get me an invite to this assumed Mr Big's birthday party. When I arrived, I joined the long line of guests at the door. Like everyone else, I had prepared an envelope filled with your money as a birthday gift and dropped it into a huge, beautifully carved, red, wooden box. We waited and waited for the host to appear. All through the cocktail party, we didn't see him anywhere. Later, I noticed someone, or something, sitting in a cushioned chair, covered completely by a red cloth. I dared not ask the other guests who, or what, it was. But as we left, everyone was saying Monsieur was healthy and doing very well. Then, I doubted myself. Who was this "Monsieur person" whom they referred to, because I never saw anyone act as host. Maybe they meant the man in the red cloth? I don't know. What do you think?'

Silently, I cursed him.

Chapter XVII

The impact of Diệu's speech on the villagers went far beyond my or the district chairman's imagination. Many Đồng villagers who had been on the fence whether to support the golf course were now on her side. Arguments and fights had broken out in the village between parents and children. Some of the spoiled children who demanded the quick money had been able to persuade their parents to sell their land, but now the parents were changing their minds, and the fighting began.

I needed to do something quick before anything worse could happen.

When the district chairman greeted me in his office, he didn't try to impress me as he usually did. Rather, he seemed nervous and immediately asked, 'When will you have the investment licence? I gave you one month. It's now been two. What are you going to do? I've done everything with the belief that the licence will legalize it all. Without it, we're liars.'

The only new information I had received about Mr Big so far had left me baffled. Sometimes I thought it was all an illusion. Maybe he wasn't a real person after all, just a phantasm concocted by swindlers. But my doubts eased when I remembered that my mother said she heard my father muttering Mr Big's name in his sleep. And then there was the letter I had received. And the district chairman had also told me about Mr Big. The district chairman was an outsider in that world, but even he knew about Mr Big from my father. All I needed from Mr Big was a nod, a phone call, a positive word, a wink of an eye, a yes and then I could accomplish my goal.

Even though I felt agitated, especially after seeing what the video had done to galvanize the opposition, I told the district chairman I would get the licence soon. He looked less angry after hearing that.

'I'm not doing all this for nothing,' the district chairman said emphatically. 'It's been one thing after another—the commune chairman, then the Đặng brothers and now that crazy law student. She must be very lonely considering how much free time she has! I was furious when my staff showed me that video. I wish I could send a gang of thugs to take care of her. Why don't you find out who she is, where she's from and who's helping her? And do it quick. Then I can accuse her of dividing the people, spreading anti-government propaganda, impeding the district's agenda, inciting violence and threatening local safety. I want her in jail, and I can make it happen. I just don't want to have to use a butcher knife to kill a duckling.'

I had only come to the district office to ask for an update and didn't intend to stay long. When he saw me stand to leave, he signalled for me to remain seated. His face was long, his chin bent, his nose grotesque, his forehead narrow and greasy, his mouth like a urinal and his eyes black like a crow's about to steal eggs from a duck.

He seemed to have something on his mind. He paced back and forth for a minute, then snapped his fingers and pursed his lips.

'I've wanted to be forthright with you,' he said, and then stopped as if looking for the proper words to continue, 'but I was afraid you might misunderstand.' Now he looked straight into my eyes. 'In fact, we've never had a formal, business agreement. We've been a bit unprofessional.'

I wasn't sure where he was headed, so I gave him my full attention.

'I want to be clear. Well, how should I say this? I should go ahead and seize all the land for the project. Throw anyone who says a word about it into jail. Remember, I'm an expert at resolving conflict. I know by heart all the theories of industrial development, productivity, the rights of the working class, labour exploitation, the cruelty of the capitalists, the Communist Manifesto and so on, but the problem we face now is pretty new to me. I used to hate terms like revenues, dividends, shares, rates of gross investment, profit and net profit, and so on, but now I have to familiarize myself with them. I didn't expect history to change so drastically.'

'What are you talking about?' I asked. 'Get to the point.'

'We are in the same boat and I hate ungrateful people,' he said. 'I want to know exactly what percentage of the profits my district will get from the project. Well, what percentage the district will get, but also what percentage *I* will get after the project is completed? What is *my* share? Will it be annual? Based on total revenue? A lump sum? After all we've gone through together, how much am I going to get?'

I should've known all this was still just about lining his own pockets. 'I'll be fair,' I said. 'Don't worry. Of course, you won't lose a single penny. We're serious people.'

'I wasn't saying you guys are not serious. In fact, you're extremely serious, but that's not enough. I mean, after you have everything you need, how do I know you won't drop me from the project? You could fill up your bags with money and forget me completely.'

I knew he wasn't joking, even though he smiled as he said that. The district chairman clearly wanted his shares in the business to be permanent so his children and grandchildren would continue to benefit too.

'After the project is complete, I'll give you a VIP membership card, even if someone else owns the course,' I said.

'Thank you, but I don't need that. If I played golf, I'd hit someone by accident. I just want the golf course to be *ours*.'

I felt a little shocked but regained my composure. This district chairman was more cunning than I thought. He had waited until this moment to say what he wanted.

'I'll never forget you,' I said, 'but it's too early to talk about these matters.'

'I don't think so.'

'Okay. That's fine. But let's come back to it another time. Today, I want to reach an agreement on land expropriation and compensation for those who have agreed to resettle. I request that you send some police officers—'

'No problem. I'll send as many as you want. Our district works for you. When you come back, we'll continue our conversation. That's enough for today.'

The district chairman stood up and assumed a cold demeanour. When he saw me remove a square parcel from my pocket, he held up his hand to tell me no.

I returned to my office, loosened my necktie and dropped into my chair. I told my assistant I didn't want to see anyone for the rest of the day, regardless of who they were.

But then, out of nowhere, Diệu appeared at my office door. She said, 'But you definitely want to see me, right?'

I looked at my uninvited guest and thought, yes, in fact, I really did want to see her.

'You're very confident,' I said, 'but, it's my pleasure to have you visit here. Please come in.'

I invited her to take a seat, and then rose to dismiss my assistant for the rest of the day and shut the door. I returned to my desk and sat in my father's old chair.

'Have you changed your mind?' she asked.

'I remember what I said when we said goodbye last time. Maybe you forgot?'

'I apologize for showing up like this. I only just learned this very moment that you are Mr Nam's son. My father sent me to say thank you to your father.'

'What do you mean? Thank him for what?'

'You haven't even asked about my father. He was kind enough to invite you for lunch.'

'I'm sorry,' I stammered. 'I didn't expect you would come here. How is your father? I promised I would come see him again because I need his help with a few things. I—' I was about to tell her I had read Bích's memoir, but somehow I couldn't finish my sentence.

'My father would have appreciated another visit. But you can't always do what you want.'

'Do you mean I can't visit your father, or something else?'

'If I hadn't gone to Đồng Village, would you speak to me in that tone of voice? I'm sure you're mad at me. You probably hate me or think I'm ruining everything. But let's talk about that later.' Diệu gave me a hard look. 'Do you want to know the truth about your respected father, Mr Nam?'

Her ferocity surprised me. I shrugged my shoulders to pretend I didn't understand, but in fact, I was trying to remain calm. Honestly, at that moment, my heart was lodged in my throat. The more serious she became, the more beautiful, elegant, kind and intelligent she appeared. No other woman had ever mesmerized me like Diệu.

'Here's a suggestion,' I said and stood up. I stepped closer to her while still keeping an appropriately professional distance. 'I don't know what business you have with me today, but whatever it is, can we please not mention it? Whatever belongs to the past should remain in the past. What I mean is, can you and I talk about something else this afternoon and for the rest of our lives? Whatever I don't know, we can pretend it never happened, and then whatever you came here to tell me today can become insignificant. Let's leave everything behind. Let's only talk about what we need from each other. Then we can walk the same path and speak the same language—' I almost said, 'of love,' but then couldn't. I was sure she could hear the affection in my voice. 'Honestly, I'm so exhausted with work. I have many regrets, but I just want to be free.'

I imagined my little speech was like something from the beautiful, dramatic scenes I'd read in European romance novels. I would give up everything, even my company, to be with her and to live a heavenly life together.

'If you want to escape, just do it,' she said sarcastically. 'No one will stop you.'

'What did I just say?' I asked. It was like I'd just woken up from a dream. I returned to my seat and looked straight into her eyes. 'Did I offend you? If so, I'm sorry.'

'Basically, you just gave me a list of the things you aren't yet prepared to do.'

I must have been losing my mind. I tried to get back to neutral ground. 'What did you want to tell me about my father?'

'First, I want to know why you came to my village so many times, and why you sought out my father. Have you been haunted by the factory your father helped build? You seem to have a lot of free time to listen to people from my village talk for hours about matters unrelated to your job.'

When I said nothing, Diệu gave a little laugh, as if judging me. 'I guess you were looking for something true that was still related to you. Such things do exist.'

As much as she had mesmerized me, I didn't like being attacked. I asked coldly, 'So, what? What do you want from me?'

'You look very weak, so don't try to pretend to be strong.'

That one stung, a knife to make my heart bleed and put her in control of the conversation.

'That's not how the son of a wealthy and successful businessman should be. But I'm not here to talk about the truths related to you. I know everything and will tell you another time, but only when you're actually ready to hear it. I'm here today because of the golf course. Why do you have to put the Đồng villagers in the middle of it?'

The question was rhetorical. I could feel more of them coming.

'Do you *have to* pursue that project and destroy the peaceful lives of thousands of people while knowing very well that the project will bring nothing good? The countryside is no place for a golf course, nor is it a place for outsiders to compete over. No one needs a golf course. Our country already has too many places that cater to the rich. Can money create a peaceful countryside? Just open your eyes and you'll see how nature is being ruined, how people descend into poverty and suffer from disease while waiting for some idyllic life promised to them by investors. I came to Đồng Village to stop the project, for which your company is the contractor. I don't want to see their farmers become poor and die tragically like in my village. Many of my neighbours still remember your father and what he did.'

Tears rolled down her beautiful, bright face. I didn't know what to do. I let her cry and turned away after pouring her some water.

'Some disgusting, greedy people want to bring home truckloads of money and couldn't care less about how others survive or suffer. Their greed is bottomless. What can they even do with so much money?' She bit her lip so she wouldn't curse.

I wanted so badly to tell her how much I loved and respected her, that I wanted to start over from the beginning again so she and I could be happy together forever. I wanted to kneel before her and confess my sincere love.

But then my mother suddenly appeared at the door. She seemed to have overheard some of our conversation. Though she looked at Diệu for a moment as if considering her suitability as a daughter-in-law, my mother was actually quite unnerved. Like she had a secret she could no longer keep to herself.

'Please stay for a second,' my mother said. 'You don't know me, but I've known you since you were a child. We owe you so much. Please accept my apology.'

Diệu bowed her head.

And then my mother knelt before Diệu, her gesture shocking me and Diệu both. Diệu covered her face with her hands and sobbed. Her whole body quivered. Awkwardly, I helped my mother stand. Diệu stepped past us and rushed from the office, though my mother called after her, begging her to stay.

'Mom,' I almost screamed, 'what are you doing?'

'I feel very fortunate to have had the chance to meet her,' she said sadly. 'I was just coming to tell you. Bích, her father, is dead. He'll never hear my apologies.'

'What? Bích is dead? When? How do you know him? How do you know he's dead?'

'Bích suffered because of our wrongdoings. Your father was not a cruel person, but he did what he had to do when the circumstance required. Your father was partly involved in Bích's tragedy, and it tormented him until the day he died. I haven't been able to sleep well ever since he told me what had been done to get the steel factory built. For the sake of profits, your father had to do as he was told. He wanted to get out of the business, but they always found ways to keep him in. He couldn't escape. He could've been murdered, and I wouldn't have been able to do a thing. Your father paid Bích's hospital bills secretly and gave him plenty of money to raise his daughter after his wife passed away. But it gave him no peace of mind. Whatever he left unfinished, I have had to continue. I told you this morning that I wouldn't be home today. It's because I went to Bích's grave and burned incense for him.'

My mind reeled. 'Does anyone else know about this?'

'Only Mr Tâm.' And then my mother whispered, 'She's such a beautiful woman. I wish her all the best.'

I dropped into my chair. My mind went blank.

I was even more in the dark than I had realized. How many more secrets must there be that I knew nothing about?

Chapter XVIII

The next morning, Mr Tâm, my chauffeur, asked me as usual where I wanted him to take me, and I answered tersely. I had to get out of the city, but I also had to stay close in case Sinh called. I decided to spend the day in the countryside just outside the city. For the entire drive, we sat silently in the car, like strangers.

My mind was still blank.

When I was abroad, I relished an occasional trip to the countryside. I loved to explore new places, meet new and friendly people, and enjoy good food and local specialties.

'I believe this is the place you meant,' Mr Tâm said after a while.

We got out of the car. I gazed at the fog-shrouded valley in front of me. The scenery was beautiful, but I felt sad.

'Don't torment yourself,' Mr Tâm said. 'I worked for your father for many years and learned from his perseverance and his ability to look courageously into his own heart.'

'What do you mean?' I asked, the agitation obvious in my voice.

'On the way here, I noticed you trying to suppress your emotions with all those big sighs. Maybe you're experiencing something troubling in your love life and it's making you sad?'

'You shouldn't make assumptions about me,' I said coldly.

'All right. Well, I do have something to tell you. I think you'll be interested.'

'Why's that?'

'Because it has to do with your father and what you're going through.'

I felt like I was already missing the blankness. I started to sigh again but stopped myself. 'Go ahead, then.'

We followed the stone steps down to a seasonal waterfall that was now dry and arrived at a creek bed full of pebbles. We crossed the dry bed into the forest.

'After the construction of the steel factory,' Mr Tâm said, 'I went to your father's office and saw him at a tea table with his head in his hands, completely distraught. He told me to go home and not to worry about him. Instead, I sat just outside his office and kept watch to make sure he was safe and didn't do anything stupid. Late that night, he went to his desk, typed something and then printed a sheet of paper. He frowned as he read it closely. After reading it several times, he tore it into little pieces.

'I thought maybe it had something to do with a mistress, but that was just a guess based on how intensely emotional he seemed. It didn't make sense, though, because I wasn't aware of his having any affairs. For the next several days and then occasionally over the next weeks, at some point late in the evening, he'd write, print and read something very closely before shredding it. He kept doing this until he got really sick. His illness shocked all of us. I was always by his side in the hospital after his visitors had left. Sometimes, he acted very strangely. He'd be terrified for a few minutes and then act normal again. One day near the end, he handed me a sealed letter and told me to keep it safe and to keep it secret, and then after he died to give it to a woman named Diệu. Her address was on the envelope. I think I'm the only one who knows about it.'

Stunned, I asked, 'Did you say Diệu?'

'I know you're surprised but let me finish. I took the letter home and hid it. I guess your mother had also been secretly watching over Diệu and helping her financially through an agent. I didn't read the letter, but I got the feeling that it has something to do with you. This morning, I stood in front of your father's altar, told him I would eventually do what he had requested and asked him to give me some more time. I've decided you should be the one to give the letter to her.'

Once again, I felt as if the earth had slipped out from under my feet. How could he have kept this from me? My mind churned with all the letter might say. 'Do you have it with you now?'

'Let me finish, and then I won't bring it up again. When you asked me to take you to Bích's village, I was surprised because your father had won construction contracts all over the country, so why would you want to go to this particular village? As you visited with Bích, I considered how I might slip the letter onto Diệu's desk unnoticed, but then, when I saw her, I lost confidence. I found myself thinking that maybe, one day, she would be your wife, though I have no logical reason why I thought that. A woman like her will bear talented and respectable children, that's for sure. Honestly, I still think she's the woman you're meant to marry, so I decided not to give her the letter because I didn't want the bitter relationship between Bích's family and your father to get in the way. If it's possible, you should ask Diệu to marry you immediately, the sooner the better, or you'll regret it forever. I can just tell that you and she are destined to be together.'

Mr Tâm wiped the tears from his face with the back of his hand. I hugged him and apologized for taking my anger out on him earlier. He pulled the letter from his jacket's inner breast pocket. 'I'm glad you have it now,' he said.

The letter had to contain secrets about my father that he wanted to reconcile with himself by confessing. I held it in my hands, staring, hesitant to open it. I lacked the courage and left it sealed for weeks.

***

In the meantime, the situation at my company became even more complicated. The board of directors was losing patience. They wanted me to be a firmer and more aggressive leader. In meetings, they implied they were losing money because of me.

I asked myself: Who are these godfathers? Why do so many of them remain hidden, and how is it that they seem to make all the important decisions? Now I knew why my father had always been busy doing things he probably didn't enjoy. He had created a system in which he wasn't the real leader.

One of the more reclusive godfathers had the nickname, the Termite Queen, though I didn't know exactly why people referred to him that way. Maybe it was because he was obesely swollen like a termite colony's matriarch, and moved as little and as slowly? If you've never seen one of these insects, you're lucky. They're disgusting. Their fat bellies spill out armies of termites that spread from the colony and destroy everything in sight.

The Termite Queen himself was also disgusting. His greasy face was pockmarked with acne scars. He had the dispassionate, intimidating look of a fighting cock, though his dry, bulging eyes resembled a lizard's. He seemed devoid of emotion and rumours suggested he would ruin anyone who threatened him but, perhaps, because of the way he looked and his poor mobility, he rarely showed his face in public.

On the day I became the company's new CEO, the Termite Queen made a rare appearance. As the rest of the board left the room, he painstakingly hoisted his corpulent body out of his chair, came to me for just a moment and lowered a heavy hand on to my shoulder.

'Try your best, handsome, young man,' he said. His rasping breath stank. His face and neck flushed red with exertion. 'Remember a powerful system stands behind you to help.'

At the time, I had thought he meant to be encouraging. Only later did I realize it was a threat to ensure my obedience. I had become a puppet the moment I sat in my father's chair.

Now, out of the blue, the Termite Queen called for a private meeting with my mother and me in the company boardroom. He asked about my work and warned, 'You must be careful. If you lose your own money, no one cares. But if you lose a penny of our money, you'll be held accountable. I hope you understand this. Kindness is, of course, encouraged, but don't make other people sacrifice. The company won't stand for it.'

My mother cast her eyes to the floor, either to hide her concern or to elude his attention. Or maybe she might have been trying to show him that she too was an outsider and not involved with any of our business.

But it was another godfather who began to haunt my sleep those days. He went by the nickname, Di Lặc, the Bodhisattva. In fact, he did look like the Laughing Buddha. He had a chubby face, red nose, and big mouth, and he was always laughing. But while the Laughing Buddha represented peace and joy, when Di Lặc laughed, it meant someone would soon be exterminated. He had no friends, only enemies. He had no partners, only rivals. He seemed truly happy only when his adversaries had been utterly defeated.

There were about ten godfathers in all in my company, and each of them held a large amount of stock. But it was their power and connections, not the stocks, that kept them in control. Rarely visible, often giving orders while staying hidden, only half of them actually attended board meetings. They decided on lucrative business contracts, investment strategies, networking and policies related to the company.

I never dared question them openly—that was an unwritten rule. I had to remind myself the survival of the company depended entirely on this incredible, invisible power with which only the godfathers could communicate. I walked in the light, while they remained in the dark. I heard them saying from the shadows, 'Stop that law student at all costs before she gives us more trouble.'

I could smell the blood in their warning.

Chapter XIX

One afternoon, I received a text from an unknown number that Sinh had been hospitalized after an incident and might not make it. The text said I'd better go to him as soon as possible. On my way to the hospital, I wondered what had happened. Did it have anything to do with our efforts to find Mr Big? I felt unsafe.

I went straight to the emergency room. The glass doors remained closed, and the staff would not allow me inside. After some time, a doctor emerged from the room, shook his head and asked if I was Việt. He told me, 'The bullets tore through too many organs. He doesn't have much time left but says he must speak to you.'

Sinh's face was extremely pale and his whole body was covered in blood-soaked bandages. They had propped up his head and shoulders on two pillows so he could breathe more easily. He opened his eyes when I said his name. He nodded to signal he recognized me. The doctor and nurses left the room. There was nothing they could do. Sinh gathered his remaining strength and spoke to me in a broken voice.

'Please forgive me for not keeping my word. I lied to you. Don't waste your time looking for Mr Big any more. I don't think he exists. I've been searching for him all these years to avenge my father's death. I always believed it was Mr Big who had him killed. But all leads went nowhere. People must have

made him up. I don't know why. I never found my father's killer.
I wanted to see his face ... to ...'
'Who was it?' I asked. I was terrified. Maybe I could help
find the murderer.
'It has been ten years, but I couldn't ...' Sinh shook his head.
'Couldn't what?'
'I ... I ...'
And then he was gone.

***

Sinh's death was no coincidence. I told Mr Tâm to drive me
straight home. I needed to know all my father's secrets. I felt
something terrible would happen soon, but what exactly or to
whom, I had no idea.

I told Mr Tâm he could go home for the night, and that
I would call him if necessary. I found myself wondering whether
I had any real idea who my father was. Could his death have
had anything to do with the secrets stored in my drawer? Who
wrote the letter to me signed, 'Mr Big'? If my father believed
there was a Mr Big, didn't that mean he had to exist? Who killed
Sinh? And why?

That afternoon, each of the major newspapers reported on
Sinh's murder differently, but they all said he had attempted to
approach a powerful crime boss at his home and his security
guards killed him as he tried to force his way through the gate.
A popular newspaper even ran the headline: 'Security Guards
Shoot a Man to Death Before He Could Murder Their Boss'.
According to the article, Sinh had made it all the way to the front
door before he was shot several times. He suffered multiple-
organ failure and severe blood loss and had died in the hospital
several hours later.

Another newspaper headline read: 'Killed by Curiosity'. It
said Sinh had lied to gain access into the mansion and when

he had been revealed as an impostor, Sinh had charged at the owner with a knife. The security guards had to shoot him to protect their employer.

One newspaper suggested Sinh might have been a gang member and that his death was probably for the best. Another speculated that Sinh was the son of a famous contract killer, and that his own subordinates murdered him either because they wanted a bigger cut of the money, or because they suspected he would double-cross them with another gang. In general, the media concluded that Sinh was a mysterious, affluent man living a reclusive life. They also fabricated wild details about his life and sexual affairs. The photo they published showed him standing beside two German shepherds as he watered a potted tree in front of an old mansion.

Normally, people were glad to hear about the death of a cold-blooded gangster. So, only the investigators were interested to discover the real cause of Sinh's death, and that was only out of professional duty. The story was soon forgotten, and Sinh's family didn't insist on any further investigation. Only I knew the secret that Sinh revealed on his deathbed. I reported the information to the police, but they dropped the case. If I decided later to reveal what I knew to the public, everyone would think I had made up the story.

That was probably why Sinh does not appear in the original *Termite Queen*.

But I was haunted by what I knew about him. On whom did he want to take revenge? Besides killing his father, what else had Mr Big done to him? Was he deranged? Did he make the whole thing up?

And who was Sinh anyway? Even this simple question could not be answered straightforwardly because in the public's view a person is simultaneously both real and unreal.

***

It took me a few days to regain my balance after Sinh's death. I needed to think about other things, like the fact that I was still alive and that I had to live for others, too. After Diệu gave her speech to the Đồng villagers, the situation was out of our hands. Most of the villagers became determined to keep their land and refused to resettle. Her ardent good nature proved more persuasive than the district chairman or I had predicted. Now only a small number of spoiled teenagers, drug addicts and gamblers supported the golf course because they needed the money. We had to come up with another strategy.

Sinh's death put a hold on my search for Mr Big, if he even existed. Sinh's last words puzzled me, but it was only after his death I realized that he and I had been puppets all along, playing the parts someone else directed.

To relax, I disappeared without telling anyone. I drove to the lake my father had taken me to so many years before. I didn't ask Mr Tâm to drive me. I needed some time and space alone to contemplate what had happened.

The water in the lake was as clear as it had been many years ago. A few pink and white waterlilies floated on the surface. On the other side stood a few cottages built during the last century. Every now and then, a bird erupted from a bush or the tall grass and flapped its wings before skimming over the water.

I sat on a nest of fallen leaves and gazed out at the lake, remembering my father skipping stones here. The circles formed by each skip spread across the lake, toward the horizon, to a place where I hoped to meet him again. Tears fell down my cheeks. The natural beauty astonished me, especially all the different colours that reflected from the water, coming together and shifting, changing, multiplying. I felt as if I had merged into the scene.

I lay down on the leaves and looked into the clear sky. In this divine moment, Diệu appeared like the picture of the Holy Mother Virgin Mary that hung in my mother's bedroom. On my knees, I begged for her forgiveness, but Diệu said nothing. She would not accept my pleas or apologies and disappeared. Moments later, she reappeared in the distance, with her hands tied behind her back, being dragged away by large, masked men. A crow in the tree above her cawed wildly. The men threw her to the ground at the feet of a big-bellied man. The whole thing reminded me of paintings I'd seen of the Catholic inquisition, with Diệu being tried as a heretic. The judge wore a black robe with a string of skulls for a belt. He looked like Satan, but with a mouth like a hippopotamus. He pointed a large, grotesque finger at her, and she burst into flames, burning to death for blasphemy.

The judge leaned forward and with an enormous tongue licked his own face. I was terrified to realize he resembled the Termite Queen.

I jerked awake, already on my feet and looking around, trying to figure out which way to run. A blast at a nearby quarry brought me to my senses. The nightmare left me deeply unsettled. It had felt completely real. I had an awful premonition that something horrible would soon happen to Diệu. The Termite Queen's disgusting face leered at me from my memory of the dream. No one could escape if he wanted to destroy them.

I had to return to my office as soon as possible.

Chapter XX

The district chairman had come up with a detailed, if unoriginal, plan. He would send the district police to coerce the families who had so far refused to accept resettlement. He told the officers they had to be mentally tough, saying, 'Your duty is to serve the community.'

In his office, he showed me a video of a recent, forced land-seizure that the major newspapers had reported on widely. An entire village had been slated to be bulldozed to make way for an ecotourism resort. Many people had refused to accept the offered compensation and would not vacate their property. They thought their land had been given too low an appraisal, so they put up fences to prevent investors and other project partners from coming into their village. The investors argued that all land belonged to the government. If the government had given them permission to convert the land to tourism, they were doing nothing illegal, and they personally had nothing to do with the rates of compensation. After many failed negotiations, the district exercised its absolute power over the people by repurposing the land.

In the video clip, hundreds of armed law-enforcement officers, who according to the chairman had been secretly bankrolled by the investors, raided the village. They marched in like a battle-tested army and frightened every living creature. Even the frogs, crickets and worms were probably terrified. Their footsteps made the ground tremble. They used ambulances, fire engines and police trucks to make their side seem even bigger, and the gaggle of reporters in tow unwittingly added to that effect. A squad of plainclothes officers infiltrated the crowd first pretending to be protesters so they could identify key opponents and get the leaders taken out first.

In the ensuing scuffle, the uniforms distinguished the law-enforcement officers from the farmers in their sloppy, colourful clothing and flip-flops or bare feet. Of course, no one dared to fight back, at least not at first. The farmers were quickly defeated. They ran like scattered ducks, trampling over one another. Their clothes were torn and their shoes and hats were strewn everywhere. It was like a battle between a rock and an egg. Only when the 'district army' moved deeper into the village were they forced to stop because some of the more courageous villagers had begun to fight back with sticks, *nunchaku*, bricks and rocks. The plainclothes squad recorded everything with their phones, from multiple angles and locations. Concerned that the situation might escalate, the uniformed officers took their time to advance, and gradually backed the farmers into a corner.

As he watched the video, the district chairman grew more and more excited. Finally, he shouted at the screen, 'Ridiculous!' Then in a more controlled voice to me, he said, 'Those law-breaking peasants shout and yell when they fight. They like to make false accusations and call themselves victims of robbery. What liars! The government would never rob its own people. They're just a bunch of ignorant, good-for-nothing, ugly peasants! The officers should beat the hell out of them!'

A voice came through on the video, sounding like it came from a bullhorn, requesting that the farmers surrender.

The district chairman thumped his desk with a fist and said to the screen, 'No need to negotiate with those stupid peasants. Just burn down the whole village and be done with it.'

He told me if he were the commander of the police during that raid, the whole thing would've been done in ten minutes. Finally, on the screen, a woman in her fifties appeared. She wore frumpy, half-unbuttoned clothes that made her look like she had just rolled out of bed. Her gaping shirt revealed her saggy breasts. She held up a bullhorn and said, 'Send someone here to negotiate. We oppose illegal coercions. We want justice and demand fair prices. No one is above the law!'

'Dirty bitch,' the district chairman said to the screen. 'They should be tough with her.'

As he spoke, his secretary entered the office and tried to hand him a stack of documents that needed his signature. He jerked his chin and told her to leave them on his desk. But the moment was over. His ardour for the raid faded and he turned off the TV. I told him again that I had already seen it several times and it was okay to not finish watching.

The district chairman told me he had learned nothing from the video other than that negotiations were unnecessary. So, he'd come up with a better strategy. He told me to come around the table and sit next to him as he turned on a projector plugged into a laptop.

'Let me show you this so you know your cooperation with me is worth your money.'

On the screen were videos of two hypothetical scenarios. In the first scenario, an actor playing the stubborn commune chairman, the leader of the protesters, was arrested; his mouth was taped shut, and he was pushed into a criminal transport vehicle. The protesters ran away. In the second scenario, the law-enforcement officers were attacked by a group of local youths who threw rocks, cow manure and petrol bombs. However, the officers remained calm and requested the protesters to surrender. One of the petrol bombs caught a building on fire, and someone shouted, 'Fire, Fire!' which caused the officers to fire their guns in the air before arresting the terrified protesters as they tried to run away.

The district chairman pressed the pause button and explained to me, 'I had my officers act out these two scenarios just to see how they'd handle something they didn't expect, but I'm not quite satisfied with how it turned out, because those idiots took the script too literally and, in reality, anything could happen. But don't worry because we have ten days to train and rehearse, and I'll come up with more hypothetical scenarios. The biggest challenge is how to deal with that law student. We have to be careful with her, because she's female, educated and beautiful . . . We have to prepare for the worst.'

The district chairman didn't elaborate, but I guessed he'd have some bastard humiliate Diệu in public, or find a way to keep her away. As long as she wasn't there when his army marched into the village, everything would be fine.

'What do you think?' he asked, hoping I would give him some encouragement. He was taken aback when I suggested he delay the operation until after he could come up with a peaceful solution to which both the district and the villagers would agree.

'Are you hallucinating?' the district chairman shouted. 'Be realistic! You can't persuade those peasants—they're donkeys. I hope you're not joking. You can't manipulate me. If you were in my position, you'd be more serious about this.'

'I need more time to think about it,' I said.

'Are you having regrets? Intellectuals like you are good for nothing. A politician once said that intellectuals are like dicks: sometimes they're soft and sometimes they're hard; they can't make up their mind. You get scared too easily. But don't worry. We do everything *for ourselves*, and not just for you.'

Then he insinuated that another business partner might do better. 'Many businesses out there want to collaborate with my district, but I keep my word and don't mind putting up with you. But never mind! If you want to withdraw, I'll be thankful.'

I wasn't surprised because I had been warned about this in a recent board meeting, but it was unimportant to me now. Since Diệu had become involved, I had changed my mind about many things, and even I didn't know why. I just needed to protect her at all costs. I could feel the danger lurking around her. I had to save her.

Before I watched the clip with the district chairman, I'd had another unexpected meeting with the Termite Queen in my office. He wore baggy clothes over his enormous frame and plodded ever so slowly with heavy footsteps. I felt very small and weak next to him. As a formality, he asked me about my plans and reminded me that to succeed in business I had to be tough and aggressive and that a shark must enjoy the smell of blood and swallow its prey without thinking. He said it was my responsibility to report to him what I had done and what I would do. I told him about some of the obstacles I had encountered, and he responded sympathetically.

'Nothing is easy,' he said. 'If it were, everybody would already be rich. It was your dad who used to say that. I'll never find another person like him again.' Then he sighed. Before he left, he placed a small box on my desk and told me to open it only after I got home.

The true purpose of his visit had apparently been to give me the box, which I left in my car. On my way back from my meeting with the district chairman, I tried not to think about it.

The district chairman seemed surprised when I didn't take his bait and beg him not to drop my company for another. I said goodbye without saying when I would meet him again.

'Anyway, we're still following the contract,' he said. 'You're my first choice. Sooner or later, I'll be promoted to the province level. No doubt about that. Don't forget to congratulate me when that time comes.'

He wanted to remind me of the long career he still had ahead of him and that cooperating with him would benefit me greatly for many years to come.

'Thank you. I have no doubt about that,' I said. 'I will definitely congratulate you when it happens.'

When I got home, I shut the door to my room and examined the box. I sensed it contained something dreadful. Flat and rectangular, it had been wrapped in yellow silk with an unusual pattern. I hesitated. Why did he give me the box on that particular day? Why did he tell me to open it at home? What did that look on his face mean? The troubled expression that always came to my mother's face any time his name was mentioned floated through my mind. The nickname, the Termite Queen, must mean something. It referred to a powerful person, a leader, someone who would spawn so many problems for others, someone who would destroy whatever and whoever was in his way.

Suddenly, my mother knocked on the door. I slipped the box under my pillow because I didn't want her to get involved in anything that might worry her.

She came in and sat on the bed beside me. 'I want to discuss something with you,' she said. 'It's time to send your sister abroad for school.'

'I've thought about that. She'll study at the best school in whatever country she chooses.'

'Also, I want to write my will,' she added.

'Is that necessary right now? If people hear about it, they won't think you're doing that only with inheritances in mind. They'll think we're covering some weakness, getting our money out and giving up. I don't want to see the company collapse. Dad spent his whole life building it.'

'In heaven, he would be overjoyed to see you so successful. But I don't want you to have a tragic ending like him.'

'Is there something else on your mind?' I asked. I slid closer to her.

'Why do you ask?'

'You've got such a worried look on your face. I've been meaning to ask you …'

She patted my knee and nodded.

'Who are the godfathers?' I asked. 'What do they actually do? What was their relationship with Dad?'

'The less you know about who they are, the better. Just remember that they, not we, run the company. They built it. They have all the power even though they've hardly invested a single penny of their own money. They contribute the secret strength of the well connected, their networks and their insiders' influence over policy—all of which have made the company rich and successful. If you were still in England, you wouldn't be exposed to these things. But you're the chairman now, here, surrounded by vultures. I want to make sure you know what your actual job is.'

'Okay,' I said. 'Tell me.'

'Listen to them and do what you are told. After your father finally figured out that his authority was just another sham, he wanted to walk away. He didn't want to be held hostage, but he was already so deep into their world, he couldn't get out.'

'What do you mean?'

'Don't be a fool and oppose them. I know you want to reorganize the company. You want transparency. But bear in mind we have no choice. You cannot do anything the godfathers don't want done. After your father's death, I thought very seriously about selling our entire share of the company, even if it meant we'd lose half of everything, or even more, just so I could live wherever I wanted and enjoy my life. You could've had a job you actually liked, and I would be free to take care of your sister without fear. Even if we lost most of our money, we'd still have plenty to live on comfortably for the rest of our lives. I just wanted a peaceful existence.'

'So why didn't you do it? You could have.'

'That's what I thought at first. But then I realized we don't even have that choice—to give everything up. I had to let you take over your father's position because of the ongoing golf course project and I couldn't tell you everything because I worried for our safety. I'm terrified for your sister and Diệu.'

My mother looked mortified when she realized the name Diệu had leapt from her tongue.

'What? What did you say?' I asked. 'What does Diệu have to do with our future? Why are we responsible for her?'

'I think of her so often because I feel guilty. That's why I mentioned her name. Never mind! She has nothing to do with us.'

'Are you being honest? What don't I know? What mistakes have I made?'

'What mistakes have you made?'

'I knew it was wrong to get involved with the golf course. I knew it was a crime, but I felt I couldn't give up because of Dad, his reputation and his wishes. If I'd known what you just told me, I probably would've acted differently.'

'How?'

'I would've given it up and helped the farmers get rich based on what they owned and what they produced.'

'What if the godfathers didn't allow you to do that?'

'They don't have as much power as you think. They're too old and their methods too outdated to control me. The situation is different now. I wouldn't be alone if I confronted them.'

My mother sat quietly and looked out the window. Then she sighed and stood up.

'I'll eventually tell you everything when it's safe to do so, but not right now. Please be patient. No doubt the Termite Queen has some horrifying plan. He has powerful methods you've not yet seen. No one can defeat him. Behind him is an invisible but all-encompassing power. At least pretend to do what he wants you to do. That's the smartest course you can take now.'

'Just tell me! Is Mr Big the "invisible, all-encompassing power" behind the Termite Queen? Or is he just a bogeyman made up to scare people away? If he does exist, who is he? Why are people so intimidated when his name is mentioned? My friend, Sinh, was murdered because he was looking for him. In fact, he tried to find him for ten years and never succeeded. Does Mr Big decide our fate, as the rumours say?'

'I don't know the answers to your questions,' she said. 'I often ask myself the same ones.'

'What about the letter signed by Mr Big?'

'Act as if you never saw it. You'll have to learn how to forget many things.' My mother stood to leave my room, but at the door, she turned back and whispered, 'Just believe what everyone else believes. If you ask too many questions, you'll be in trouble.'

Then she slipped into the hallway and shut the door.

My mother was afraid and with good reason, but I was no longer a little boy. I wouldn't be manipulated. I wouldn't let rumours control my life. I used a knife to open the box.

Inside was a photo of Diệu, crossed out with red marker.

I snapped the box shut and sat shivering as despair rose up my spine. I had to do something. I rushed out and found my mother getting ready to go to the Buddhist temple. She looked at me as if she already knew my question.

'I've got to go soon,' she said. 'Do you need something?'

I held up the box and by the look in her eyes I knew she knew what it was. I showed her the crossed-out picture of Diệu.

My mother's face turned pale and she murmured, 'He's decided to get rid of her. Goddamn that Mr Big!'

'What did you just say?' I almost shouted. I was shocked. 'Say it again, Mom!'

She gulped and swallowed, realizing her mistake. 'Did I say something? Oh, I think I'm not making any sense. Never mind!'

'I can tell you're trying to protect me. Just tell me everything! Did Dad die because of him?'

She closed her eyes tightly and shook her head, not as a response, but to the debate raging within her. 'Do you remember,' she said at last, 'many years ago, you once saw such a box in Dad's office. It was wrapped in yellow silk and tied with black ribbons. Later, out of curiosity, you opened the box after your father had unwrapped it. You saw a photo of a man whose face was crossed out with a red marker, and a note that said, *final solution*. You were terrified. You asked me about it, and I made something up to calm you down. Later, the man in the photo was psychologically tortured and went insane. And then your father's company won a huge contract. The fact that the man never vanished could've been because he was lucky, or because maybe your father had intervened somehow. On other days, other boxes appeared on his desk. One contained a photo of an old man. He disappeared suddenly and it was as if he'd never existed. Your father received many such boxes.' She sighed and slumped, finally free of this secret, but still terrified that she had told me.

'How many boxes were there?'

'I don't know. Your father was haunted by them, just like I am, and now you.'

'We can't live like this, having our whole life manipulated by cruel people who lurk in the dark. We have to redeem ourselves.'

'What do you mean? We ourselves have done nothing wrong.'

'Yes, we have!' I cried. 'We've been complicit with the terrible, evil things done to Bích, Diệu and thousands of other people because we wanted to be rich. They lost their land, lost everything and died with their lives in ruins. Diệu is right— it's not *development*, it's *suicide*. Most people never see justice, not even on their deathbeds. They resent and hate us. Dad couldn't live the life he wanted because he felt he had to protect us. He got endless amounts of money but lost everything else.' I paused to let the words sink in. 'Who is Mr Big? Is he the Termite Queen?'

'He's a larger-than-life, terrifying person,' my mother whispered, now staring straight into my eyes. 'He's more dangerous than a seven-headed snake. Honestly, I'm not sure whether he's the Termite Queen or if there's still some other Mr Big behind him, but you can't defeat them. You're too young and inexperienced. I couldn't bear to have you vanish one day like the others. Please, I beg you.'

I looked away from her beseeching eyes. 'The Termite Queen is probably Mr Big. He spawns the unbearable pressure on others to get rid of the people in his way. He had Sinh's father killed, and now he's threatening to kill the woman I love.'

My mother said nothing, her face like stone. I could tell she worried whether I'd be able to survive after knowing all this.

'Fuck him,' I said. 'He's a goddamned devil in human form. But he doesn't have as much power as you think.'

In a whisper, she asked, 'What can you do?' Then she shook her head and said in a quavering voice, 'No. There's nothing you can do. No one can defeat him.'

Chapter XXI

The district chairman scheduled a date for the land takeover, despite my request for an indefinite delay. I later found out he had scheduled it for his birthday because he wanted the confrontation to be extra special. He said he had done everything according to the law, and if there was a mistake, it wasn't his fault. It took me many months to realize he had rushed the whole thing, regardless of the risks, and for his own benefit, not ours. But, by this point, none of it mattered to me because I had already made up my mind to abandon the project and face whatever dangers arose for refusing to do as I was told.

Sinh's desperate deathbed-confession weighed on me. He had spent his entire life looking for Mr Big without considering that the Termite Queen was right next to us all along. Sinh had wanted to find out why his father had been killed. Mr Big had to be involved. I had no evidence, but it turned out Sinh's father had owned a substantial share of stock in our company, and it would be too much of a coincidence if the Termite Queen had nothing to do with it. I would not be surprised if he had sent Sinh a crossed-out photo of his father in a box.

I pushed everything aside so I could focus on how to save Diệu. I didn't tell her someone was scheming to murder her. She probably would have assumed I was just trying to scare her into backing down. But also, if she knew I loved her and believed what I said, it might only make things worse.

I pretended not to know the secrets my mother had told me and tried to appear to be carrying out all the Termite Queen's requests. In meetings, I feigned enthusiasm for pursuing the golf course. I emphasized the importance of removing the two obstacles that stood in our way: the commune chairman and the law student, Diệu.

But my mother was right. I was not strong enough to rival the Termite Queen. I put on a good show, but nothing escaped him. Somehow, he even knew about our intention to leave the company when the time came, which he regarded as a threat to his profits. It seemed he, the Mr Big I was certain he must be, could even read my mind. Maybe that was why he had given me the box when he did. It was all too easy for him to discover my weaknesses and take advantage of them. Still, his carefully orchestrated scheme to get rid of Diệu shocked me when I finally learnt of it. Fortunately for me, at the last minute, one of his minions had also had a crisis of conscience and asked me to help. He revealed the entire plan, leaving me just two hours to take action.

The plan assumed Diệu would, as she had for the past several weeks, show up in Đồng Village on Wednesday evening to meet with the young people who supported the commune chairman and to discuss strategies to protect the Đặng brothers and stop the golf course project. The Termite Queen would have Diệu murdered right then and there. To save her, I had to be there fifteen minutes earlier. It was raining heavily, and it would take me two hours to get there if I took the main road. I asked Mr Tâm for help and explained the urgent situation and my plan to save Diệu. He suggested a shortcut and assured me we could make it. I could've called her and told her about the murder plot, but I was afraid she wouldn't believe me or assume that I was trying to intimidate her.

Mr Tâm understood my dilemma at once and chided me for not having told him about it sooner. Though I had known Mr Tâm for years and thought of him like a second father, I didn't actually know much about him. He immediately became a different person—no longer the passive and punctual driver I knew. He told me to stay calm. He would take care of everything. I wasn't entirely sure he knew what he was doing, but I had no choice but to rely on him.

When we got into the car it was raining heavily. Mr Tâm drove us to a plot of land outside the city with a tall garage and ten or so old military vehicles parked outside it. He told me to wait in the car while he went into the garage. When he returned, he was driving a UAZ Russian jeep with a tall man about his age whom he introduced as Mr Nhanh, the owner. They had both been commandos in the American War, and after his friend had been discharged, he'd begun collecting damaged UAZs and repairing them. I thanked him for his help and climbed into the back seat. Mr Tâm was no longer the calming presence I was accustomed to. The way he set his jaw reminded me of a cowboy gunfighter from Hollywood movies. The UAZ's souped-up engine roared as we raced into the canyon.

Deadly serious, but with a light in his eye, Mr Tâm seemed excited to be reliving his wartime days as a military driver. Mr Nhanh was excited too, whooping through the tight turns and urging Tâm to go faster. We turned on to an even worse potholed road, and then dipped into a canyon. I stayed quiet, not uttering a single question. I held my breath as the jeep launched into the air from a rise, and when it spun and roared. The modified suspension took care of most of the bumps, though we did bounce up and down a lot and once nearly careened off a cliff.

Đồng Village did not have streetlights. According to the man who called to tell me about the murder plot, Diệu was likely to be on the seven o'clock bus, which was due any minute.

We hit the main road outside the village, drove through the darkened town and continued a kilometre or so in the direction from which the bus would come. Then Mr Tâm turned around, angled part way off the road and turned on the emergency blinkers. I grew anxious as our wait dragged on. The headlights of each approaching vehicle sent shivers up my spine. I worried we were too late—maybe the bus had already gone past—or that we wouldn't be able to convince her to come with us. I was so nervous. I had fully committed to give up everything just to have her in my life and protect her from danger.

Mr Tâm told me to stay in the UAZ. I wanted to shout and to ask him why he was acting so mysteriously, but he looked so intimidating I didn't dare. He had transformed into a menacing gangster. He and Nhanh got out and had a quick conversation I couldn't hear clearly. I opened the door and said I wanted to help, but he yelled, 'Stay where you are!' so forcefully, I did.

I could see the bus coming toward us. Mr Tâm and his friend jumped out into the middle of the road. They pulled down their hats to hide their faces and waved handkerchiefs to signal the bus to stop. The bus driver pulled over. Mr Tâm and Mr Nhanh boarded the bus and as Nhanh spoke to the driver, Tâm made his way down the aisle, looking at each passenger. I could see Tâm speak to a young woman, then drag her screaming out of her seat and up the aisle, berating her all the while. His loud scolding drowned her out, so it was hard to hear exactly what she was screaming. Nhanh carried her off the bus in front of him like a hissing cat, despite her valiant struggle. The passengers sat quietly, their eyes averted. Mr Tâm spoke with the bus driver again before he stepped down, and then the doors closed, and the bus groaned away.

Nhanh pushed Diệu into the back of the UAZ next to me. In a surprisingly kind voice, he said, 'I'm very sorry, Miss. We just wanted to save you.'

When she recognized me, her mouth fell open in surprise. 'You!' she cried. 'What the hell do you think you're doing?'

'I'm so sorry for scaring you,' I quickly replied. 'It's not what it looks like. Whether you believe me or not, for now please cooperate with us.'

'Cooperate with a kidnapping?'

I didn't answer her question. Mr Tâm had started the UAZ and begun to speed along the road, back the way we came. We passed the bus stopped in the village, and then a little way down the road turned wildly onto a rutted lane. Diệu's hand moved towards mine as she tried to keep from bumping her head. I placed my hand over hers and gripped it firmly. At first, she seemed uncomfortable, but then relaxed as she seemed to register my sincerity.

When I noticed Mr Tâm looking repeatedly into the rear-view mirror, I turned and saw headlights right behind us. The Termite Queen's hired killers somehow knew Diệu was in our jeep. Maybe the bus driver had told them. Even with our souped-up engine, we couldn't outrun them. The killers would try to force us off the road and then shoot all of us. I trembled as I pictured how it would play out, and Diệu was sensitive enough to notice my alarm.

Despite the terror I felt, Mr Tâm and his friend looked calm. Confident in his control of the situation, Mr Tâm drove without appearing to worry about the kidnappers following us. When their headlights drew close to our side, he deftly manoeuvred so they couldn't cut us off. Their driver must have been skilled too, but he failed to sneak around us and the narrowness of the road forced him to slow down.

The rain had made the winding, dirt road slippery, and if either driver was careless for even a single second, his vehicle could flip over or hurtle off a cliff. Our UAZ shook violently, and the other vehicle nearly slammed into our side. Then abruptly they had to slow again to avoid hitting an outcropping of rock alongside the road. We raced forward and Mr Tâm suddenly let out an excited cry.

'Hold tight!' he shouted as we accelerated toward a sharp turn. The headlights behind us sped up, too. At the edge of the turn, just a few metres from the precipice, Mr Tâm cut the lights, cranked the wheel furiously, slammed the brakes and spun the UAZ like a top. We came to a stop and Mr Tâm hit the lights just in time to see the killers' Humvee plunge over the edge of the ravine.

'Okay!' Mr Tâm said with a big sigh. 'We're okay now. Loosen your grip on that poor girl or she won't be able to breathe!'

Only then did I realize that I'd been holding Diệu's body tight against mine. I could smell the scent of her hair and became suddenly conscious of her warm body pressed against me. Despite the danger, I almost wished the drive had been longer so I would have had more time to keep her safe in my arms.

'I'm sorry,' I whispered and slid away.

Diệu said nothing and still looked terrified.

We returned to Mr Nhanh's garage, and when the three of us had transferred into my car, Diệu turned away from me and stared out the window for the entire ride back to the city.

'I hope you don't blame us for acting so abruptly,' Mr Tâm said. 'If Mr Nam were still alive to see what a smart and beautiful woman you've become, he'd be very happy.'

'Thank you for saving my life,' said Diệu, 'but I need to return to the village. I still have work to do there.'

'I don't want to interfere in your work,' Mr Tâm said, 'but may I suggest that you stay at my house for a few days, just to be safe, and then you can do whatever you want?'

'Thank you for your kind offer, but there are a few things I must take care of. I can't do them if I stay at your house.'

'You can't do them if you're dead either,' he said. 'Please reconsider, and if you change your mind, just let me know, and I will come get you at any time, day or night.'

Back in the city, Mr Tâm stopped the car in front of Diệu's apartment building near the university. I opened the door and helped her out. I'd said nothing while she spoke with Mr Tâm. Diệu absent-mindedly pushed a strand of hair from her face, looked at me and said, 'I want to speak with you.' Then to Mr Tâm, she added, 'Thank you again. Please excuse us.'

Mr Tâm nodded, and I thanked him for his help and told him he should go home and rest. I would take a taxi later.

I suddenly felt as if Diệu and I had been on some strange date. In the dim light coming from the park across the street, her beautiful face looked mysterious.

'I want to thank you personally,' she said.

'In fact, I should be the one thanking you.'

'Please don't make this harder than it already is,' Diệu said and smiled sadly. 'I owe you something—something one cannot truly repay.'

I stepped closer and caressed her face and gently tilted it toward me.

'I beg you,' I said. 'Please give me the chance to redeem myself. I know I can't make you trust me, and I completely understand. My father was a reluctant accomplice in your family's tragedy and the tragedies of many others in your village. I'm only learning about it all now.'

Diệu swiped my hand away and asked, 'Who was behind it all, then? And what do you know? That your father's wicked scheme caused my father's paralysis? That hundreds of my neighbours almost chose to die rather than to live in poverty and fear? Your father brought us nothing but disaster, filled his pockets with heaps of money, made us all suffer and disposed of us like trash. That steel factory not only poisoned our land and water, but our very lives. Nothing can survive there now. No one. He gave away our futures like bait to bloodthirsty sharks. Do you really think I can forgive crimes of such magnitude by accepting your apology? Let me tell you—there can never be a friendship between us. You're a rich money-maker and everyone else is just a slave who cleans up the trash you leave behind.'

'What if what you just said was untrue, or only partly true? What if your curses aren't warranted? History has deceived both of us. I don't mean to deny my wrongdoings, if I committed any. I can't give back what was stolen from you, but what if there are other truths?'

'The more you say, the more motivated I feel to do the work I must do. I don't need you to grant me mercy. There will be more confrontations between us. Go ahead and do whatever you want.'

'There'll be no war between us,' I said, looking across the street to the lights and dark trees of the park. 'I've decided to give up everything. I won't be involved in whatever happens next, so please don't blame me. I apologize for all that's happened. And please take every precaution to stay safe. As long as the Termite Queen lives, real danger can reach you at any time. Let me know if you need anything.'

I stumbled away as sad as I had ever felt in my life, as if a whole mountain had slid down and buried me.

But then I stopped because I could feel Diệu's eyes still following me. I ran back to her, knelt at her feet and held her hands against my face.

She caressed my cheeks and said, 'I believe you are sincere, but we cannot be friends. There are more awful truths that you don't yet know. You would not survive them.'

'I love you,' I said. 'That's the most important truth. I don't need anything else but you in my life. I'll wait however long it takes to change your mind about me. The Termite Queen is behind everything, and my father was his victim the same as all the others he destroyed. He won't rest until he gets rid of you, and then I'll be next. He's the devil himself. But I won't just accept it. I won't accept his death sentence like my father did. I will fight back. It will be a fight between an experienced, old tiger and a defiant, young man. I'll need your help.'

Diệu said nothing, understandably caught between sympathy and an inability to forgive the sins of my family.

I stood and took her hands and squeezed them gently. Then I walked away, leaving her standing there like a lone, stone statue.

Chapter XXII

I had been collecting every scrap of evidence and information I found related to Mr Big since all this started with the hope that it would somehow help me determine who he really was. Now I had to figure out how to use it all against him. If I didn't do something, neither would anyone else, and we'd be his puppets forever.

I told my mother what I intended to do and asked her to tell me everything she knew about the Termite Queen. She hesitated at first, but agreed when I insisted that I would move ahead even without her help.

At the beginning, she told me, my father had been the IT manager at a quarry, which gave him a solid background in both information systems and construction. Even as a young man, the Termite Queen had been very large and very strong, and therefore was always one of the most productive workers at that same quarry. Back then, exceptionally hardworking, efficient and productive workers earned the Soviet title *Stakhanovite*, and often got slotted to be promoted to the head of their unions. The Termite Queen was no exception. But he had dropped out of school and couldn't read or write well so, when he needed help with paperwork or guidance on how to behave properly in various business situations, he relied on my father for help. When the Termite Queen had to give a speech to the quarry workers, he asked my father to write it for him.

My father had the office secretary type it up and make three copies so the Termite Queen could practise and be sure to have a copy when the time came. The typist handed the Termite Queen the three copies without explanation. On the day of the speech, at the podium, in front of all the workers, the Termite Queen read all three copies, apparently never realizing he had repeated himself. The audience lowered their heads and hid their giggles behind their hands. The head of the union had a lot of power, so the workers were afraid he'd take revenge on them for laughing. When the meeting ended, he criticized my father for writing such a long speech. My father didn't want to embarrass him with the truth and instead agreed and apologized.

That was the start of their friendship. The Termite Queen needed my father's tact and intellect, and my father needed the Termite Queen's growing power and reputation. At a party one night, after having drunk too much rice wine, my father told him the story about his parents. The Termite Queen advised my father not to tell anyone else about it, but even so, my father had already foolishly made himself a hostage. Back then, if a person's family background was unclear or unsavoury, they'd never get promoted and might not even get hired for a job in the first place. By the time the Termite Queen had been promoted to run the quarry, my father was completely in his power.

Rung by rung, the Termite Queen climbed the career ladder. Heading the quarry union led to other, regional and then national union leadership roles. He used those connections to start a research institute for construction materials, funded by the government and managed by my father. Though the Termite Queen wasn't a high-ranking official, he was conniving and knew how to network with the influential and powerful figures above him. Once the Termite Queen climbed above the need to take part in day-to-day operations, my father used his patronage to start our company, which specialized in civil engineering in the post-war era. Under the government's supervision, it relied on the Termite Queen—by now, well on his way to becoming Mr Big—for networking and illegal transactions. He was very good at it. He knew how to manipulate the system and succeeded at making our company the only candidate for many enormous and lucrative construction contracts. Thus, our company grew very fast and took in vast revenues. During that time, if a person knew how to take advantage of an opportunity, they could become unbelievably rich overnight.

With its enormous capital and clandestine support from powerful people, my father's company started to eliminate its opponents. When the government privatized in accordance with the enterprise law, my father, with Mr Big's assistance, bought the workers' stocks at very low prices. The number of the company's stockholders diminished every year since it constantly lost money as it overextended to buy dissolved state companies' huge properties at fractions of their real values. That was all part of Mr Big and my father's brilliant strategy based on a much grander vision. Our company grew into a giant construction empire as the value of the properties skyrocketed. But by then, Mr Big, my father and just ten other people held all the stocks. On paper, my father was the president and CEO of the company but, in reality, everything was run by an advisory board comprised of the godfathers and secretly chaired by the Termite Queen. Board meetings were always private, bordering on clandestine, and never did all the godfathers attend at one time. They did everything they could to shroud their identities and involvement.

But then a war broke out among the board members. It started with some disagreements over investment strategies, business goals and the distribution of profits, but turned into a bitter battle between Mr Big and another godfather nicknamed the Guillotine. According to my mother, the Guillotine was

Sinh's father. She claimed he was unmatched in his ability to vanquish rivals thanks to a group of loyal and merciless gangsters who worked for him. Just when it looked like he was about to overthrow Mr Big's leadership, the Guillotine died unexpectedly atop the naked body of a beautiful woman. He had been poisoned.

Mr Big manipulated the media into reporting that the Guillotine had died of a heart attack. At that time, Sinh was living an extravagant life abroad. When he returned to Việt Nam to attend his father's funeral and take over his father's affairs, Sinh was nearly killed in a car accident. Several suspicious incidents followed after that. He sold all his stocks, abandoned the company and holed up in an old mansion, telling everyone he simply wanted a peaceful life. But in truth, he had secretly begun his search to discover who had murdered his father. Since his father had sat on several such boards, it could have been any one of dozens of these powerful men, all who had taken great pains to conceal their true identities.

Much later, I learned that on the day of the funeral, Sinh also received a note of condolence signed by Mr Big. Sinh felt there had to be some connection between this person and his father's death because the note ended with, 'I'm very near you'. Sinh grew obsessed with Mr Big, certain that he had murdered his father. His long journey to find the killer stretched out over the years, until Sinh eventually became so exhausted and discouraged that he finally gave up. But then a detective he had hired told him that I was also looking for Mr Big, which confirmed to Sinh that Mr Big actually did exist. When Mr Tâm and I came to his old mansion and spoke to his servant, Sinh secretly observed us the whole time. He said he would help me find Mr Big, but in fact he was hoping I would help him.

I had stacks of notes on Mr Big filling my desk drawers, but I had to admit none of it meant anything. Nothing I found could actually serve as evidence of Mr Big's crimes, and as the clock ticked down for Diệu, I also grew desperate and exhausted. It was then that my mother appeared at my office with a folder and an envelope. The look she gave me somehow seemed both happy and sad.

'You're all grown up now,' she said. 'I'm very proud of you. Your father in heaven must be smiling. I can see that you are committed to a just and moral path, and that your love for Diệu means nothing will turn you from it.'

'That's true, but even so, I'm not sure what to do next. I have no real proof of what Mr Big has done.'

'That,' she said, placing the folder on the desk in front of me, 'is why I'm here.'

The folder held dozens of documents and a stack of photographs.

'Your father prepared these to protect you once he was no longer with us. He meant them to be a weapon for self-defence.'

I quickly examined the documents. My father must have foreseen the situation might eventually come to this, so apparently all along he had been secretly collecting evidence of Mr Big's crimes. In his situation, he couldn't have outed Mr Big without destroying himself, so he collected the evidence to protect my mother, my sister and me. My mother had been reluctant to reveal the files because she had been afraid I was too inexperienced to use them wisely and would fail if I tried to fight back.

I took the folder home and locked it in a safe beneath the floorboards of my bedroom.

I decided what I needed to do before anything else was to apologize to Mr Bích at his grave and also to his relatives. That was not an easy thing for me to do.

It had been two days since we rescued Diệu, and I hadn't spoken to her since. Every night, I wanted to call her, but

I told myself I shouldn't. Without telling her, I had hired some top-notch bodyguards to protect her, but I was still anxious. I imagined Mr Big chopping her into pieces that he'd wrap into gifts and send to her relatives and close friends. If that ever happened, would I receive some part of her on my desk? I wondered if Mr Big knew that Mr Tâm had helped with the rescue.

He had been given the nickname the Termite Queen because he was the most powerful person in my company, and also because a termite queen gives birth to an endless army of blind workers that will destroy everything in their path. I imagined if I ever saw him lying naked on a chaise lounge with a satisfied grin on his face, he would look exactly like a grotesquely swollen termite queen. He was rotund; his skin was smooth and shiny. Some of the photos of him that my father had collected showed him having sex with numerous women at the same time, and the other godfathers had probably nicknamed him the Termite Queen either out of fear or out of admiration. His large, repulsive penis made me think of destruction rather than reproduction.

The Termite Queen's ability to neutralize his emotions terrified me. When he had stepped into my office to leave the box that suggested he would have Diệu killed, he did so with the relaxed and tired demeanour of someone who had just walked out of a brothel.

Before I could put any plan into action, two developments attracted the media's attention. The Đặng brothers were accused of resisting arrest and disobeying a government order, but a stay order required the district to withdraw the expropriation and allow the brothers to continue to use the marsh until the matter was settled. The government, due to public pressure, also ordered a pause on all golf course projects across the nation to reconsider whether too many were underway.

I heard the news on the radio on my way to visit Bích's grave. I wasn't surprised. In fact, I felt relief. I eagerly anticipated the chance to give Bích this news, to apologize and also to tell him that Mr Big had always been behind everything and that my father had also been a puppet controlled from above.

Mr Tâm and I found the village cemetery without trouble. I intentionally chose to arrive during the late afternoon to avoid the villagers' attention. The countryside had once been bustling but now it was quiet, desolate even. Most of the young people had left to earn a living elsewhere, though I had heard many ended up lost to gambling and drugs and other vices. The elderly had to do most of the work. They walked the fields and lanes slowly, their backs hunched. The sight of a stranger would make them suspicious.

We followed a dirt path through tall grass for a few hundred metres to reach Bích's grave. The date on the headstone reminded me he had died less than a month after I'd visited him at his house. I wondered if he had carried everything he had written in his memoir to his grave, and a deep sadness settled into me.

Someone had recently left fresh incense. The sticks had burned down to only a third and emitted a pleasant smell. I looked around but saw only grass and birds flitting from stone to stone. My heart beat faster.

Mr Tâm and I arranged our offerings on a platter that we had carried with us. I planted burning incense in the censers at his grave and at the graves around his. The scent reminded me of stories my father had told me in my childhood that suggested the souls of murdered people don't reincarnate or rest in peace. Those unfortunate souls would wander their villages as angry ghosts, cold and lonely. Only if their living relatives prayed repeatedly and sincerely could souls like that find peace. Maybe Bích's soul was wandering right then and there. Would he see and recognize us? Would he register our sincere repentance and accept our apologies? Would he forgive us?

My eyes filled with tears, as did Mr Tâm's.

By twilight, the incense had burned halfway. We lit paper offerings and left fruit and rice wine on the grave.

I started to return down the dirt path to the car with my hands clasped in prayer. I felt a little lighter. Then, on an impulse, I ran back to the grave and pulled out the unopened envelope Mr Tâm had given me earlier. I suddenly felt I must burn it at Bích's grave too because it no doubt contained my father's explanations for what he had done. I hoped Bích would forgive him and they could become friends in the afterlife. Mr Tâm saw what I intended to do and as I knelt at the grave, he grasped my shoulder gently and reminded me, 'The letter wasn't meant for you.'

He was right. My father had written the letter to Diệu. She should receive it, not me, and not Bích. I guessed my father was watching me from above. Mr Tâm held out his hand and I gave the letter back to him.

Then a woman's voice startled us, saying, 'But you can burn this one.'

We turned and saw Diệu standing as still as a statue not far from us. She must've seen everything we had done at her father's grave. Without meeting my eyes, she thrust a wooden box wrapped in yellow silk into my hands. Maybe she had brought it here to burn but had hidden herself when she saw us.

'Either take it home with you,' she said, 'or burn it right here.'

I held the box in my trembling hands, wondering what might be inside. Was it another picture of her? Of me? Mr Tâm? My mother? As I froze considering these possibilities, Mr Tâm snatched the box from me. Then, saying nothing, he piled up some dry grass and lit it, and when the fire was big enough, placed the box in the flames. He added more dry grass and twigs to make sure the box burned completely. I glanced at Diệu's tearful face.

As the flames consumed the box, Mr Tâm handed Diệu my father's letter. I didn't need to explain anything to her. The light, dry wood burned hot and fast and quickly turned to ash. We left the graveyard without saying a word. At a fork in the path, we went one way, Diệu the other. I watched her from the car gliding through the tall grass until she vanished around a bend. Everything inside me urged me to run after her, but Mr Tâm grasped my shoulder and said, 'Be patient. It's not the right time.'

Chapter XXIII

That night, I was plagued by nightmares. In one that kept haunting me even after I awoke, I placed the folder that contained the evidence of Mr Big's crimes on the desk in front of him.

'So, have you finally made up your mind?' he asked in a dead voice without looking at me.

'Do you think it's too late?'

'No. You're right on time. Tomorrow, call a board meeting, and we'll agree to let you quit. You threw away our money like seashells. You sacrificed all our and your father's work just because of that country girl. Maybe you forgot diamond cuts diamond?'

'Or maybe you did.'

'You should be smart enough to understand the fact that whoever has all the money is king. Unfortunately, in your father's will, he didn't tell you this one, simple truth: this company is an iceberg. Even your father only knew the part above water. That tiny bit is nothing more than the tip of my finger. The vast portion underwater is immensely bigger and has always only had one true owner.'

'I have evidence that proves you're an imposter, a liar and a thug who relies on a network of gangsters to threaten and murder people. You steal the state's and citizens' property in equal measure. You collaborate with greedy officials, corrupt politicians and opportunistic middlemen to ruin this country. You really are a termite queen!'

'Very well articulated,' he said, and then yawned. 'Maybe you should be a politician or a news reporter. Do you think your little folder can scare me? Let me guess: it contains your father's accusations and a few lines written by witnesses whose lives have been ruined because they're stupid and unlucky. None of those photos show me doing anything illegal. You say I plotted to murder that pretty, little law student and Sinh's promiscuous father, but what evidence do you have? You can't have any proof unless you've gone straight to hell and asked Satan himself. Even if you do have some lousy piece of evidence, you can't touch me, because I hold the law in the palm of my hand. I can punish or reward anyone I want.' He rolled his shoulders and yawned again, as if tired of the conversation. 'Do you know anything about banana trees? Their trunk and leaves mean nothing. It's the bulb underground that is the real thing. I'm the bulb.'

He was certainly bulbous, that much was true.

'You are no longer needed for the golf course project,' he said. 'Your name will be dropped from the list of the company owners. If you think you have too much money and want to do charity work, go ahead. The company will be restructured and sell all the in-progress projects to other companies. If you don't want to lose everything, go home and convince your mother to sell all your stock to us. We'll give a decent price—maybe a third of their value. I can be very kind, you see. But if you don't sell, I'll have no choice but to be cruel. I'm sure you're aware I have ways to seize all your holdings without paying a cent, or to reduce their value to nothing. You know it's not an exaggeration. I *am* the Termite Queen.'

Finally, he brought his eyes up to gaze into mine. They were tiny. Alien. Dead.

'So, what then?' he said. 'You have something more to say? Or is that all? If so, go play now so I can work, you little shit.'

I realized then I had been a fool to take him on. My mother was right.

I tried to hide my weakness beneath my own deadened gaze. As I picked up the folder and began to walk away, the Termite Queen hauled his gargantuan carcass out of his chair and shoved another small wooden box across the desk toward me before plopping back down. It looked just like the one Diệu had given me at her father's grave.

'I've kept this for years,' he said. 'It's yours now. Want to know what's inside? You can open it right here if you like.'

I looked at the box with curiosity.

He tapped his fingers on the desk. His assistant appeared immediately. Mr Big jerked his chin at me and said, 'Open it for him.'

With its narrow, rectangular proportions, the box looked like a little coffin. Inside, it held an effigy that resembled my father, with a long needle pierced through its head.

I felt dazed. My eyes blurred.

'Are you scared?' the Termite Queen scoffed. 'Pathetic.'

I bit my tongue and glared at him. But my body quivered with fear.

'Let me tell you where it came from. The farmers who lost their land because of the steel factory made it to curse your father. To them, then, now and forever, Nam was a heartless and greedy devil. Every family in that village has a box like this containing an effigy of your father. They consider him a criminal, which is in a way true, even if it was me behind everything. But of course, I can't tell them that and no one knows. And even if I did, or you did, no one would believe it. Now that no one cares about who your grandparents were, I could tell my power over him was no longer absolute. So, I made him the scapegoat.

What a poor fate! Similarly, I'm sure the Đồng villagers feel the same way about you because of the golf course. Better watch out! They could try to kill you at any time. And they might! Just so we're clear, let me tell you this directly—you are just our stupid, little puppet. You've wasted company money bribing insignificant people, just as your father did, but it was me who encouraged you to do so, just to see you dig yourself deeper and deeper into the mire. It only cost me pocket money. It doesn't matter. Now we just wait for this little squall to blow over and the investment licence will come through and the golf course will still get built and the villagers will still blame you. Don't even begin to think you'll have a share in it. All that money will be mine. I'm sure your father never told you about his many failures. You and he are so similar. Arrogant and stupid.'

I'd heard enough. 'You're disgusting! You're wrong if you think I'll let you win like my father did. I'm young and ethical. I have a long road ahead of me. There are many people tired of your kind of business who will work with me for the well-being of this country. You're ancient, from a disgusting past. No one is afraid of you any more. Trust me! You're too blind to see you're at the end of your road, standing at the edge of a cliff. You live for no one. Haven't you realized yet that you're too old to spend all the money you've stolen? Heaven will punish you for your crimes, even if no one else does. I'm sure you have no idea how much money you have and know even less about the real world. You've got a rotten, disgusting stench about you and you're just too blind to see you're actually dying.'

'Everyone's dying, you little shit, even you. At least I'm better than all those patriotic chumps who act like monkeys. Have you ever seen a circus monkey? After each show, the trainer feeds it candy. If not, it won't perform again. It'll misbehave, even piss in the audience's face and all over the trainer. How many people in this country are like circus monkeys? I'm not smart and can't count to a thousand, so help me. If you don't give them houses, benefits and titles to put on a show, they'll betray everyone, even their own benefactors, and embezzle, steal, or sell whatever they can. They'd sell the entire country, its peoples and ideals if they could. I used to be a quarry worker, but my vision is clear, isn't it?'

The Termite Queen burst into a laughter that sounded like the roar of a lion grown tired of playing with its prey. He pulled open his trousers and an endless stream of plump, milky white termites swarmed forth. With their sharp, strong teeth and blank expressions they blindly devoured the desk between us. Everything around me began to disintegrate.

'Look!' he shouted. 'If I say so, within seconds, my termites can overwhelm the entire country. I can order them to devour everything in the blink of an eye.' He jerked his chin forward. 'Show him what you can do.'

Instantly the army of termites swarmed all over my body and beneath my clothes. They chewed through my skin and into my flesh. Within seconds they had gnawed me down to the bone.

***

I woke up in a cold sweat, panting. And yet, in that inexplicable way our subconscious minds work, the nightmare revealed to me what had been in the box we burnt with Diệu. When she told me to either take it home or throw it into the fire, her facial expression had been soft, maybe even kind. I hoped she wanted me to leave the past behind so we could start a new relationship with one another. Hopefully, she had forgiven me. With my heart pounding, I got dressed and put on a blue tie my mother had given me. Blue felt like a lucky colour. I opened my wardrobe and took out the small wooden box I had prepared. This one was lined with velvet, and inside, it held a diamond ring my mother had given me with the instruction to 'Give this ring to the girl you love most.'

I decided the time now must be right.

Just as I was about to leave home, one of the security guards I'd hired ran up to the front door. He looked pale and said in a rush, 'Sir, we've just heard something terrible has happened. Someone . . . just died . . .'

'What?' I asked, thinking he referred to Diệu. 'A man or a woman?'

'A man.'

I sighed with relief. But then I thought maybe the dead person was the commune chairman. If the Termite Queen had failed to murder Diệu, maybe he'd have the commune chairman killed instead.

Mr Tâm drove me to the address where the security guard said the crime had been reported. It was the Termite Queen's main house in the city. A crowd had already formed in the street in front of the enormous mansion. All the security guards were speaking of an attempted murder. They knew me from the times the Termite Queen had come to the office and ushered me into the bedroom where he lay dying.

But it was too late. The Termite Queen never got the chance to say his last words to me or his family. He scowled as if unable to find someone who could understand him. He must have wanted to say something serious. Blood spilled from his mouth. His breath came in gasps. I could hear the air suffering in and out of this throat. His gaping mouth revealed big, gold-crowned molars.

On his deathbed, his face was swollen like a balloon and had taken on a sickly grey hue. His drum-like belly appeared larger as he writhed in agony. His back curled like a shrimp, and the veins popping and writhing beneath his skin looked like fattened leeches. He panted heavily, and pissed and shit himself at the same time. Then his face turned as dark as an old kettle. While the paramedics tried to hold his enormous body down, he squirmed like a python, and then, all of a sudden, his eyeballs popped from their sockets like bullets shot from a gun, or corks from bottles of champagne. Everyone was horrified. A noise that sounded like a paper bag popping came from his groin. The paramedic said, 'His scrotum has exploded,' and two testicles that looked like boiled and peeled goose eggs rolled down his thighs. His most loyal servant, wearing a black suit and a red tie, rushed forward and caught them. He held them in his hands as if they were precious, and then put them in a box, presumably so that they could be set within the Termite Queen's coffin, and in hell no one could ridicule him for having been castrated.

But according to the paramedic, the Termite Queen was not yet dead. He was still breathing. His big toes writhed up and down.

'He wants to say his last words,' someone said. 'Get his family!'

I had no intention of giving him the satisfaction of speaking to me then, so I left. But according to rumours, later that afternoon, the Termite Queen had still not died but his body was already starting to rot, and because he hadn't yet said a word, his relatives lost patience and left his side. A doctor was brought in who later said that at midnight, the Termite Queen suddenly sat up, his black eye-sockets writhing with worms. His lips were swollen and his nose looked as if it had been eaten by termites. One rumour said a baby snake wriggled out of the hole where his nose had been. His entire body was rapidly decomposing. His head lolled back and forth like a broken melon. Maybe he was looking for something to take with him to his grave. The terrified doctor said that suddenly the eyeless, noseless, earless and thick-lipped Termite Queen had sat up and shouted, 'My money, my . . . money . . .' and then fell back on the bed and died. The housekeepers who cleaned up afterward said the bed and floor were soaked with a viscous, yellow liquid that had oozed out of his decomposing body.

Chapter XXIV

The Return of the Reaper (chapter from the original *Termite Queen*)
Seeing that Việt would not act, the Termite Queen had ordered a man nicknamed the Grim Reaper, accompanied by two other gangsters, to kill Diệu. The Reaper would kidnap her and then arrange to make her death look like an accident. He planned to snatch her at the bus stop after she disembarked to meet her Đồng Village friends to discuss legal strategies to prevent the construction of the golf course.

When he arrived in the village and learned that some strangers had waylaid the bus and kidnapped Diệu before it made it to the village, the arrogant Reaper took offence. Now, it was personal. There were rivals to take out besides the girl. The only direction the strangers could have gone was toward the city via the back route through the canyon. The Reaper raced toward the turnoff, and sure enough, a UAZ matching the bus driver's description was there on the road ahead of them. The Reaper and his accomplices whooped and cackled like hyenas, hot on the scent of blood, ready to tear apart their prey and devour its flesh.

Let's take a moment to talk about the Grim Reaper. The Reaper owed the Termite Queen for saving his life after he had been arrested for murdering another gang leader. With the Termite Queen's connections, the Reaper had not only stayed out of jail, he'd even been commended for defending himself and ridding society of such a terrible criminal. The Termite Queen had been the one to give him his nickname after they had worked together for a short while, since no one survived once the Reaper knew their name. The Termite Queen rewarded his loyalty and obedience with a gold-plated gun and several special privileges. For instance, any time the Reaper needed to lie low, there was always a room at the boss's mansion available to him. He was the only person with such unlimited access to the Termite Queen's residence.

The Reaper had a beautiful wife who had once been a popular beauty-pageant winner. At some point, she spiralled into using drugs, and then became a wanted criminal after taking part in a trafficking ring. The Reaper had wiped out the drug-dealing gangsters, brought the beauty queen home with him and gotten her through rehab. She came to rely on him for protection and a safe, comfortable life, and eventually they married. When the Reaper was around, she always called his boss by the respectful pronoun, 'Grandfather', but it was rumoured she was having an affair with him. Every time she came home from a visit to 'Grandfather's' house, she had on some new expensive jewellery. Gold rings, diamonds—even a Cartier jade necklace that must have cost tens of thousands of dollars. This enraged and terrified the Reaper, whose sleep was frequently haunted by nightmares featuring the gifts she had received from his boss. He forced himself to think that the Termite Queen's adversaries must have concocted the rumours to try to drive them apart. After all, the Termite Queen was always surrounded by women much younger and more beautiful than his wife. What time or need did he have to flirt with an older married woman?

Despite his jealousy and scepticism, the Reaper always did whatever the Termite Queen ordered without question, reminding himself that without the Termite Queen, he would be dead or in jail. When the order came to murder Diệu, he designed a careful plan. He would drive up next to her, one of the accomplices would roll down a window to ask for directions, and then they'd drag her into the Humvee and take her to a pass where they would throw her off a cliff or shove her from the bushes into the path of a speeding truck. Things like that could easily happen on such a dark and rainy night. But one of the Termite Queen's young servants had seen Diệu on the news and when he heard the order to have her killed, he'd had a panic of conscience and revealed the plot to Việt, the young chairman of the company. When the Reaper learned that the woman had been taken from the bus, he realized he had been betrayed and swore he'd find the rat and take revenge. Whoever interfered had endangered him, his crew, and his boss. They would have to die a miserable death. But first, he needed to take care of the woman.

Flying up the canyon road, the Reaper revelled in the power of his armoured Humvee. But each time they drew near, the UAZ would accelerate and narrowly avoid getting caught. He managed to pull up alongside the UAZ, but then they scraped the guardrail around a hairpin bend and he had to slow down. 'Son of a bitch!' the Reaper shouted. 'I'll get you!'

The two vehicles swerved and jockeyed dangerously on the narrow winding road in the heavy rain. The Reaper drove like a maniac. Each minute that he couldn't catch them made him all the more crazed, willing to take even greater risks to overtake his prey. The other driver must have sensed his desperation and suddenly began to pour on the speed. The Reaper floored the accelerator. That old piece of shit couldn't compete with his Humvee in a flat-out race. Besides, he had never let the Termite Queen down before. This time would not become the first. Suddenly the UAZ's lights went out and it just disappeared from the rain-soaked road. Before he knew it, the road disappeared too, and the Reaper's Humvee launched over the edge of the ravine and tumbled down, rolling over and over again before it came to rest.

The Reaper lay in the car unconscious for several hours. When he woke, his entire body ached. His face burned like it was on fire. His legs felt like they were chained to heavy rocks and when he tried to move them, he gasped with pain. The rain had finally stopped. A quarter moon had come out and insects chirped all around. Not far from him, he saw his two accomplices lying motionless on the ground where they had been thrown from the vehicle. They were completely drenched and unconscious, probably dead. He'd been lucky. The driver's airbag had saved his life.

The Reaper clawed his cell phone from his pocket and called the Termite Queen to tell him what had happened. His boss seemed displeased but less so than expected, and even comforted the Reaper before asking where he was. The Termite Queen told him not to worry and to wait at the wreck for the guys he would send to help get him out of there. The Reaper's legs hurt badly, but they were not broken, and he was a strong and experienced man who had disciplined himself with martial arts, so he was able to drag himself toward his companions. But it was too late for them. He pushed the dead bodies together to lie side by side and wiped the dirt from their faces. Then he propped himself against the upside-down vehicle and waited for the rescuers. He could see only the silhouettes of trees in the ghostly darkness and hear the rush of strong winds. After a while, on a hunch that something terrible would happen soon, he drew himself behind a rock and held his gun across his chest.

Around midnight, two large men arrived at the scene of the accident. In the dim light the Reaper saw them approach the overturned Humvee. When they passed by, in the moonlight he saw they had drawn their guns and he smelled gasoline. Still concealed behind the boulder, he heard one say to the other, 'Where is he? Look around.'

After a while, the first one said, 'He must've gone back up to the road. Let's wait to burn these bodies and the car. We can't tip him off. Leave the gas here and we'll search back the way we came. Be careful.'

They had been sent to kill him. The realization hit him like a bucketful of cold, filthy water in the face. A seething rage began to boil within the Reaper. He waited until he had a clear view of both assassins in the moonlight and quickly fired two rounds. He hobbled over to them. One was still moving. He shot the other in the head to make sure he was dead and then sat on the first's chest, making him groan. 'Why did he send you to kill me?' he asked. 'Answer quick, or I shoot again.'

The survivor groaned, 'The boss wants your wife for himself. You must know he's been fucking her.'

The boiling rage inside him exploded in a hot, white flash. He shot the man in the face, and then picturing the Termite Queen with his wife, he shot the dead man again and again until he emptied the clip. He searched the men for their keys, took their guns and then dragged their bodies toward the two others. He poured gasoline on the four corpses, opened the cap to the Humvee's tank, and splashed gas down the side. He lit a bundle of grass with his cigarette lighter and tossed it on to the bodies and then, ignoring the pain, staggered away up toward the road as fast as he could. He was halfway up the slope when the gas tank blew and knocked him flat. Then he got up and kept climbing.

The Reaper drove the would-be killers' SUV through the dark canyon back to the main road. It started to rain again. In the pre-dawn darkness, he pulled over just before a bridge. The river roared, swollen from the storms. He nosed the car down the bank, put it in neutral and set the brake. He got out and found a rock to jam the accelerator, released the brake and dropped the transmission into drive. The car jerked as the racing engine caught and plunged the vehicle into the river. Within seconds it was gone.

He sat on the riverbank and let the rain wash the blood from his face and clothes, and then he limped into the next town. At dawn, he rented a room at a truck-stop motel. He needed time to recover and to think carefully about how to get to the Termite Queen. He showered and dried himself and then slept all day. He made no calls, and left the motel only to buy food and listen for news. Lying on the bed, he couldn't stop himself from imagining the Termite Queen's bloated naked body atop his wife's lissom frame. He imagined her moaning and the Termite Queen grinding his teeth. He imagined his boss's grotesquely huge penis gushing little, white termites all over her. Infuriated, he punched his own chest and bit his lip. He smoked and drank bottle after bottle of the cheap rice wine sold at the truck stop. Only after he blacked out could he stop the plague of torturous images.

The Reaper's thoughts turned to suicide. He could no longer bear the shame caused by his own imagination. He had nothing to lose, nothing to regret. Tears soaked his pillow.

Five days passed, and still no one had heard anything from the Reaper. Then, late into the night of the sixth day, he appeared at the door of his home. He went inside, took a shower, shaved and asked his wife to help him dress his wounds. When she asked him where he'd been and how he'd been injured, he forced a smile and said nothing. Upset by his silence, she went straight back to bed without him. The sun started to rise, and the Reaper looked obsessively at the clock.

He drank a bottle of wine and smashed the empty bottle on the floor. Hearing the crash, his wife came downstairs and pleaded with him to stop drinking. If she could get him to go upstairs, she could open the front door, run out and ask the neighbours for help. But the Reaper could read her mind.

The sight of the expensive, jade necklace above the sexy, low-cut neckline of her nightgown finally pushed him over the edge. He shot her in the chest and popped the cork of a champagne bottle with his thumb. She crumpled to the floor and took her last breath. The Reaper smiled a grim smile and poured the sparkling wine down his throat. 'Goodbye, you cheating bitch,' he said. 'You won't have long to wait for me and Grandpa Termite Queen in hell.'

His emotions finally burnt out, the Reaper reloaded his gun, the gold-plated one the Termite Queen had given him all those years ago, and slipped out the door as quietly as a ghost.

As a habit, the Termite Queen always started his day at six. He got up, brushed his teeth, took a few deep breaths and ate an enormous breakfast. After his divorce, he had decided not to remarry and lived alone with several trusted servants. Only women were allowed in his bedroom, and he had hired a team of strong, young men who knew how to shoot and fight to be his drivers and security guards. Anyone who came to see him had to be searched first.

The Termite Queen rarely left his mansion, unless it was absolutely necessary. He thought not wasting time or energy would let him live longer. With his royal ambitions in mind, he had the place designed like a Chinese palace.

After breakfast, he drank a cup of tea and plodded into the garden. He wore a royal yellow, silk gown like the emperors of the Nguyễn dynasty, and slippers that had been embroidered with auspicious patterns and red dragons, embellished with Indian sapphires. The sash to his gown had a pearl buckle and was encrusted with thirty-one red rubies. In his royal outfit, he loved to stroll around his spacious home and courtyards, imagining himself to be authoritative and powerful like an emperor at court. He would sit on his throne and command his bodyguards to leave him alone. With his eyes closed, he enjoyed the feeling of being alone under heaven, far above everyone else. A long, long time ago, a fortune-teller had told the Termite Queen that he was born under a lucky star and that the dragon governed his destiny. Việt Nam was no longer a monarchy, the fortune-teller had said, so he would never be an actual king, but he would have infinite power. Even so, the Termite Queen never gave up his dream of becoming an emperor, knowing that would mean he'd receive endless blessings from heaven. Thus, he had an elaborate throne constructed and installed in his favourite courtyard. He loved to use the word *royal* when he referred to his possessions: his *royal* car, his *royal* pen, his *royal* ashtray, his *royal* signature. It was his second favourite word, next to *real*.

That morning, as he sat upon his royal throne, he began to wonder what had happened to the two men he'd sent to murder the Reaper. It had been six days and they weren't back yet. As if an answer to his unspoken question, the Reaper appeared in the courtyard wearing a simple olive-green uniform instead of his usual field coat. Astonished by the Reaper's sudden entrance, the Termite Queen at first thought it must be his mind playing tricks on him. But then the Reaper slid the door shut behind him. A terrified look flashed across the Termite Queen's face before he quickly regained his composure. 'So, you're still alive, huh? Where are the other good-for-nothing guys?'

'You want to know where they are? They're waiting for you in hell.' Then he smiled his grim smile. 'If you wanted my wife, you should've told me. No woman should have come between us. I would've divorced her and gotten out of your sight. You didn't have to play this terrible game with me.'

Before the Termite Queen could say a word, the Reaper drew his gun and shot his boss in the head, then the chest and finally the groin, though the last bullet hit his thigh instead of his enormous penis. The Termite Queen fell from his throne with a thud. The Reaper heard footsteps from the next room, so he charged into the house and shot the Termite Queen's most trustworthy servant too.

It all happened in less than three minutes.

Epilogue

In history, the end of a regime often leads to a positive change for a nation, or even the world, and sometimes a person's death gives birth to a new and better era. With this book, the real *Termite Queen*, I hope I have laid to rest many of the unfair and inaccurate misrepresentations that appeared in the original *Termite Queen*, and now, with this task accomplished, I believe my days as a writer are over. As for my company, the regime that the Termite Queen had established finally and officially came to an end. With him out of the way, my mother and I sold all our shares of the company in a public offering, hoping that the light of public ownership would clear away the rest of the shadows.

I was glad Mr Tâm gave Diệu the letter my father had written and rewritten for years. I would soon learn that he tore himself apart mercilessly in it. But even before I read it, I hoped the letter might help close a tragic past that had not directly involved Diệu and me, but that had nevertheless turned us both into victims and enemies.

For the full week following our meeting at the cemetery, we had no contact with one another. With the Termite Queen's death, I no longer worried about her being murdered. I ached to see her and to tell her all I had not yet been able to say. I dialled her number several times but lacked the confidence to send the call through.

Consumed by a mixture of anxiety, disappointment and longing, I desperately hoped she would call me. And then, one late afternoon, Diệu appeared at the door to my home. I invited her in, but she would not enter, and so we faced each other through the doorway. She looked at me calmly and warmly.

'I brought this to return to you,' she said, handing me the envelope. 'You can open it and read it if you like. Thank you again for everything you have done for me.'

I glanced at the unopened envelope, and I think the look on my face must have said I didn't know what to do with it.

'Please keep it,' Diệu said, her voice gentle but serious. She hesitated a moment before continuing. 'I'm trying to accept what you said the other day, that your father was not a bad person. It's better for me to think of him through you. Please give my greetings to your mother. Also, the commune chairman wanted me to tell you that he's doing fine and will never give up. Take care, Việt!'

I looked straight into her eyes, which were like the vast sky, and said, 'Can we write a new chapter together—a story about light, love and forgiveness? The main characters will be you and me, as well as the millions of other people to whom we are indebted. We are both young and hopeful. We still have our dignity. I need you in my life. You don't have to answer now. We still have a long future ahead of us. I hope you can feel my sincerity and give me the chance to ...'

I swallowed to try to ease my dry throat. My pounding heart felt as if it might shatter my ribs. I started again, 'I deserve whatever you decide. It's fair. But we can't live with hatred in our hearts for the rest of our lives, especially hatred caused by someone else. We can't let ourselves be victims of a past governed by ignorance and greed. Let's not let those cruel people continue to hurt us. Let's build a new life together and raise the most beautiful, intelligent and moral children the world has ever known.'

I flushed, and had to stop for a few seconds before asking, 'Can we be together, please?'

Diệu lowered her head slightly and said nothing.

I felt like a crazy man mumbling to myself. I almost started to cry.

She could feel that without looking at me. That was why she turned her face away to hide her emotions, I thought. She seemed to want to say something, but couldn't, or decided it wasn't the right time, so she sighed. Then Diệu looked at me very deliberately and very kindly but still did not speak. She backed away, hugging her chest with her arms, and then hurriedly got into a waiting taxi and disappeared down the street.

I stood still, like I had been turned to stone, watching Diệu go. I felt then, as now, that she was an angel sent to save me from ignorance and greed.

At midnight, after I burned incense on my father's altar and asked for his blessing, I finally read the letter he had written to Diệu, which of course does not appear in the original *Termite Queen*. If it did, maybe that narrative would have treated him more kindly. My eyes welled with tears. My throat was dry. The final paragraphs of the letter read:

> My childhood was traumatized by the terror of death coming from out of the blue. So I understand what you must feel when you fear harm from individuals who lurk in the shadows, and it is to my undying shame that I am partly responsible for making you feel this way. You likely hate, even loathe such shadowy villains, and I deserve to be cursed along with them. But I, too, am their victim. I feel disgusted with myself when I say that, but it is the truth.

Every day, I punish myself by writing this letter to you. I want to repent for my wrongdoings, and I pray for your safety. I hope you will become a beautiful and forgiving person. Each time I type this letter, tears fall from my eyes, and by now I cannot remember how many times I have cried. I know I can't ease the sorrow in your heart, but I sincerely believe justice eventually triumphs, and a fair judgment awaits us all. I wish none of this had happened. I wish I could fall sound asleep, and that when I wake, you will already have become my daughter.

Despite the past, I wish you a rich and fulfilling life. I wish you all the best!

The next day, I took the letter to my father's grave and burned it. In the white ashes fluttering into the air from the fire, I thought I saw Diệu's gentle and forgiving eyes.

And in the vast, blue sky above, I'm sure my father was smiling.

Acknowledgements

The translators would like to thank Tạ Duy Anh for entrusting us with the joyful task of translating *The Termite Queen* into English. Special appreciation goes to the Humanities Institute at the University of Montana for supporting Quan Manh Ha with a research grant to finish this project. Thanks also to Joseph Babcock, Nguyễn Phan Quế Mai, Julie Stevenson, Võ Hương Quỳnh, Amber Caron, Ben Gunsberg, Jennifer Sinor, and Michael Sowder for their friendship and encouragement. We gratefully acknowledge the support of Nora Nazerene Abu Bakar and Usha Surampudi at Penguin SEA; they recognized the importance of this book and made it the best it can be. We are especially grateful to Ben Kerkvliet for writing the essay to contextualize the very real issues addressed in the novel. And finally, our most heartfelt thanks go to our beloved family members for their unflagging support: Đinh Thị Hải, Noel Harold Kaylor, Jennifer Peeples and Owen Waugh.